TWISTED LOVE

TALES OF REVENGE & WOE

EDITED BY
CHRIS BARTHOLOMEW

TWISTED LOVE

EDITED BY
CHRIS BARTHOLOMEW

STATIC MOVEMENT

TABLE OF CONTENTS

Burning Love
Dorothy Davies

"How much do you hate him?"

The words seemed to shock the young man. He pushed his tousled hair back with one hand, an obvious time wasting exercise to give him a moment to think before responding. Shock gave way to a glimmer of understanding.

"As much as you."

I laughed, showing him white teeth set amid blood red lips and tongue. No matter his apparent exhaustion, he still twitched. I saw it.

"You can't, my beloved, you can't. I hate him with every fiber of my being and no one can hate more than that."

"Janetta, my darling..." He reached for me but I rolled away, savoring the smell of crushed grass as I did so. Nature at its most basic. Grass crushed beneath a human body.

"Enough, enough! You were wonderful, you are wonderful, my joy, my heart, my life, but no more tonight. I need to think..."

"We've made our plans."

"Randy, you made plans, I am not sure we can go with them just yet."

I rolled over onto my back, gazing up at the velvet night sky, wondering how many stars there were and whether anyone had succeeded in counting them. The thought that each one was a fireball intrigued me, as fire itself intrigued me, the colors, the flickering of the flames, the greed with which it consumed whatever it could find, wood, coal, paper, cloth, flesh, hair, bones...

Those thoughts were best kept very secret indeed. I had Randy where I wanted him, to some degree, but not enough to let him in on my thoughts and dreams and ambitions. Somewhere an owl hooted, close by the undergrowth rustled and I caught sight of a fox loping quietly away, mouth open so it had caught nothing – so far. Well, that makes two of us, my friend, I mused and laughed silently.

1

"I'm getting cold." Randy got up and began swinging his arms around to generate some heat. Reluctantly I got up, without his help. Lithe and sinuous as I am, I could get myself up from the ground without assistance. It was something he said he admired, my independence, which translated to my inability to accept help. I thought it was a drawback; there were times when a little help would not come amiss.

"I'm going home," I announced with an edge on my voice that said 'no argument.' Randy nodded, a movement I could just about see in the darkness caused by the huge oak.

"Then let's go."

We walked along the edge of the cornfield, the ears ripe and ready for harvest, the wind stirring them so they spoke in sibilant whispers to one another. I wondered if anyone could speak the language of the corn and if they could, what they would learn. Then I berated myself for stupid thoughts. Hold on to reality, I told myself. There is one big thing to do and the sooner you do it, the better.

Randy left me at the steps leading up to the house. He walked off without once looking back, just as I had told him to do, so why the tinge of disappointment that he hadn't turned round once to look at me? What good was a lover if they didn't act like one? Even if it meant breaking the rules I had given him... but then, had I not chosen him because he was compliant, meek and obedient?

I hurried up the steps, my footfall silent in expensive leather pumps. The door eased open without a sound and I slipped through the gap, all but holding my breath. There was no member of staff around that I could see. With a sigh of relief I climbed the stairs to my room, where I locked the door behind me and threw myself on the bed, only then realizing I had been actually been holding my breath all the way up.

Hate.

An all-consuming emotion that blinds people to reality, reasonable thought, often reasonable behaviour. Hate. Hatred. Loathing. Detestation. Whatever the name, whatever the word, the object of that hate became unbearable.

And Stuart Edward Philip De Vere Walston, my husband

of ten years and three days, if I was counting – which I surely was – had become unbearable to my vision, my hearing and my touch. His voice grated on me, his platitudes were a patronising condescension – if I could phrase it thus – and all I wanted, dreamed of, visualised over and over, was plunging a sharpened steak knife into his starched shirt front, seeing the richness spill out and stain the white and then the black of his ubiquitous evening suit. The problem: that vision was swiftly accompanied by the one of the police arriving, arresting me and taking me away in handcuffs, incarcerating me in some ghastly prison cell for years and years.

Even hate has a price, a step it is impossible to take for the sake of sanity.

Oh, but there are other ways to wreak revenge.

I sat up, reached for a cigarette and then remembered I had quit smoking a week earlier. No, that was the wrong term; I had decided to delay having a cigarette. The 'delay' had now gone on for just over a week and it was getting easier, although I missed the feel of the slender tobacco packed tube in my fingers, the flare of the lighter, the flame which brought instant relaxation and pleasure. Ignore the ash, the tainted breath, the smelly clothes, the tarred lungs...

Stop it, I told herself. Stop it! Anyone can do diversionary tactics like that.

Face facts.

My husband, the local squire, land owner, Master of the Hunt, benefactor to the local community, is a two timing nasty piece of work.

Under the clothes, no one can see the bruises from the vicious pinches or sly jabs with an elbow, hard enough to damage.

He thinks I don't know about his dalliances, his one night stands, his longer term affairs, thinks I can't see the looks he gives to the current one who has caught his attention, someone who will be bought off when he's bored, in about three weeks, judging by the rate he gets through them.

And I get Randy, a farm hand, a rough and ready laborer. The thing is, Randy is always ready and if he is sometimes rough, it doesn't matter.

Randy professes to hate my husband as much as I do. I disbelieve him for his home, where he and his older brother still live, is owned by the farm and by my husband. His job is dependent on my husband. He can tell me he hates him but I disbelieve him and know that apart from me, no one hates him for no one sees him as I do. But he's useful, he's discreet, he's young, he has staying power and he's good looking. And in awe of me. What more could I ask?

Well, peace of mind for one.

How to get it is something else.

I am not letting my husband continue to get away with endless affairs, which he flaunts in front of me, knowing well that I am aware of them. Is it my fault he scorns my room and my bed? Is it my fault I am no longer the young woman he courted and married? Does it not occur to him that he too is ten years older and sagging in places?

I know what I want to do. I know it well enough that I can see it happening and, with the right circumstances, no one will know anything about it until it is over. None of this hacking at his chest with a steak knife and having witnesses to the act. No, nothing as crude as that.

Hit him where it hurts. In the bank account.

All I have to do is work out the very best way of doing it...

***

I was the model wife for some weeks. Entertaining guests, running the house, supervising the perfect meals, I did nothing that he could criticize in any way, shape or form. He did not visit my room, for which I was grateful, for I would have found it difficult to respond with enough ardor to satisfy him. That I saved for Randy and nights on the edge of the cornfield, with the rustling sound of the corn talking to itself as background to my cries of passion.

It was then the seed of an idea came to me.

The first task was to find out where my husband conducted his dalliances with his latest paramour. Slut, whore, two timing friend... the names could go on forever but were futile, he had power, money and status, she had ambitions and that I understood. My revenge was not going to be against someone he had managed to entrap, but against him, the monster, the ogre, the bane of my days and my existence.

I bribed a stable lad to follow them one night, to find out where they went when she visited our estate. Simple, he said, they were so engrossed in one another they had no idea he was following. They went to a small cottage on the outskirts of the land, one I had seen many times when out riding but ignored. It was tumbledown, in drastic need of renovation and repair and I never thought about why recently the roof had been patched, the windows replaced, the door shutting properly. Foolish woman that I am, I thought perhaps he planned to put a tenant in there. Instead he was using it to put a part of him into her. I wondered what it was like inside the cottage, how much effort he had made, without actually wanting to find out. Mixed up feelings fighting for precedence and none of them winning.

He spoke at dinner about the money we would reap – I use the word advisedly – when the harvest was gathered in, mentioned the high price of corn, the heavy crop we had raised this year together with the barley and the wheat. He spoke of a new carriage, we could afford it, he said, when it was sold and the money banked safely. I sat and listened and nodded and said 'yes' in the right places and smiled at him as if delighted with the fact we could have a new carriage and money in the bank, as if that made up for his philandering right before my eyes. I saw nothing but my need for revenge. I ask now, do you blame me? Have not countless women – and men, come to that – felt the same over the centuries, when they find the love of their life has been dallying with someone else? My problem was, he was not the love of my life in the first place, but he was *my* husband, the fact I didn't care about him was immaterial. Possession is everything. He chose me before he chose them. Illogical I know, but to me it was perfect feminine reasoning.

I chose a night when Randy was full on ready in every sense of the word. We met at our trysting place, the base of the oak, where undergrowth had created its own enclosure. We met and we loved intensely for some time. Then I complained I really needed a cigarette and pulled the box of matches from my pocket. Randy laughed; he had never seen me smoke and could not believe I did, or that I owned such things. I had a cigarette with me but had no intention of lighting it. Instead I struck the match, missed the cigarette, to his amusement, and threw the lighted match onto the patch of fuel I had quietly placed in the corn an hour or so before we met.

It was spectacular. An entire cornfield went up in flames in no time at all, the corn no longer whispered, it shrieked in its dying throes. At least, that is what I heard, the dying of the corn. I could almost hear my husband shrieking at the loss of income from the harvest.

It was only when the flames had died down that the source of the shrieks was discovered. Instead of using the cottage that night, he and his paramour had chosen a place in the corn.

I had my witness in Randy who swore that I had thrown a match away that I shook to extinguish the flame before I threw it. I had the staff who spoke of my husband's dalliances with all and sundry and how he normally used the cottage but this night had seemingly changed his mind.

Revenge is a dish best served cold? No, revenge comes in flickering flames, intense heat and the sure knowledge that the memories will live with you forever.

I ask you, how many women get to burn down a cornfield – and their cheating husband with it?

The corn has grown again and it whispers its secrets. I am grateful now that no one understands the language that it speaks.

About the author: Dorothy Davies is a writer, medium and editor who lives and works on the Isle of Wight, a small island off the south coast of England. She is a full member of the Fictioneers, has contributed to many Static Movement anthologies and is in the process of editing a few as well. Her book *Death Be Pardoner To Me*, the life of George, duke of Clarence, is to be followed by *Thirty Pieces of Silver*, the life of Judas Iskariot, in about Spring 2011. She hopes her novels and her work with Static Movement will continue for many years.

American Fugitive

Adam Francis Smith

Veronica stood before the television, one hand raised to her face, feeling the bruise left there by her live-in boyfriend, Leon.

Leon left for work hours ago, but she could still feel the slap. It had been days since he had last struck her and she thought that maybe he had somehow softened. But he came after her with fury in his eyes this afternoon when he realized his work clothes hadn't been pressed.

"I'm sorry," she pleaded. "There wasn't time. I had the shopping and the cleaning to do and the trash bin was full."

His hand was fortunately open when he connected with the soft flesh of her cheek.

"Stop with your excuses! You're lazy and you don't care how I look. I'm going to look like I sleep in my uniform. You are useless, pathetic."

At least her favorite television show, 'American Fugitive' was on tonight. Seeing Bruce Callaway on the TV each Tuesday was reason enough to carry on. He was so handsome and classy. Veronica dreamed that someday she would meet him. She just knew he'd fall in love with her at first sight.

***

Flashy prime time music issued forth from the speakers as slick graphics introduced the upcoming show's cast and crew.

"Tonight, America, we are on the trail of a real killer. He's accused of beating his wife to death..."

Veronica wasn't paying attention to the words. She simply stared at Bruce Callaway on the screen. His tight curls and dimpled cheeks were so inviting. She imagined kissing his smooth, clean-shaven face.

The picture switched to a photo of the current featured fugitive. "If you've seen this man," announced Bruce from off-screen, "call our toll-free number. Remember folks; do not

7

attempt to approach this man. He is a vicious killer and is considered very dangerous."

Veronica knew the next announcement by heart: "Anyone who calls with information that leads to the arrest of tonight's fugitive will be flown here to our studio to appear on an upcoming episode of American Fugitive."

She thought how wonderful it would be to capture a fugitive and have Bruce Callaway thank her personally. With that in mind, she focused on the face of the killer.

Her knees nearly gave out as blood rushed to her head. The face on the television belonged to Leon! She was certain of it. Her mind was a sudden flurry of disjointed thoughts:

Can that really be Leon? Should I call the toll-free number? Will I be a hero? What will Leon do if he finds out I called? Can that really be him? A killer? Wait. Calm down. Look at the picture.

She peered closely at the screen. It sure looked like Leon. Bruce was giving some background and Veronica tried to focus on the words.

"... married in 1997. Neighbors say that Maxwell and Jessie often had violent fights and the police were called out on several occasions. On May 4, 1999, the police arrived too late; Jessie Ferguson was dead, beaten to death in her kitchen. Maxwell was arrested, but was able to slip his cuffs and make a bold escape by stealing a police squad car. The car was found minutes later, but Maxwell was gone."

When the show paused for a commercial break, Veronica moved to the sofa and sat. She thought back to when she had met Leon in a bar on Thanksgiving Day in 1999. His pick up line was that he was traveling cross-country, seeking employment, but he would consider settling down for the right reason. His wink had won her over.

"We're back folks. Now pay close attention to this next piece of information. A former neighbor of the Ferguson's reports that Maxwell Ferguson has a birthmark on his right shoulder. It is apparently in the shape of the letter E. Keep in mind that it is relatively easy to cover or hide a birthmark, but we are trying to provide you with all the information we currently have available."

Oh my God, thought Veronica. *Leon has a birthmark exactly like that. I've got to get out of here!*

"Remember, viewers, anyone who provides information leading to the arrest of Maxwell Ferguson will appear on an upcoming episode of American Fugitive."

Veronica's panic was pushed aside by a sudden thought: *What if I captured Leon? Bruce would be so impressed!*

She began to devise a plan. Leon would be home from his night watchman job in just a few hours. There was little time to waste.

***

Veronica was not good with tools, but in about two hours she had managed to rig a simple trap. Inside the front door, suspended from four plant hooks, hung Leon's hammock. A long electrical extension cord ran down the wall and across the foyer into the dining room. One end of the improvised rope was attached to the hammock and the other was held tightly in Veronica's left hand, ready to be yanked hard when Leon entered the house.

In her right hand she held a heavy mallet. The plan was simple: Leon would enter and Veronica would pull the cord. The hammock would come down over Leon's head, trapping him long enough for Veronica to run up and whack him with the mallet. As he lay unconscious, she would tie Leon up with the electrical cord and then phone the toll-free number to American Fugitive.

Time moved slowly forward while Veronica waited. *What if Leon had been watching television at work? Surely he wouldn't come home, knowing the show was her favorite program?* Oh, that would ruin everything! She quickly decided the odds were slim and steadied her resolve.

Perhaps I should clean up the tools? She noted the screwdriver, stepladder and miscellaneous screws and hooks that littered the foyer. Before she could decide whether to clean them up, the front door swung open. Leon stepped in and quickly took note of the mess in the foyer.

"What the-" he began. Veronica yanked hard on the orange cord. The end disconnected from the hammock and fell to the floor. The hammock itself remained attached to the hooks above.

"Veronica! What the hell is going on here?"

Panic again began to take hold of Veronica, but she could hear the voice of Bruce Callaway inviting her to appear on his show. She dropped the end of the cord and squeezed the mallet tighter. Before she could change her mind, she raised the weapon and charged into the foyer.

"Yaaaahhhh!" She swung the mallet at the dumbfounded Leon with all her might. He raised his arm in defense and blocked the blow, immediately striking out with his other hand. His heavy punch sent Veronica reeling. She crashed into the wall and crumpled to the floor. Leon grabbed the mallet.

"What is this all about?" he asked while she whimpered.

Veronica sniffled, "I saw you on TV tonight. You killed your wife!"

Leon contemplated her words for a moment before replying. "So? You were going to kill me with a hammer?"

"I was going to capture you. I was going to be a hero!"

"Well, that won't be happening, will it? What do you think I'm going to do with you now?"

Veronica looked around for anything that could be used as a weapon. The only thing within reach was the electrical cord. Leon stood between her and the other tools.

"Get up, Veronica," he ordered. He pulled her up by an arm.

Veronica twisted and dropped until Leon's grip slackened. She dived toward the tools while Leon grabbed for her and missed. She picked up the screwdriver and held it before her, turning to face him.

"Now what good do you think that is going to do?"

"Don't come near me! If you do, I- I'll kill you!"

Leon laughed and tossed aside the mallet. "Come on then, Sweetheart! Kill me!" he taunted.

Veronica considered throwing the screwdriver at him and

making a break for it. But she knew she couldn't put enough force behind the throw and he'd simply knock it away and come after her.

She thought about Bruce again and imagined sitting across from him in a fancy Hollywood restaurant. If she fled, the dream would never become reality. She couldn't let that happen, she needed Bruce.

"Yaaaahhhh!" she found herself screaming and charging again. She held the screwdriver before her with both hands.

Leon was ready and easily batted her arms aside. The force of her charge carried her into a spin as her arms swung around. She added as much force as she could to the spin and brought the screwdriver back into play. Leon was unready and the point of the screwdriver scraped his neck from chin to shoulder blade. The tip stuck on a loose wrinkle of flesh and Veronica forced it in and down.

Leon shouted expletives as the metal sank into the base of his neck. He swung wildly at Veronica but adrenaline afforded her the strength to absorb the blows. She pulled and jabbed the screwdriver into Leon's neck and shoulders. Again. Again. He finally landed a hard elbow to her temple.

She found herself on the floor once more, waiting for the final blow that would end her life. Leon crashed down beside her, now clutching at his neck, his hands a sticky-red mess.

Veronica fought to stand but the floor was slick with Leon's blood and she couldn't make it to her feet. She skittered backwards, away from the dying man, afraid that he might be able to lash out again and harm her. But as the flow of blood lessened, she saw Leon's eyes roll back and his eyelids flutter. He opened his mouth to speak, but she could not make out the words.

When he stopped breathing, Veronica made her way to the door and used the handle for support as she stood. She stepped carefully across the foyer, avoiding the pooled blood. In the kitchen, she reached for the phone and pulled the handset from the receiver.

The tone hummed in her ear as she struggled to remember the toll-free number to American Fugitive. It came to mind along with an image of the handsome Bruce Callaway. He had just introduced her to America and added that he was pleased to announce that she had consented to become his bride. "Ladies and gentlemen, the future Mrs. Callaway!"

She dialed the number.

The busy signal continued unnoticed as she played the dream like a movie in her head.

About the author: Adam Francis Smith was born and raised in Chicago, Illinois. He is a product of the Chicago Public School system. Of CPS he often says, "I learned more in the halls than in the classroom." He is a watcher of people and writes about what he sees. Perhaps you'll see a little of yourself in one of his stories.

Beyond Black Marsh

Stephanie L. Morrell

Gabby slid across the floor of her bathroom until her back was against the wall. She knew that removing the knife would only make her injury worse, but she was all alone and without a weapon. She took a deep breath, closed her eyes and grabbed onto the handle with both hands. She started to pull out the blade and the sensation was far more painful than when it first entered her body. She fought hard to remain conscious as the knife slide through her muscles and re-tore her flesh. It exited the wound with an excruciating serration. Gabby used all of her remaining strength to hold onto the bloody knife for protection. Soon the doorknob started to turn a few times and then it rattled loudly against the lock. She was terrified as to who was on the otherside and wondered how long it would take them to break in.

This is it. Gabby thought. *I made it through what happened earlier tonight and now my life is going to end here, in my own home.* She gritted her teeth, stood up on shaky legs and stepped to the right, behind the door. *Well I'm not going without a fight.* She gripped the bloody knife more tightly and held the blade towards the door. Gabby's blood loss was coming in streams and it hit her with a grave force. *Not without a fight.* She told herself. *Not without a fight.*

***

Earlier that evening...

"Hey there, Gabby. I missed you at lunch this afternoon." Randy grabbed a Samuel Adams, popped off the top, and placed it in front of her. "What are you doing here at this time?"

"I was in the middle of writing and couldn't stop myself so I decided to come by for an early dinner instead of lunch." She shook off her umbrella and removed her coat. "It's really coming down out there." Gabby took a few swallows of beer and then patted her lips with a cocktail napkin.

"Do you want the usual, kiddo?"

"Of course," she laughed. "Chicken fingers and fries."

"I'll get Frank on it right away."

***

Randy was in and out of the kitchen when Seth Davis waved him over. Randy jokingly referred to Seth as, Pretty Boy, from time to time because of his good looks.

"What's up, Seth?"

"Who's that woman you've been talking to?"

"I don't know who you mean. There are a few women in here."

"Are you going to make this difficult for me, Randy?" Seth's dark eyes narrowed. "You know who I mean."

"Can't say that I do, pretty boy."

"You are a ball buster, old man." He shook his head. "I'm talking about the small brunette with short hair and rather large...well you know." He didn't want to finish the sentence.

"Large what," Randy egged him on with the question.

"You know...she's rather chesty."

"You mean Gabby." He started to laugh. "I know you're always a gentleman, so I just had to hear how you'd put it."

"Happy to amuse you." Seth took a swallow of beer. "What would your dear Kathy say about this conversation?"

"The wife loves Gabby so she'd probably just laugh."

"So what's her story?" Seth asked the question in seriousness.

"Well, she's a writer and a real smart gal. My wife is reading her book and really likes it. Apparently the book is doing well because Gabby was finally able to quit her day job. She comes here for lunch every day and she's a very nice girl; however, I think she likes her privacy because she lives way out beyond Black Marsh...and you know there's nothing out there."

"So what is she drinking," Seth asked. "I'd like to send one over to her."

"Samuel Adams, but she usually only has one drink with lunch. Also, she seems to be kind of a loner so don't be offended if she turns you down."

"Oh." Seth took out his wallet. "Well, I'm going to try and get through to her." He looked at Randy. "I want her dinner to be on me."

"You got it." Randy nodded. "I'll just add it to your tab and let her know."

***

"Hello there, Gabby. "I'm Seth."

"Hi." She smiled. "Randy said that you would be stopping over."

"And here I am." He offered his hand to her.

Gabby accepted the gesture and felt a spark as his long slender fingers wrapped around her tiny hand. She examined his face and was taken by his appearance. He was tall and slender with a broad chest and muscular arms. Seth's olive skin and dark hair gave him a movie star appeal; however, it was his dark eyes that made Gabby blush.

"It's nice to meet you," she told him. "Please have a seat."

"Thanks."

"Actually I should be thanking you. Randy said that you covered my meal. You really didn't have to do that."

"It was my pleasure." His dark eyes gleamed. "Randy says that you're a writer. What types of books do you write?"

"I have published over a hundred short stories, mostly horror," she told him. "The book I have out now is a psychological thriller about a serial killer."

"Really?" Seth raised an eyebrow. "You look so sweet. I can't imagine your mind going to such a dark place."

"I am just full of surprises." She giggled. "What do you do?"

"I put myself through college by working construction, graduated with a master's degree in business, and now I own a small, but successful, construction company a few towns over. I usually stop by here a few evenings a week after work. I'm considered a business man but I still enjoy getting my hands dirty at the construction sites whenever I can." He gestured towards the front window. "As you can see by the weather, today was not one of those days."

"I guess not." She listened to the rain.

"So are you seeing anyone, Gabby?"

"No'" she answered softly. "Actually, I am not."

"Then would you like to go out with me sometime." His eyes never left her face.

"Wow, you are very direct." She chuckled.

"Is that a yes or a no?" He asked the question with a smile. "I was told that you are somewhat of a loner so I am prepared in case you turn me down."

"Really," she continued laughing."

"Let me think about it." She tilted her head playfully. "Do I want to go out with you?"

"Wow, you are tough. Please just put me out of my misery and..."

Seth's comment was cut off by the sight of Randy and Frank being led out from the kitchen at gunpoint. Behind them walked a man with a shotgun in his hands, and a ski mask covering his face.

Seth, Gabby, and the nine other patrons were ordered to sit down on the floor in front of the bar. A second gunman had already seen to locking all of the doors and then quickly collected cell phones from everyone in the bar. He didn't want any 911 calls going out to the cops.

"I want everyone to keep their traps shut. We don't want any heroes so do what you're told and maybe you'll all get out of this alive," said the first gunman." He shoved Frank to the floor with the others.

"Maybe, we'll get out of this alive," Gabby whispered to Seth nervously.

"Shh. Relax and stay calm. They just want money and will probably get out of here as fast as they can."

"All right Boss," the first gunman looked to Randy. "I came here for a reason, so make my life easy and just do what you're told."

"Sure, sure," Randy said quickly. "Just take it easy. We don't want anyone to get hurt."

"You need to shut your mouth and take me to that safe of yours."

"All right. The safe is in my back room."

"So get up off your ass and take me there," the first gunman ordered.

"Okay." He slowly stood up and walked towards the bar.

"Looking for this, old man?" The second gunman held up a handgun. "Found it underneath your bar. It will go nice as a side arm to my shotgun."

Randy stood silently with his eyes wide and his face as white as a sheet.

"Let's go." The first gunman grabbed Randy by the back of the neck and led him to the back room.

***

"You don't think they'll hurt him, do you?" Gabby kept her voice low. "He's a grandfather for God's sake."

"I don't think so," Seth told her softly. "Like I said, they just want money. Randy does his drop-offs to the bank on Wednesdays so his safe is pretty full tonight. There is a lot of cash and these scumbags just want to get their hands on it, I'm sure."

"How do you know that?"

"Know what," asked Seth.

"How do you know when Randy drops off his money," Gabby asked suspiciously.

"What does that matter?" Seth frowned.

"All right," the second gunman shouted. "I want everyone to give me their wallets and cash." He scanned the group with his eyes and set his gaze on Gabby. "You." He pointed at her. "Come here."

"Why," she asked in a shaky voice.

"Just get up and get the hell over here," he told her. "You are gonna collect for me."

"Oh." She was visibly shaken.

"Please," Seth broke in. "Just don't hurt her."

"What did you say to me?"

"Just don't hurt her. She's no threat to you." He kept his dark eyes fixed on the gunman."

"No heroes," he shouted and then lunged at Gabby. He pulled her up from the floor by her hair"

"Don't be so rough." Seth tried to keep himself calm.

"You just don't get it, do ya?" The gunman looked to Gabby and then pointed the shotgun at her head. "Unbutton your shirt." He growled.

"What?" Her eyes were wide.

"Open up your shirt and show me those huge tits of yours."

"No," Seth cut in.

"I am doing this because of you, Hero." He cocked his gun. "Every time you open your mouth I am going to take it out on your girl. Say another word," he dared Seth. "Say another word and I will shoot her for the hell of it." The look in his eyes said his threats were sincere.

"Please don't do this," Gabby Begged.

"Open up your shirt or I'm gonna do it for you." He looked to Seth. "I want you to say something. Just say something so I can get into her pants."

Seth looked to Gabby and caught her gaze. She pleaded with her eyes for him to remain quiet, and so he did. Seth's expression was a look of suppressed fear and rage; however, he understood that trying to defend her would only make the situation worse.

"Now for the last time...open up that shirt, bitch." His voice was loud and loosing control.

"All right." She cringed. "Just please don't shoot me." She closed her eyes and bowed her head towards the ground.

No," said the gunman. There will be no hiding that pretty face of yours." He used the barrel of the shotgun to lift up her chin. "I want everyone to see you." He started to laugh. "This is a show and I am in charge so open your eyes and look at the audience."

"Please…"

"Do it." He screamed and then pressed the gun against her temple.

"Okay," she said through tears. "I'll do it." She looked up at the other patrons and saw Seth.   He locked his eyes with Gabby's and held her gaze with a gentle expression. His eyes told her that everything was going to be all right.

"I want you to look at me," said Seth. "Just look at me." His tone was soft and soothing. "Keep your eyes on me."

Gabby slowly unbuttoned her black top, exposing the able white breasts filling her soft pink bra. The humiliation and fear was overwhelming and it caused her to sway. The idea of doing this at gunpoint, and in front of strangers, sent a sick feeling into the deepest pit of her stomach.

"Nice." The gunman stared down at her chest. "What about what's under that bra," he asked ruthlessly.

"Please don't make me do this." She begged the gunman while keeping her eyes on Seth.

"You're not in charge here, bitch." He pushed the gun harder against the side of her head.

"I know," she said fearfully.

"Then do it or I'll blow your freakin head off.

"Just keep looking at me." Seth told her. "There's no one here but you and I." He spoke the words soothingly as if trying to hypnotize her into forgetting the horror of the situation. "Just look into my eyes and nowhere else."

Seth's words were having a calming effect on Gabby and the gunman noticed it.

"This is bullshit," he shouted at Seth. "Keep your mouth shut." He then focused on Gabby. "I want you to look at me and take off that bra right now."

"What the hell is going on out here?" The first gunmen entered the room with his gun pointed at Randy.

"Nothin," the second gunman said angrily.

"You're a freakin idiot." The first gunman said to his partner and then shoved Randy down with the others. "I told you to get someone to collect all of the wallets and money, not to watch a strip show." He looked to Gabby. "Put you tits back in and sit down with the rest of them."

Gabby hurried down next to Seth and tried to close her blouse. Her hands were shaking uncontrollable and this made it impossible for her to button up.

"It's all right," Seth said soothingly. "Just relax and let me do it." He started with the top button and was very gently. He was careful not to be intrusive after what she had been through.

"You," the first gunman pointed at Randy. "Go around and collect everyone's wallet and don't try anything stupid." He cocked his gun. "Hurry up."

Randy looked up paleface and weary.

"Do you hear me talking to you old man?"

"Yes," he told the first gunman, and then stood up carefully. "I hear ya."

"Good. Then do it." He was growing impatient. "Get the wallets and cash before I start to lose it like my partner over here."

"I am so ashamed," Gabby whispered. "I was standing there for everyone to see and God only knows what would have happened next."

"It's all right," Seth reassured her. "I've got you now," he whispered. "It wasn't your fault, Gabby. I just wish that I would have done something to stop that son of a bitch."

"No," she said quickly. "It only would have made things worse. He would have made me take off my pants and then..."

"Don't do that." He finished buttoning up her blouse. "Just try not to think about it." He looked into her frightened hazel eyes. "I don't think he will be bothering you again."

"God, I hope not." She leaned her face against Seth's firm chest. "I just want to get out of here."

"I know," he whispered. "I know."

Seth placed his hand around Gabby head and gently stoked her soft hair with his long slender fingers. He could feel her tiny body beginning to tremble through her sobs and so he held her tightly in his arms.

***

20

The police were called after the gunmen fled the scene. Officers questioned the patrons; however, little information could be gathered. Both men were masked and no one caught a glimpse of their car. The patrons were concerned by the fact that the gunmen had their wallets; therefore, they knew everyone's home address. The officers believed that the gunmen would most likely leave town, but they told everyone to report their stolen cell phones and credit cards.

***

Gabby waited for the officers to leave and then she headed for the door.

"Please wait." Seth placed a gentle hand on her shoulder. "Are you going to be all right getting home?"

"Yes." She took a deep breath. "I just want to get out of here."

"I could drive you."

"No thank you, Seth."

"Oh." He was visibly disappointed. "I have to confess that what transpired here tonight made me feel less of a man." He looked to the ground. "I was unable to protect you from that scum and it kills me."

"It's all right..." She tried to sound reassuring. "Good night."

"Wait. I know this is a terrible time to ask, but could I have your phone number."

Gabby did not reply.

"I am worried about you and would feel better if I could call and check up on you tomorrow." He ran his fingers through his dark hair and fixed his gaze on hers. "I know that we just met, but I really want to see you again."

"I'm sorry but I just really need to leave now." Gabby thought about what the gunman made her do, wrapped her arms around her chest, and then shuttered. "Goodbye Seth."

Gabby ran out into the rain, got behind the wheel of her car and then drove off into the storm.

TWISTED LOVE

***

One hour later...

The rain came down in buckets as lightening lit up the sky in bright flashes of electric blue. Thunder rolled on in loud crashes causing Gabby to jump at every sonic boom. After leaving the bar she wished for a safe quiet night at home, however, a loud crash resonated outside and caused her electricity to go out.

"Oh please, God...not tonight." She took out her flashlight and went to the front window.

Gabby recognized the sound and knew that it wasn't the thunder this time. A car had crashed into the pole down by the base of Black Marsh. The pole was hit hard enough to knock out the power and that meant someone might be hurt. Gabby's landline was out do to the storm and her cell phone was stolen so she could not call 911. She grabbed her flashlight and umbrella, and then headed down the path to see if she could help the driver.

***

Someone stumbled out of the disabled car and climbed up the embankment. He placed a hand to his head and tried to focus his thoughts.

A bright round light was coming towards him through the dark and the rain.

"Hello," said Gabby. "Are you all right."

"I think so," answered the driver. "My car hydroplaned around the bend and sent me off the road and into the ditch where I hit that pole."

"How can I help," she asked.

"Could I use your phone?"

His voice and his stance were familiar to Gabby. She took a few steps closer and shown her light directly into his face.

"Seth, is that you?"

"Gabby?" He held his hand up to the light and narrowed his eyes. "It is you."

"I can't believe this." She stepped up close to him and

touched his forehead. "You're bleeding."

"Am I." He reached up and touched his fingertips to the wound. "Looks like I am."

"Come on," she insisted. "Let's get you inside where it's warm and dry. We are both going to catch our death out here."

***

Seth sat silently and studied Gabby face closely. He took in the loveliness of her fair skin, soft full lips and bright hazel eyes.

"You are freezing." Gabby cleaned Seth's wound. "Maybe you should get a hot shower while I dry off your clothes.

"Are you sure it's all right."

"We are both without phones so you will be stuck here until public service hears about your accident and fixes that power line."

"How?"

"I'm sure that some other homeowner has a cell phone and will call the power company."

"That's not what I meant." He offered a charming grin. "I was wondering how you are going to take care of my clothes without the use of a dryer. The power is out, remember?"

"I know that." She couldn't help smiling back at him. "I will hang them over the fireplace while you're showering. Besides, they aren't saturated or anything."

"All right." He leaned in close and kept his dark eyes locked onto hers. "Thank you for taking me in." He spoke the words softly.

"You're welcome," she said trying to hold his deep gaze.

Seth leaned in and gently placed his lips onto Gabby's mouth. He drew her in with a slow deep kiss and then pulled back. He looked into her face and waited as she finally opened her eyes.

"I think I will take that shower now."

"Of course," she said breathlessly. "Let me get things set up for you."

The bathroom was lit by several candles so that Seth could make his way around the room. Gabby set out a clean dry towel for him and then removed the pile of wet clothes once he was hidden behind the shower curtain.

Seth took a long hot shower and thought about the kiss he had shared with Gabby. He wanted more than just to kiss those soft full lips, but she had gone through an ordeal and he wasn't going to push her. She had invited him in for the night and that spoke to the fact that she didn't fear him.

I have to pay close attention to Gabby and read all of her reactions to me. He thought as he showered. *Every time I am close to her I have such a strong urge to feel her body against mine. It was more than luck that brought her into the pub for dinner tonight. Now I just have to make her feel the same way about me.*

***

Gabby changed into a dry pair of blue jeans and replaced her black shirt with a warm pink hoodie. She zipped up the front of her top and then went out into the front room. Gabby felt Seth's clothes as they hung in front of the fire. They were completely dry and warm so she gathered them up and placed them onto the brown chair across from the sofa.

Seth's face and the kiss that he offered was the only thing on her mind.

What is he doing to me? She asked the question of herself. *I have always been a solitary person who is more than cautious when it comes to dating. I am almost forty years old and have never been so immediately attracted to someone.* She thought about the situation at the pub earlier and the vulnerability that she felt at the hands of that gunman. *What he forced me to do at gunpoint could have gone further and been much worse. Still, it was a horrible feeling and Seth got me through that. The look in his eyes and the sound of his voice had such an effect on me. It was as if he was putting me under some kind of spell and I still haven't come out of it yet...*

"Gabby," Seth called out from the bathroom and interrupted her thoughts of him.

"Yes."

"I have finished up in here and was wondering if my clothes were close to being dry."

"Oh."

"It doesn't matter if they are still damp," he told her. "I will still put them on."

"No. They are dry." She walked to the bathroom and leaned up against the door. "Is it safe to come in?"

"Yes," he answered softly. "Please come in."

Gabby opened the door and saw Seth standing there with a towel wrapped around his waist. He was slender and long wasted with tight abs and well-defined arms. His chest and shoulders were muscular as well, and the sight of this made her turn away.

"Here you go."

Gabby held out the clothes and felt Seth's hand brush against hers. The sensation of his flesh against hers made her tremble. He accepted the clothes, placed them down onto the vanity, and then took her hands in his.

"Thank you," he said keeping his eyes on her face. "I appreciate all that you have done tonight."

"It's all right," she answered shyly staring down at the floor.

"Look at me, Gabby."

"I can't." Her face was flushed.

"Please just look at me for a moment."

Seth spoke in the same soothing tone that he used at the pub earlier and Gabby could not resist. She looked up at him and gazed into his deep brown eyes.

"I just want you to know that everything is going to be fine. You are going to get past what happened tonight, and I would like to help if you will let me."

"Oh. I don't know." She tried to maintain eye contact. "But I appreciate the offer." The sight of him in the towel aroused her to the point where she had to excuse herself. "I will see you in the other room."

***

"You said that you have never been married, right?"

"Yes," Gabby told him. "I just never found the right person."

"I got married right out of college but it didn't work out. We divorced soon after."

"Sorry to hear that."

"It's all right," he assured her. "It was so long ago. Almost eighteen years, in fact."

"Now here we are, almost forty, and single." Gabby chuckled.

"Actually I am past forty. Forty-one to be exact." His dark eyes caught the flames from the fire.

"Forty-one is good." She watched the light dancing in his eyes. "Everything about you is good."

"Really," he asked the question with a smile. "You can go on if you like."

Gabby just giggled nervously.

"It's all right."

Seth held Gabby's gaze and then gently pulled her face towards his. He kissed her on the mouth with the same passion displayed earlier, however, this time, he didn't pull back. He ran his hands down the small of her back and pulled her body tightly against his own. The two of them remained in an embrace until a banging from the back of the house cut through the silence.

"What was that," Gabby asked with wide eyes.

"I don't know." Seth stood up. "Let me go and check it out."

"I'm coming with you."

"No." Seth held up his hand to her. "You wait here while I make sure everything is safe. I will be right back."

Gabby sat on the sofa and waited. She heard another loud bang followed by a thud as something crashed heavy against the wall. A few seconds of silence rang out and then there was movement.

"Well Hello," said a familiar voice. "Nice seeing you again." It was the voice of the gunman who threatened her earlier, and he wasn't wearing the mask. He entered the room with a shotgun pointed at Seth's head. "I want the two of you to sit down and shut up. I especially don't want any trouble from you, Seth." The gunman shoved him towards the sofa.

"Seth?" Gabby stood frozen from fear. "Oh my, God. How does he know your name?"

"I don't know." He looked to the gunman. "Where is your partner?"

"We had kind of a falling out and so I had to put him down." The man looked to Gabby. "Then I thought of you and decided to stop by for some fun."

"Leave her alone."

"Don't tell me what to do, Seth. You have to share her."

"You know him, don't you?" Gabby backed away from Seth. "You are in this with him."

"That's not true, Gabby."

"Then how does he know your name," she asked nervously.

"Maybe he overheard it at the bar tonight. You said my name a few times."

"Maybe not," said the gunman. "Seth Davis, you're in construction and you live over in Moorestown." He started to laugh. "We know each other all right." He looked to Gabby. "It's just a shame that you've seen our faces. Guess I'll have to kill you when I'm done screwing you."

"He's lying, Gabby. I don't know him. We have never met."

"That's how you knew about the drop-off for the money." She continued to back away.

"No. You have to trust me, Gabby. This guy is full of shit."

The gunman reached out, grabbed Gabby, and tore at her shirt. She tried to fight him off but he pointed the shot gun at her face and she froze. He had already killed his own partner, so killing her would mean nothing to him.

"Let her go." Seth lunged forward and tried to grab the shotgun.

Gabby was sent to the floor during the siege and then crawled past the two of them and into the kitchen. She pulled a large knife out of the drawer and then crawled towards the bathroom.

Seth got a hold of the shotgun so the gunman pulled Randy's handgun from his back pocket. He smashed Seth in the side of the head, knocking him to the ground and putting him out of commission.

Gabby made her way down the hall, but not before the gunman came up on her. He wrestled the knife from her grasp and plunged it into her abdomen.

"I don't want you dead just yet," he told her, blood pouring from her belly. "There a few things I am going to do to you first." He got down on the floor next to her and smiled. "This going to be fun." He played with the knife handle and watched as she cried out in pain. "I think this will be so much more fun if I leave that knife inside you."

The gunman undid her pants and started to pull them down when Seth came up on him. Seth's head was still reeling from the blow and bleeding heavily, but he fought to get his bearings straight. He was able to pull the gunman back, and at that point, Gabby crawled into the bathroom and locked the door.

There were sounds of a violent struggle followed by a gunshot. Gabby pressed her ear to the door, heard the sound of a loud thud...and then there was silence.

***

Gabby slid across the floor of her bathroom until her back was against the wall. She knew that removing the knife would only make her injury worse, but she was all alone and without a weapon. She took a deep breath, closed her eyes and grabbed onto the handle with both hands. She started to pull out the blade and the sensation was far more painful than when it first entered her body. She fought hard to remain conscious as the knife slide through her muscles and re-tore her flesh. It exited the wound with an excruciating serration but Gabby used all of her remaining strength to hold onto the bloody knife for protection. The doorknob started to turn a few times and then it rattled loudly against the lock. She was terrified as to who was on the other side and wondered how long it would take them to break in.

This is it. Gabby thought. *I made it through what happened earlier tonight and now my life is going to end here, in my own home.* She gritted her teeth, stood up on shaky legs and stepped to the right, behind the door. *Well I'm not going without a fight.* She gripped the bloody knife more tightly and held the blade towards the door. Gabby's blood loss was coming in streams and it hit her with a grave force. *Not without a fight.* She told herself. *Not without a fight.*

"It's me," said Seth. "Please let me in."

"No. I can't. I don't trust you."

Gabby wanted to remain standing but her body would no longer allow it. She fell hard against the wall and tried to use its stability to support her. Within seconds her mind began to reel and the dizzying feeling spread throughout her entire body. The strength in her legs waned completely as her body dropped to the hard tile floor with a thud.

"Gabby," Seth called through the door. "Talk to me Gabby."

She moaned in response and prayed that he wouldn't get to her. She rested her head back against the wall and fought to keep her eyes open. When Seth broke into the room she still had the knife in her hands and the blade was pointed at him. Seth got down on the ground, removed the knife from her weak grip and then held her face in his hands.

"Open your eyes, Gabby. Just open your eyes and look at me."

She struggled to force them open, and as she did, the sight of him close to her was terrifying.

"You're going to kill me now," she coughed out weakly. "I've seen your face and now you're going to kill me just as you did your partner in the hallway."

"No, "he whispered softly. "I would never do anything to hurt you."

Seth pulled a bath towel down from the metal rack and used it to apply pressure to Gabby's knife wound. She cried out in pain and fear, unable to take her eyes off of Seth for fear of what may come next.

"He isn't my partner," Seth assured her.

"Then why didn't he just shoot you? Why did he let you live?"

"He wanted to make me watch," Seth said softly. "He told me that I was no hero and would have to watch as he raped and murdered you. After that he was going to kill me too. I just got to him first."

Gabby wanted to believe him but her mind was so unclear. She was unable to focus her thoughts and now Seth was in control. Trustworthy or not, her life was in his hands.

***

The following morning...

Gabby opened her eyes and saw a bright white light that was blinding. She squinted and tried to focus, and then slowly the voices were coming in clear.

"How are you feeling, Gabby," asked a familiar voice.

"I..." she blinked a few times and the faces came into focus. "Randy?" she turned to the person standing next to him. "Kathy?"

"The wife and I heard what happened and we had to make sure you were all right."

"What happened," she asked in confusion. "Where am I?"

"Don't you remember, dear?" Kath stepped next to the bed. "You're in the hospital. You needed surgery for the knife wound, but everything went well. The doctor has been in here twice to explain it."

"Oh." Gabby frowned at the overhead lights above her bed.

"Guess you were still pretty out of it from the anesthesia and pain meds when the doctor spoke to you." Randy patted her lightly on the shoulder. "We're just so glad that you're all right."

"How did I get here?"

"Someone heard gunshots out by Black Marsh and called the police." He turned to his wife. "See Kathy. That is why I want you to get a cell phone. Emergencies can come up anytime."

"All right," she said with exasperation. "Maybe I will get one."

"Finally," Randy sighed.

Gabby got a kick out of their marital banter, but could not get Seth out of her mind. She wanted to ask about him, but was afraid. The two gunmen were dead, and if Seth had a hand in things, she would find out sooner or later. The ordeal they endured was intense and now her feelings for him were strong. She decided to keep those feeling to herself and go on with life trusting in one person, herself.

***

One month later...

Gabby was working on a second novel and hadn't been to Randy's since before the robbery. She decided it was best for her to lay low, but then a letter arrived in the mail. It was a hand written letter and the contents of it greatly moved her.

Dear Gabby, Perhaps I am overstepping but I wanted you to know that I spoke with Seth. He told me about your fears and suspicions that he had involvement in the robbery and your attack. Well he didn't. Seth knew about the drop off day to the bank because I confided in him and he warned me that it was dangerous to have a weekly drop off. He told me to make smaller deposits throughout the week to prevent my place from being targeted, but I'm old and stubborn. The gunmen had apparently cased my place for a while. That's how they knew about the money in my safe and the gun beneath my bar. The gunman who broke into your home had worked briefly at one of Seth's construction sites. That is how he knew Seth's name and where he lived. Anyway, I hope this letter finds you well. Warm regards, Randy.

***

Gabby wanted to see Seth but her mistrust of him surely

31

had an impact. He too stopped going to Randy's and did not try to call or contact Gabby.

How he could ever forgive me, she thought. *And would I be able to forgive him if the situation were reversed?* She asked the question knowing what the answer would be, and that was, no.

Gabby decided to leave Black Marsh and start over somewhere new. She visited the local realtor and placed her house on the market. Someone was watching from across the street as she left the realtor's office and she recognized him at once.

"Seth?" She whispered the word out loud.

He continued to stare at her with a saddened expression, and the sight of this made Gabby tear up. The traffic light on the corner flashed the go ahead for pedestrian crossing but Seth, did not cross. He remained still in his stance. Gabby then watched as he slowly turned and then disappeared around the corner from which he came. The traffic light finished the pedestrian countdown and then flashed a red hand in warning. Cars rushed by in an endless string leaving Gabby to stand on her own.

***

"Excuse me," said a voice that was breathless from running.

Seth turned to find Gabby behind him.

"I know that doubting you was a terrible mistake and I can't expect you to forgive me." Hot tears fell from her eyes. "You were so wonderful to me on the awful night and I couldn't have survived without you."

His dark eyes never left her gaze as the sunlight lit them up like black diamonds. The expression he wore was impossible for Gabby to decipher so she continued to plead her case.

"You were there for me emotionally during the robbery and then put your life in danger back at my home. I will be forever grateful for that and eternally sorry for how I treated you in return. I understand why you may never forgive me but I have to ask for it." She took a deep breath and tried to compose herself. "I also want to say, that along with the gratitude, I feel something else and that is something I would like a chance to explore that with you."

Gabby waited for Seth to respond, and when he didn't, her heart sank. She turned and ran down the sidewalk, wanting to cross to her car and escape forever. Before she reached the corner a hand took her shoulder and held on tight.

"Wait," Seth said softly. "Look at me."

Gabby turned to him, and slowly looked up; the expression in his eyes drew her in.

"I would never hurt you, and of that you must be certain."

"I am," she looked to the ground in shame. "Please know that I am."

Seth pulled Gabby in close, kissed her softly on the lips and then held her in his arms.

"The police found the body of the other gunman in the woods not to far from your home. Both men were deceased and Randy recovered all of his money."

"Thank God." Gabby said wearily.

"I still think you're tough and probably would have had nothing to do with me if our first night together had not been so intense."

"That's not fair Seth, besides, it looks like you've got me know."

"Looks like I do."

Seth thought about all of the trouble he went through to find the right guys to hold up Randy's place. Everything went just as planned. Gabby was singled out, he was her hero, and in the end, both gunmen were killed. There were no witnesses and now he had a strong hold over a woman he had been following for over a year. He had read all of her short stories, studied her online profile and realized that she would be hard to crack. Still, he did what he had to in order to make her his, and no one was left alive who could spoil this.

About the author: Stephanie L. Morrell is married and lives with her husband, Chris, in New Jersey. She has 55 short stories published. 9 are in online horror magazines and 46 more are published in print books from, Static Movement Imprint, Pill Hill Press, Wicked East Press, Blood Bound Books, DFE Quarterly, and Daily Flash Publications. She has an author's page on facebook and her author's website can be found at stephaniemorrell.com

CREATIVE JUICES
Ken Goldman

At daybreak the sky changed from deep purple to chipped porcelain, as if the world had turned upside down and all the color had drained out of it. Arthur Argent grasped...

... The sun deck railing in a stupor, afraid his legs might give out the moment he let go. In the bedroom Chrissa pounded against the locked closet door with an enraged succession of heavy thuds that suggested she had begun to fling herself against it. Unable to silence the screams that had increased to a piercing series of shrieks and howls, Arthur pressed his palms flat against his ears as his legs folded beneath him. He shouted back at her until his throat felt raw, hoping to block out her screaming. Above him the early morning seagulls screeched to one another as if mimicking the echoes inside his head.

He knew he could not keep his wife imprisoned much longer in her own home. But the howling creature he had locked inside the bedroom closet the night before was not really Chrissa anymore.

Three weeks earlier Arthur had believed he loved his wife more than anything else in the world.

He was wrong.

***

Three weeks earlier - a lifetime ago - Arthur...
... sat behind his IBM keyboard gulping down his third cup of coffee. He knew he might sit at his desk all day waiting for words that might not come.

An old saying he remembered went : *'Writing is easy. You just sit and think until beads of blood appear on your forehead.'* Arthur had just about reached that point, and in another hour he might be wringing out his brain like a sopping sponge. He lit

35

his last Marlboro and pulled the curtain from the window to let in the breeze coming off Barnegat Bay. The first day of June had begun without him.

Outside on the sun deck Chrissa's easel faced the bay, the canvas covered by an old flowered sheet. She had just pulled her Toyota into the driveway below. Arthur watched her unload half a dozen tubes of paint and a handful of new brushes onto the stand alongside her easel, supplies she had bought to put the finishing strokes on the seascape she had been painting for her Long Beach Island exhibition on July 4th. Chrissa waved to him from the deck and sat at the easel mixing her paints.

Arthur tugged the blank roll of paper from the carriage of his printer and rolled it into a ball, pulled up the window screen and aimed the wad at his wife below. It hit her square on the top of her head.

"Working hard?" she called up to him. "Paper wads seem so junior high, don't you think? You want to come down here so you can deliver your work to me in person?"

He answered from the window, "Sorry, no can do. That paper in your hand represents the entire bulk of my work for this morning. But if it's a special delivery you want..."

When Arthur reached the sun deck he was smiling. Approaching Chrissa from behind he placed his hands on her shoulders and nudged her neck. "Yes indeed, there's something about a woman with a smudge of blue paint on her nose that drives a man wild. You feel like getting rid of that smock for a while?"

She rose from her easel with the paintbrush still in her hand, the cool sea breeze blowing honey colored wisps of Chrissa's hair into Arthur's face as he took her into his arms. "I thought you were working on the great American novel up there. Whatever happened to the guy who once told me that in this state a wife's disturbing her husband while he's writing is cause for justifiable homicide?"

For a moment Arthur felt like a kid who had been caught cutting class. Without meaning to, he looked away from her.

"First that guy has to write the great American sentence. And expressing myself doesn't seem my strong suit these days.

36

Chriss, maybe I had only that one novel in me. I just can't — I can't find the right-"

She sensed the red flare he was sending her and led him to the bench in front of her canvas. She squeezed his hand without saying a word and sat silently by his side.

He kissed the tip of her nose and lifted the sheet from Chrissa's canvas. "Okay, I've used up my bitching privileges for the day. Let's have a look. These paintings of yours might determine whether we get to keep this outrageous retreat by the bay we call our home."

Arthur looked at the canvas without speaking. No doubt about it. He had married a woman who was as talented as she was beautiful. He forced a smile, aware of the effort it took.

"I still have to do the gulls,"she explained, almost apologizing.

"If Van Gogh were alive, I swear the man would send you his other ear. Chriss, this is so damned beautiful. How do you —?"

She stopped his words with a finger to his lips and smiled as she moved closer to him. "You want to know my secret? You think I see a seagull and suddenly I'm inspired? I'll tell you something about inspiration, my love. Right after I get rid of this smock for a little while."

"What about the seagulls?"Arthur asked.

"Screw 'em," she answered.

***

At noon Arthur told his wife he wanted to take the jeep for a spin to goose up his muse, or failing that, maybe stop into Jimmie's Surf n'Sun Tavern in Beach Haven to pick up some cigarettes and a coed or two. She reminded him that the only woman they had ever seen in that watering hole had looked like Bella Abzug.

"Well, then maybe I'll just get tanked," he answered. He kissed her and hopped into his Scout.

***

Nothing inside Jimmie McLaughlin's Surf n'Sun Tavern gave the slightest indication of surf or sun. The pub...

... defied the tourist-pandering trend of other South Jersey shore bars, making no attempt to establish a motif. The bar's decor consisted chiefly of sparkling beer mugs and wine glasses suspended over the bartender's head, three ceiling fans, and five booths with wooden seats for which Jimmie had never bothered to buy cushions. Chrissa had once called the pub a classic study in minimalism.

The tavern had a nondescript ambience that seemed to elude the tourists, yet there was something basic and uncluttered about it. Even in the middle of the afternoon, Jimmie kept his place dark. Arthur liked that.

Three years ago when Arthur first strolled into the Surf n' Sun Jimmie had confessed that the only book he had ever read all the way through had been *This'll Kill You*, a mystery novel by a promising thirty year old author named Arthur Argent. With that admission the bartender had won a patron to his pub for life.

Jimmie McLaughlin never talked much about his past, but Arthur felt certain he hadn't cultivated that order-a-drink-or-die look judging beauty pageants. From the patchquilt of conversations they had, Arthur knew that Jimmie still played a mean sax, carried a chunk of shrapnel in his rump that he had received on the first day of the Tet Offensive, that he had lost a teenaged son to a drunk driver over ten years ago, and that he was on his third wife, Veronica, a classy blond Art Major who had attended Boston College and who had an ass as shapely as a cashew nut.

But you had to love a guy who could scare the bejesus out of a kid who was trying to pass a fake ID to him, then wink at a customer before sending the kid off with a load in his BVD's.

The moment Arthur walked inside his surprise struck him dumb. Bright workmen's lights hung snake-like from the rafters, and carpenters sawed away at ply boards in the back of the tavern. Except for him, no other paying customers were inside.

Jimmie stood smiling behind the bar. Arthur took the stool directly in front of him and the bartender poured him a mug from the tap.

"So? What d'ya think?" he asked, the words wrapped around a grin that bordered on shit-eating. He unrolled a blueprint on the counter next to Arthur's beer. "Closin' down for two weeks this afternoon, so kiss this subway tunnel goodbye. That whole back wall goes, and I'm puttin'in some tables with linen tablecloths and a hundred gallon fish tank in the wall behind the bar. I even hired a guy to sculpt me a mermaid."

Arthur looked around, then turned to the bartender. "Jimmie, tell me this is a joke. Three weeks ago you insist that yours is the only bistro on the Jersey shore that has any character, and now you're turning the place into Sea World? Hell, why not cover the room in anchors and fishermen's nets and start serving creme de menthes with the little umbrellas?"His words sounded bitterer than he had intended.

Jimmie watched him chug-a-lug the beer without the mug leaving his lips. He leaned toward Arthur, as if sharing a secret he didn't want the men working in the back to hear.

"Listen, Artie, I'm not givin' this place a facelift for the sole purpose of pissin' you off. The tourists'money is good on this island, so what's wrong with courtin' some of it?" He looked at Arthur's empty mug, and studied the expression on his customer's face. "You keep drinkin' like that, my friend, and your liver will doggie-paddle right out of your mouth. You want to talk about that beehive you're sittin'on?"

With a surgeon's precision, the bartender had opened a vein.

"Sorry. It's been a rough morning, Jimmie. Chrissa's canvases are selling faster than she can paint them and it's like she's not even trying. Every day I watch her paint these incredible masterpieces while I can't write word-one to save my life. Some mornings I feel like I just want to chuck every one of those damned canvases into the Atlantic. God, I hate myself for thinking like some sort of—"

His voice had taken on the tone of a confession, but already he had said too much. He attempted a fast break to another topic. "Speaking of creativity, whose idea was *this* layout? I thought your idea of interior decorating was to tape Miss February to the mirror."

Jimmie smiled the knowing smile of a man not easily fooled by underhanded compliments. He rolled up the blueprint and went to the refrigerator. He took out a quart of what looked like orange juice in a clear plastic container and carried it to Arthur.

"Listen, keep this to yourself. Hell, I haven't even told Ronnie because she'd laugh herself sick. I liked that book you wrote, and you damn well deserved your place on the New York Times Best Sellers'list. And I think I can clean out some of those dust balls in your head."

Arthur looked at the quart of liquid the bartender had placed in front of him. "Jimmie, speak English. I don't have the slightest idea what you're talking—"

"-Artie, you've known me for, what, three years? My present wife is a pretty talented interior decorator, did you know that? Ronnie's not like the last two twinkies. But me? Hell, I've never been creative enough to piss my initials in the sand. Then along comes this stuff and I feel like I could repaint the Sistine Chapel."

He stroked the container. The gesture seemed almost loving.

Jimmie poured the liquid into a shot glass. It looked too thick and mustard-colored to be orange juice, more paste than liquid. A little of it slid down the edge of the glass, and the bartender caught it with his finger, then licked it. "This stuff is expensive. Don't like to waste it. A little goes a long way. Here..."

The liquid clung to the glass like a thick batter. Arthur took the glass and held it to the light as if he expected to see something swimming inside it. "Just how *'expensive'* are we talking?"

Jimmie reached under the counter and rifled through some papers, handing him a business card. "That squirt is on the house, if that's what you mean. A hundred bucks for the first five quarts if you order. The people who make this stuff don't advertise, not in the usual sense. I got a few of these cards when Ronnie sent me to that fat farm last month. I don't know what they put in it, but I tried some while I was there and that convinced me to call. The results were — well, come back to my bar in two weeks and I'll show you the results in mermaids and fish nets."

Arthur looked at the words on the card.

***

Creative Juices Natural Vitamins for the Mind
1-800-DRINKITNOW

"Vitamins? Jesus, Jimmie, I already take every damned vitamin known to Western civilization. This airplane glue better not grow hair on my palms." He sipped the juice. It tasted too sweet for him to identify any recognizable fruit in it, although it had a thick apricot after-taste. He downed the rest in a gulp and pursed his lips. "What'd you say this goop does?"

Jimmy returned the container to the refrigerator and turned to him.

"I'll let you answer that for yourself, Artie. Just wait until you face those blank pages again..."

Natural Vitamins for the Mind . Arthur considered the words as the Scout sped down Ocean Drive. Well, why not? So many middle-aged body parts today seemed either liposuctioned out or silicone-injected in, so who could say what was 'natural' anymore?

With the sticky sweet undertaste still on his tongue, Arthur *did* feel pretty good compared to thirty minutes ago. Damned good, in fact.

Arthur thought of Chrissa, and suddenly he wanted her so badly he almost ached. He hit the gas pedal, his hormones singing *Mammy* all the way home. When he urged Chrissa from her easel, this time he did not wait for her to remove her smock. He took her on the living room floor.

Creative Juices... Natural Vitamins for the Mind .

... And points South, Arthur thought as he pulled his wife's body to his.

An hour later and drenched in sweat, as Chrissa headed for the shower upstairs; still breathing heavily she stopped to turn to Arthur.

"Lover, just what is Jimmie McLaughlin putting into his beer lately? If you'd apply some of that creativity to your writing that you just showed me on our rug, people would forget those clowns Hemingway and Fitzgerald."

He felt the energy of an electric current crackling inside him. Her words hit him like a revelation from God.

... Just wait until you face those blank pages again.

"Jesus, you're right! Why didn't I think of that? Chriss, I feel like I could write a freakin' epic!"

He scrambled for his jeans and stood up without putting on his shirt. Whether inspiration had come from Jimmie's wonder juice or from going belly to belly with Chrissa made no difference. He headed toward the study, and joined her on the staircase. "The next sound you hear will be my muse singing her heart out!" He patted her bottom as he passed her.

"I had no idea your muse was Dr. Ruth Westheimer!" she called from behind him.

Even before Chrissa turned on the hot water, Arthur's muse had begun her aria. He tapped her words upon his IBM keyboard going full-tilt boogie as those creative juices bubbled hot inside his brain. He played the computer keyboard like a possessed pianist for the next twelve hours.

At 2:15 a.m. Arthur finally leaned back in his swivel chair. The ideas had come in such orgasmic bursts he could hardly write them fast enough. He stopped, not because the rush of inspiration had stopped, but because his fingers ached.

He walked downstairs and picked up the bowl of chicken salad Chrissa had left for him, and stepped outside to watch Barnegat Bay shimmer in the moonlight.

Writing was so much like giving birth, he thought. He had no doubt that the thirty-three pages he had written contained the embryo of a best seller. The birthing was nowhere near complete, but tonight he had finally given his new novel a heartbeat.

For the first time in weeks he savored the bay's beauty, and considered waking Chrissa, hoping she might share the moment with him. He had always wanted her to paint the Barnegat under a full moon such as was out tonight. His resentment of her talent had gone, and he felt glad to have sent those thoughts packing.

He looked at her easel, remembering she had expected to complete her seascape today, and he wanted to see her finishing strokes. He removed the flowered sheet and looked at her canvas reflected in the moonlight.

It took a moment for the realization to register. She still had not added the seagulls. Chrissa had not touched the painting since they had made love that afternoon.

***

Nor had she touched it by June 21st. As he did every morning during those three weeks Arthur lifted the...

... covers gently getting out of bed, careful not to awaken Chrissa. She had been having a very bad dry spell lately, and had been feeling depressed about her approaching exhibition.

In three weeks Arthur had consumed all five quarts of Creative Juices and had polished off the last of them the morning before. Yesterday he had called for a new delivery to arrive this morning. The frosty voice on the other end sounded like a nun's whose celibacy had finally gotten to her, but she assured him delivery would be before noon.

Arthur expected the same balding red-faced wisp of a man who had come three weeks earlier. The man had introduced himself as Mr. Howard Goode, but otherwise kept the niceties minimal. The salesman looked like he could use a vitamin supplement himself, or maybe a good laxative. He had handed Arthur a clipboard to sign, carried the cardboard box to the front door, smiled politely, and sped off in a dusty Ford station wagon in bad need of a new muffler.

On that morning Chrissa had gone for a run on the beach. Arthur knew any explanation he might offer her would make him sound like a man ready to cut out paper dolls in a rubber room. How could he explain spending a C-note on five bottles of sticky gunk whose only listed ingredients on the containers were some cryptic vitamins called CSF?

The plastic quarts went immediately behind several six-packs inside the cooler in Arthur's study. Jimmie had advised keeping the liquid's existence a secret, and given how much the stuff cost, that advice seemed pretty sound. Even as Arthur had gulped down the last glass he felt uneasy about the secret he had kept from his wife. Like a man disposing of damning evidence late at night, he walked two blocks to the dumpster where Lilac Street met the bay and discarded the last empty container while Chrissa slept.

He knew his new shipment would arrive before Chrissa awoke. During the past week she had been sleeping past noon, and during two of those days she stayed in bed until late in the afternoon. She had good reason to be so exhausted, given the sexual decathlon that had been going on between their sheets several times a day. Still, until recently Chrissa had been an early riser and lately she seemed tired most of the time. Perhaps this had been her way of calling time out.

He poured himself a cup of coffee and sipped it as he sat on the swivel in his study. Better to concentrate on the novel, he thought. Maybe he could get a few pages done before breakfast.

He read through the final paragraphs of last night's draft and smiled. *Missing Persons* he intended to call his novel about medical students who steal morgue cadavers and exchange their body parts for good grades. As a college journalist Arthur had written an article on the inefficient tag-'em-and-bag-'em attitude in city morgues, so the medical school equivalent of a chop shop was not so far-fetched.

He had written four hundred and fifty pages of *Missing Persons* in just three weeks, and the ideas still wouldn't quit. Arthur asked himself the usual 'What if . . .?' and knew Ms. Muse would soon fill in the rest with her usual serendipity of ideas. He leaned back and waited for her song to begin. He waited for thirty minutes, but the muse sang nothing.

Arthur turned off the computer. He knew what he needed, and until that joyless little turd arrived with the delivery he might as well save the electricity.

He wondered if his dependency on the vitamin-fortified glop hadn't really been a bad case of simple meatballheadedness. How many otherwise clear thinking types became hooked on placebos that contained nothing more potent than Nutri-Sweet? Mind over matter, self-hypnosis, power of suggestion, there were lots of buzz-words for this sort of self- deception. The props varied from rabbits' feet to french kissing the Blarney Stone, but it all came down to one thing: if it made you feel better, it worked.

Was gulping down a magic fruit juice so different? This gluey liquid *worked*. Vitamin CSF, whatever in hell it was, *worked*. He didn't care how and why. If he were fooling himself, he could laugh about it while sipping pina coladas in the Carribean.

But a snarling pit bull growled in a darker cavity of his mind. He had been making voracious love to Chrissa ever since he had started taking the vitamins. Sex had become - he could think of no other word - *necessary*. Like an elixir, the stuff had transformed his lovemaking into some sort of primal urge. At first his wife shared the same supreme pleasure as he concerning the sudden frequency and intensity of their times together. But lately her enthusiasm had flagged with her energy.

The urge burned inside him every day like hot acid. Like the secret inside his refrigerator, he did not share his reasons for his persistence with his wife. But *he* knew his reasons. He knew them well...

... Arthur never wrote more eloquently in his entire life than during the past few weeks after he had made love to Chrissa...

... And Arthur never needed to make love to Chrissa more urgently than after he had downed a frothy glass of Creative Juices.

***

He heard the muffler of the old Ford even before he looked outside. As the station wagon pulled into his driveway...

... Arthur hoped the sound would not awaken his wife. He draped the blankets over her and shut the window just to be sure.

Stepping out to the patio Arthur expected no formalities from Mr. Howard Goode and received none. The man looked like a scarecrow in a cheap suit as he stood by the cardboard box of containers wiping his forehead with his sleeve. Although it was shaping up to be a hot day, the salesman said nothing about the weather.

"A hundred dollars for five quarts, right?" Arthur asked because he could think of nothing else to say. He held out a fistful of twenties.

The man looked at the money in Arthur's hand as if he had just offered him a steaming turd.

"Mr. Argent, I'm afraid there has been a misunderstanding," he said, still wiping his forehead. "You see, one hundred dollars is our introductory price for new customers. But it isn't our standard price."

Arthur felt like grabbing the skinny weasel by the throat, but he knew he should have seen this one coming. Smart consumers had a term for this sort of thing... *Bait and switch* . And smart consumers had another term for the kind of guy who fell for it... *Schmuck* .

"And just what *is* the 'standard price'?"

"One thousand dollars," Goode answered, returning Arthur's leer with his own. "In cash."

For a moment Arthur laughed, thinking the scarecrow had a sense of humor after all. He almost said, "That's a good one, Mr. Goode. Now, seriously . . ."Arthur stared at him, stared at him hard. The expression on Goode's face clearly indicated he had not made a joke.

"Are you crazy? What makes you think I would pay that kind of money?" Arthur practically spit the words at him. "I don't even *have* that kind of—"

"-I'm sorry, Mr. Argent," Goode interrupted, scooping the carton in his arms. "I was hoping we could do business. Most of our customers usually see the benefits of our product. Well, you have our card if you should change your mind..."He slid the carton into the back of the dusty station wagon, and got into his car.

Arthur remembered the half-finished novel inside his IBM and prepared to swallow a mouthful of crow. He leaned toward the driver's window. "Listen, how about just one quart? Let's say a hundred for one quart . . .?"

"I'm sorry," Goode answered without looking at him. He rolled the window up and pulled out of the driveway.

Arthur stepped into the street behind the accelerating old Ford. For a moment he considered picking up a rock and heaving it at the battered station wagon with the belching muffler. Instead he shouted, "Go to hell, you damned thief! I hope you drive into the ocean!"

Suddenly he stopped shouting, dimly aware that he had just committed one mungo screw-up. He turned and looked to the sun deck of his house where Chrissa stood, watching him.

***

Had someone then asked Arthur Argent to explain his reasons for jumping into the jeep, he could not have done so. Chrissa deserved...

... the truth. Later he would try to explain the importance of the vitamins to his writing and hope she did not file for divorce or have him committed. He would show her what he had written and pray she understood. With any luck they would raise two glasses of Creative Juices and together toast *Missing Persons*.

But right now Arthur had a novel to write, and something more urgent waited for him inside the plastic containers in the refrigerator at Jimmy McLaughlin's tavern. He'd lay it all out for Chrissa later, but first he had to lay down some tracks to Jimmie's.

Arthur had not been to the Surf n' Sun since Jimmie had closed for renovations, but he knew the bartender was good for a container or two, and Jimmie would not act insulted if offered money. Better the money should go to him than to that wet fart, Goode.

Jimmie had remodeled the bar front in natural quartz, and Arthur felt he might owe the barman an apology. The renovations clearly were an improvement after all, and good taste had prevailed.

But with a closer inspection something was not right. The large new stained glass window along the front wall outside the tavern had a lengthy crack that ran diagonally in a jagged line from top to bottom, and masking tape traced the crack's path. The glass tiles punched out from the bottom corners made the gaping holes resemble missing teeth. The glass had also been removed from the entrance door's smaller window. Arthur wondered if maybe some local vandals had taken a field trip to Jimmie's to do some remodeling of their own.

He pushed the door open and walked into complete darkness. Arthur could not see ten feet in front of him.

"Jimmie? You in here?" His voice echoed ghost-like in the room. The tavern's silence matched its darkness. "Jimmie?"

He heard a stirring from behind the bar. A flashlight snapped on and shone directly into Arthur's face. He jumped back so quickly he hit the wall with a thump.

"Artie, is that you?" Jimmie asked from his stool behind the counter, his face a half moon in the murky light.

"Jesus Christ, Jimmie! You scared the living shit out of—" Groping the wall, his hand hit the light switch and he snapped it on. Arthur squinted in the semi-darkness to verify that what he saw was really there.

Jimmie's new wall-length fish tank was now a gaping hole framed in shards of broken glass. Dozens of multi-colored tropical fish lay scattered motionless on the floor surrounding Jimmie's stool like assorted gum balls. Several had flopped midway across the room, and Arthur felt one mash beneath his Nike as he approached the counter in the dim light.

Behind Jimmie a headless sculptured mermaid perched precariously alongside the mirror that itself had several massive cobweb cracks as if it had been struck repeatedly with a mallet. The mermaid's wooden head lay in the sink.

Every beer mug and wine glass hanging above the bar had been shattered into fragments. Several wine glass stems dangled overhead. The bar counter had been walloped and gashed.

Tables lay on their sides, and the new bright red seat cushions in the booths had been sliced open and gutted, their stuffing hanging from them like cotton intestines.

"Jimmie... Jesus, Jimmie, what happened?"

"Ronnie. It was Ronnie," he said, as much to himself as to Arthur. The bartender absently snapped the flashlight off and back on. "When she came into the bar after I closed last night— she just went— she just went crazy. She had my kid's baseball bat with her and this steak knife in her pocketbook, and for a moment I thought— I thought she was goin' to—"He reached for the flask under his counter. "She didn't break *this*. It's about the only thing she didn't get to with that damned bat... And my stuff in the cooler," he added with a pained smile. He took a long swig from the flask and swallowed hard.

Arthur carried a battered stool behind the counter and placed it next to Jimmie's. "Did you have a fight? Where is she now?"

"Artie, I wish I knew. I'm afraid to go home, afraid what I'll find there. It's been comin' for a few days. I saw it comin' but I just—I just—"Suddenly his eyes widened as if a mine had exploded inside his brain.

"Artie! Jesus, Artie! Have you been takin' that vitamin stuff, that Creative Juices stuff I told you about?"

"Yeah... In fact that's why I'm—"

"—Jesus H. Christ, Artie! Spill that stuff the hell out! Don't come near it! Oh God, I'm so sorry I ever—!"

Jimmie didn't have to say another word. Somehow Creative Juices, Inc. had a connection to Veronica McLaughlin's rampage.

"Tell me everything," Arthur said, not certain that he really wanted to know. Jimmie handed the flask to him.

"You'd better take a good swallow of this first," he said. Arthur did, and handed it back. Jimmie took more than a good swallow. "I'm sorry about not tellin' you how much money the bastards wanted after the first order, but I only wanted you to get back to writin', and I figured after you sold your book, the money wouldn't—"

"It's okay, Jimmie. Tell me about last night."

"Artie, that juice built this place, you know that? I drank two quarts the first week and did the blueprints myself in one night. And I haven't touched a damned blueprint since I took shop in high school. Suddenly I'm goin' around the house playin' the kid's guitar and listenin' to classical music, for Chrissake. Artie, I hate classical music and I'm listenin' to Beethoven's friggin' Fifth Symphony! And suddenly I've got this brontosaurus in my pants. Two months ago doctors were playing pin ball with my prostate, and suddenly I'm bangin' Ronnie six ways from Sunday like I'm some kinda rabbit!"

Arthur remembered his first taste of the liquid and what followed with Chrissa on the living room floor that same afternoon. He reached for Jimmie's flask." But that much was fine by me,"Jimmie continued. He leaned toward Arthur to grab his shoulder. "You can't blame a guy for wantin' to reawaken the old horn dog, can you? So I keep takin' more of the stuff, and I order enough to see me through the turn of the century. Screw the money, right? I'm havin' me one hell of a time. But I'm so busy creatin' and makin' the beast with two backs which transformin' this pub into a cocktail lounge, and I don't see what's happenin' with Ronnie."

"She suddenly is losing *her* energy..." Arthur added absently, remembering the missing seagulls on Chrissa's canvas.

Jimmie looked at him out of the corner of his eye. "Not just her energy, Artie. She's losin' her damned *talent*. I'm married to Veronica for five years now, and not a day went by that she wasn't designin' somethin' in that portfolio of hers. Suddenly my wife can't draw a line, can't get her ass out of bed. She's cancelin' appointments, watchin' t.v. and shovin' potato chips into her face all day without leavin' the couch! And the pisser is, the more I'm bangin' her, the worse she gets... and the better *I* get! I'm tellin' her to turn off the friggin' t.v. so I can *read,* for Chrissake!"

The bartender looked at the author and laughed bitterly.

"Last night Ronnie shows up here just after last call. Says she wants to see how I'd fixed up the place, 'cause I'd done it myself, though she offered her help before all this stuff started. The last customer leaves, and she says she's got a surprise for me in the car. When she comes back she's got this bat in her hands and she just starts swingin' at everything in the place, everything she can manage to hit — and when she's done swingin' she takes out this knife from her pocketbook and cuts the chair cushions to ribbons. I tried to stop her but I couldn't get near her. She looked like she would do to me what she did to those cushions, but instead she ran out of here screamin' like a banshee."

"What snapped in her?" Arthur asked.

He stopped and grabbed Arthur again. "I think Ronnie was pissed that I took somethin' from her, and she wanted it back. But it's the juice that did it! You know what I think that juice *does*? I think it turns you into some kind of blood sucking leech or a damned vampire bat. Except it isn't blood you suck out—You suck out a little piece of a person's *mind* every time you hit the sack with 'em! Jesus, that's what I think I did! I drank so much of that stuff my wife has practically no mind *left*! Artie, I want you to get this shit out of here now! Take it all! Get it the hell out of my life! I don't want it in the same room with me!"

"Okay, Jimmie. Calm down, okay? I'll take care of it." Arthur opened the refrigerator where an entire carton remained unopened. "Jesus, an hour ago that prick Goode wanted a grand for this stuff."

"There's more in the storage room freezer," Jimmie added. "I just hope it hasn't poisoned us already. I don't even know what's in it."

But Arthur no longer thought of the cases of Creative Juices his friend wanted to unload. He looked at the ruins of Jimmie's Surf n' Sun Tavern, and he thought of Chrissa surrounded by her unpainted canvases, alone, waiting for him...

***

Arthur found Chrissa where he had left her, standing in her robe on the sun deck and watching the sailboats on Barnegat Bay. When he opened the sliding door behind her...

... She did not turn toward him. He stood beside her and took her hand. It felt cold and lifeless.

... she did not turn toward him. He stood beside her and took her hand. It felt cold and lifeless.

"I read the first four chapters of your novel," she said

without changing expression while looking at the bay. "I think it's the best writing you've ever done."

The compliment brought no sense of pride with it. "I wanted to show how sometimes good people do the wrong thing."

"Yes," she agreed and turned to him. "Sometimes they do. Like a good man keeping secrets from his wife." Her words struck like a hard slap.

"And sometimes they get a second chance," he added. He stepped to the sliding door and opened the carton he had carried from the jeep. He poured a tall glass of Creative Juices and brought it to her.

"Vitamins for the mind?" she asked. Before Arthur could respond, Chrissa interrupted him. "I found the card in your wallet while you were out last night. I wondered why you were so secretive about getting rid of those containers in the middle of the night. Two weeks ago I felt like a beer, and I found four containers of this stuff behind your six packs." Her eyes bored into his. "Arthur, I had hoped that after all these years you would have realized that you didn't marry a fool. It's not as if I give a damn about the money but — When you and that bony stranger had your little tiff in our driveway this morning, I made a call. A thousand dollars is an awful lot to pay for Love Potion Number Nine, isn't it? You could have at least asked—"

Arthur handed the glass to her. "Chriss, there's a whole lot more to it than that. I'll explain it all to you, I promise. But I want you to drink this for me now. It'll make you feel better, and it'll make *me* feel better. Will you do this for me?"

"I suppose you'll be wanting us to crawl back into bed for the usual parallel parking, then?" she asked. "Arthur, I'm sorry, but I don't think I have the strength to—"

"I don't think that's going to be a problem," he interrupted, thinking, "... *Not ever again.*"

Chrissa studied the pasty liquid. "You poured only one glass. You're not going to join me?"

"Only in bed... if that's okay with you," he added, as he watched her drink.

The blond woman in the tailored knit suit stared over her Caesar salad at the young woman with the honey-colored hair, as if debating whether to approach her table. The younger woman looked up...

... from her glass of wine and smiled politely. "Excuse me, but do we know each other?"

"You're Chrissa Argent, the artist," the blond woman said, revealing a slight Boston accent as she spoke. She carried her salad to the young woman's table. "I'm Veronica McLaughlin. Your husband and my husband..."

"Jimmy McLaughlin's wife! Yes, I remember you! My husband and yours were good friends," she said. "I guess you and I have some pretty awful things in common. I was so sorry to hear about Jimmie."

"Thanks. I was sorry to hear about Arthur." The woman looked over her shoulder, and lowered her voice to practically a whisper. "The papers didn't tell it all about Jimmie's death. The story got pretty distorted, and people just wanted someone to blame, so I caught a lot of it. But the truth is my husband used to tell me that he never felt like he had amounted to much. The crazy thing is that he spent thousands fixing up that bar of his trying to prove something to himself, then trashed it all in one night. His mind just snapped like a twig. The media fell over one another reporting how the next day he doused himself with the gasoline he took from our lawn mower and threw a match on himself right on our front lawn. I heard one reporter there call it a creative way to die."

She took a hasty drag from her cigarette and plunged her fork into her salad.

"I suppose it's fortunate the papers left out the details. Toward the end our marriage wasn't so great. I don't think we would have made it had he lived. Jimmie resented my work, and in turn he shared nothing in his life with me. The man even used to hide his expensive vitamin juice from me when I was sick, and he had a truckload of the stuff. On the night before he died when

I found some hidden in the refrigerator in his tavern, I drank a whole quart of it just for spite while he was in the can. I told him about it when he came out, and said, 'C'mon, Jimmie. Why don't you take me right now on top of the counter?' I never saw him so furious. But we did it anyway."

For a moment Chrissa almost winced, but a year living in Manhattan had taught her the art of the quick recovery. "I read in House Beautiful that you're living off Central Park West. I'd say you've done pretty well for yourself since Jimmie's death. That's quite a lovely home you redecorated in the Hamptons. The article said you're all the rage among the New York senators' wives."

Veronica pushed a crouton around in her salad bowl. "Well, I suppose that's my cue to act modest now. But actually I showed that issue to everyone I ever knew. I hate to say it, but they would never have done that piece on me when I was married to a bartender." The woman's confession had opened a door, and Chrissa sipped her wine as if measuring her next words. "Veronica, I'd like to share a secret with you too. My husband was the same way. Arthur felt such resentment over my paintings; he'd blame me when he couldn't write. His writer's block finally proved too much for him, I guess, and your husband's death pushed him over the top. On the night after Jimmie died Arthur locked me inside our bedroom closet. I screamed for hours, and when the police finally showed up in the morning, they found my husband on the concrete beneath our sun deck with his neck broken."

The two women stared hard at each other and smiled knowing smiles.

"Our stories have much in common," Veronica said.

"Yes. Strange the way they seem to parallel and intersect one another as they do."

"No one could make up two stories like that."

"No one..."

Again the two women smiled.

"It's funny,"Chrissa added, "but as much as I thought I loved Arthur, I never painted better in my whole life than after that happened. My July 4th exhibition got me started, and that was barely a week after Arthur died. And then, of course, there was my novel."

Veronica smiled. "A best seller too, I hear. I promise to read it the first chance I get. What's it called again?"

"*Creative Juices,*" Chrissa said. "I guess I got the idea from my husband. On the day he died the police found his jeep filled with cartons of those same vitamins Jimmie used to take. Of course, the police wanted to know why a man would kill himself who had enough vitamins to last him into Social Security. I told them what Arthur had told me, that Jimmie just wanted to get rid of the stuff and gave the whole load to him." "I remember," said Veronica. "The police came to ask me to verify that a few weeks later, and asked me the same thing about why Jimmie would have built a brand new bar. I told them maybe Jimmie just wanted to get rid of his vitamins for the same reason he took apart his bar. They say suicides do that, like taking care of unfinished business. The police didn't ask any more questions after that."

Chrissa sighed. "Well, at least something good came out of it because all that emphasis on those vitamins gave me the idea for my novel. There's these medical students who steal cadavers because they discover CSF creates a powerful fortified vitamin. Guess I've become something of an expert on vitamin supplements considering the stockpile my husband left in his Scout. I've got to admit the stuff works pretty well, too, when taken with a twenty-five year old male chaser."

"I'll second that," Veronica said, smiling. "But just what is CSF supposed to be, or do I have to buy the book?"

"Cerebral spinal fluid," said Chrissa as she took a cigarette from a silver holder. "It's used as a kind of shock absorbent, the liquid that surrounds and flows through the brain..."

About the author: Former teacher Ken Goldman, an affiliate member of the Horror Writers Association, has homes on the Main Line in Pennsylvania and at the Jersey shore. His stories appear in over 565 independent press publications in the U.S., Canada, the UK, and Australia with over twenty due for publication in 2011. He has written two books, "You Had Me At ARRGH!!" (Sam's Dot Publishers) and "Desiree" (Damnation Books).

Another Piece Of The Pie

Shea Hennum

"Why?" I asked.

"Because I love you, of course," she replied, her head tilted, her smile wider than the Grand Canyon.

"That's insane," I said.

"And you are free to have your opinions," she replied.

"It doesn't strike you as crazy?" I shouted.

"Oh, hun," she said, putting her arms around me. "You don't think I'm crazy, do you?"

I pushed her away, shouting: "Of course you're fucking crazy!"

She frowned, a faint scent of anger pouring off her. "What?"

"You're clearly..." I noticed her fist tighten and her forehead crunch. I decided not to finish my statement.

"You don't love me more?" she asked—the most frightening thing was the sincerity with which she said it.

"What?" I asked.

"You don't love me *more*?"

"Why would I love you more?"

"Because I'm the whole pie now."

"You're what?"

"Love is like a pie, and now I'm the whole pie."

"The whole...? What does that even mean?"

"You were giving your love away, and not to me, so I took it."

"You took it?"

"I wasn't getting one-hundred percent, so I took what I wasn't getting."

"You say that like it's no big deal!"

"It's not? I *deserve* all of your love."

"I don't give a fuck what you think you deserve," I shouted, "you can't fucking kill people!"

"But now we can be together, for all time," she said,

56

grabbing me by the collar and pulling me close, a very sensual smile on her face.

"No," I said, pushing her away again. "I can't... I gotta turn you in, this is... I have to do *something.*"

"Oh, you're silly. The police won't find anything," she said. "Now," —talking off her shirt as she says it—"Marci won't be back for another three hours, so we have the whole place to ourselves." She flashes that smile, again, that off-kilter smile that I can't seem to shake.

"They won't find anything? What? What does that—" She kisses me with some newfound vigor and interrupts me.

"I" —kiss—"made sure" —kiss—"there" —kiss—"wasn't—"

"Stop!" I shouted, pushing her back. "Stop it! We're fucking through! This isn't right. This isn't fucking right!"

"Oh, you don't mean that, silly," she said, coming back at me.

I pushed her away, a third time.

"No, I do!" I shouted. "You burned my fucking books—"

"They were a distr—"

"And I don't even want to know what you did to Mark!"

"He was a distraction, too." Her voice is perpetually monotonous.

"A distraction from what?" I shouted.

"From me, of course." That smile...that fucking smile.

Her teeth bared like a deranged dog, her tits out like some macabre porno.

"And what about my parents?" I asked. "What the fuck are you going to do when they visit? You gonna burn them in a fucking trashcan on the front lawn, too?"

"God dammit!" she shouted. She knocks a vase off the table and flips it, shouting: "God dammit, God dammit! God dammit!"

She's screaming and thrashing and trying to destroy anything and everything within arm's reach. I grabbed her by the shoulders and turned her around.

"Jesus Christ!" I shouted. "Calm the fuck down!"

She begins to cry, her face going pale and her cheeks

going cherry red, tears streaking down her face. "I'm sorry, I'm sorry! I just want to make you happy."

"You did, before you started doing God knows what to my friends, to my fucking stuff."

"But don't you see?" she shouted.

"See what?"

"They were taking you away from me."

"Stop saying that."

"It's true!"

"It's not true," I said. "It's not true. We were solid 'til you jumped off the deep-end."

"I didn't jump off the deep-end," she defended herself. "I was doing what was best. And I will deal with your parents, and then you will see."

"Are you hearing yourself?" I said. "This is fucking lunacy."

"It's fine," she said. "I know you love me"

"I can't do this," I said. I let go of her and made my way to the door. "Don't bother bringing me any of my shit, you can have it."

"No!" she shouted, grabbing my arm and pulling me back. "No, no, no! You have to stay! J-just stay, a-and, and when I get rid of your parents—"

"Listen to yourself!"

"When I get rid of your parents you'll be all mine, and then we'll be happy!"

"Have a nice life, you psycho bitch. I'm out."

"No!" she shouted, pleading. "Please don't go!"

"Are you kidding me?" I asked. "I should've left the second you used 'left' and 'no' in the same sentence."

"You just need to think for a while," she said, exhaling deeply trying to calm someone—I'm not sure if her target was her or me—down. "Tomorrow your parents will be out of the picture and you'll realize that loving only one person is so much more fulfilling. You'll see, I just know it!"

"What about me?" I asked, pointing at myself.

"Huh?" she asked.

I chuckle—out of fear? —"I'm the most egocentric person

I know!"

She looks confused, perplexed.

I laugh harder now. "I love myself as much as I loved Mark, my parents, much more than any of that shit you 'got rid of.'"

Her smile disappears into a look of zoned-out confusion.

"This relationship has clearly been screwed since Jump Street, I was just too stupid to notice."

I turned around and pulled open the door. I heard the 'clink' and 'clank' of porcelain on porcelain. I heard a wail, and before I could step through the door I felt sharp pain in my back. I tried to turn, but felt a sharp stab in the base of my skull that overwhelmed me before I got a chance.

"That's...?" I asked.

"Uh-huh," the reaper said.

"Wow," I said.

"Yeah," the reaper mumbled.

"I really look like shit," I said, tilting my head.

"Everyone thinks that," the reaper said. "Its fine, you look good."

The reaper takes me by the shoulders and turns me around the face the bright, shining door.

"She really was a psycho, right?" I asked. "Like, I wasn't just imagining it, she was crazy, right?"

"Oh, God yes," the reaper said with a laugh.

About the author: Shea Hennum is a young writer whose work has been featured in/on Shrunken Wool, Pulp Empire, www. BleedingCool.com , Redcarpetcrash.com, and is scheduled to appear in Make Something.

X

Cutter Slagle

Thursday, September 17, 2009
1:00 PM

Staying two steps behind in her new, snakeskin Manolo Blahnik stilettos, Maxi Porter followed the man that she had been instructed to kill by the end of the day.

The *click, click, click* her heels made on the clean, white concrete was anything but soothing. Any other day, the sound would have been like music, and Maxi would have tried to find a rhythm as she strutted down the street. But not today. Today, the clicking was annoying, painful even. Like nails down a chalkboard.

The blistering sun began to beat down and under her blonde bob wig she began to sweat. Like a raindrop, a clear trickle ran down the left side of her face, but before it could sting her dark eye, she swiped at it with her perfectly manicured fingers. Already fall and the California heat still hadn't taken a vacation. Beverly Hills seemed to be a sauna, and the strip of Rodeo Drive was starting to feel like red hot coals.

As she continued to follow, passing crystal clear glass storefronts and tall, expensively priced item buildings, Maxi made notice of the less than crowded streets. Thank God, she sighed. In this sweltering weather where not even the large, money green leaves of a Palm tree could offer shade, the last thing she wanted was to be surrounded by a huge amount of people. Or worse, tourists.

Mr. X, as she referred to the man whose life she was going to end, never turned around. Maxi knew he wouldn't. He was someone who never looked back, just always forward, and that had been one of the qualities that she had come to admire most about him. His confidence. Most multiple Academy Award winners portrayed different characteristics. Cocky, shallow, maybe even a little immature. But not Mr. X. No, he was smart.

He was passionate. He was proud.

Maxi placed the suit he was wearing, well half a suit. The jacket was missing, but the black pinstriped pants were intact, along with a crisp, button down white dress shirt rolled at the sleeves. His smooth, blonde hair was slicked back, and she knew he would be wearing his Ray Bans to shade his light gray eyes from the glowing sun.

Watching him, admiring him, Maxi thought she might be sick. She clutched her large brown Louis Vuitton bag even tighter, feeling the weight of the gun at the bottom of her purse. She was almost sent over the edge. Tears instead of sweat ran the course of her face this time, and she didn't bother to clean them up. Instead, she let her large, dark sunglasses conceal her sorrow and desperation.

How? She asked. How did I get to this place in my life? Maxi stopped, turned, and struggled to look at herself in a shop window. Wig covering up long, brunette, locks, off white button down rain coat that stopped at her knee, bought just for this occasion. Trembling, tanned bare legs. She didn't recognize herself. Didn't know herself. Didn't *want* to know herself.

I thought I could do this, she thought. But I can't. I don't want to, I won't! But ultimately she knew she had to. Maxi Porter was a woman who no longer had a choice.

Saturday, March 14, 2009
7:30 PM

"Another Vodka Martini, dirty, please." She didn't feel the buzz yet, but desperately wanted to. Who in the hell does Richard think he is? Maxi thought. Perhaps it was the anger coiling through her that was causing the liquor to take a slow effect. Probably, she considered. Because Maxi wasn't just angry, she was downright furious. Her cheeks flushed, she knew not because of the alcohol. Her hands clenched, almost on their own it seemed, into fists, and she felt her brow forward.

Maxi sat at the Polo Lounge Bar in the Beverly Hills Hotel—alone. The high wooden chair with small cushion didn't offer much comfort, causing her to grow more aggravated. The large, rectangular black and white horse portrait behind the bar prevented her from seeing her reflection. But Maxi knew that with an off the shoulder, solid black dress, black pumps, and hair pulled back into a twist, that she definitely looked the part. She recognized the stale scent of cigar smoke from a nearby booth overpowering that of her Chanel Number Five, and wanted to scream.

"Your drink, miss." She nodded at the bar tender, only really noticing the murky, wet beverage and round, electric green olives. As if on cue, her mouth began to water, and once fisted hands, now relaxed and reached out eagerly to begin nursing her cocktail.

"Rough night?"

She turned to her left, halfway through her drink, and still cursing Richard for making her come to the benefit alone. Maxi didn't need a proper introduction; she knew the man standing beside her in the tailored tux was David X.

"You could say that, Mr. X." She saw confusion spread across his face, form wrinkles, and almost laughed.

"I'm sorry, do I know you? Have we met?"

"Not formally. Hi, I'm Maxine Porter." Maxi thrust out her right hand, using more force than she had intended. Legs on the chair quickly began wobbling, and she thought she might spill out of it. That was until David interfered, and she felt him reach out with one hand and grab her, preventing the fall.

"Whoa, you're drunk."

"Yes, more so than what I had thought," she willingly admitted. The fact still didn't stop her from finishing the last of her Martini.

"So, Maxi Porter, as in Richard Porter?"

"Exactly as in Richard Porter, the director from your latest project." She watched him nod, take a sip of what appeared to be Scotch on the rocks, and then clocked his ring finger even though she knew it wasn't vacated. A solid gold band winked back at her.

"And where is Richard tonight?"

Maxi's shoulder's rose into a shrug. "Toronto, I believe. Filming a new masterpiece of some sort."

"Aw, I see."

"And what about you, Mr. X? Have the night off from shooting or are you between roles at the moment?"

"David, please, and it's the latter," he said. "Earning a second Best Actor Oscar garners me some vacation time. I believe so, anyway." Her eyes never left him as he threw back the rest of his drink, and placed the small stemless glassware down on the granite bar. Maxi wondered how much *he* had had to drink.

"Not to mention," he continued, "my last experience filming left me stressed and quite exhausted."

"What do you mean?" Maxi asked, titling her head sideways in curiosity.

"Your husband's a prick to work with."

"Funny, Richard said the same thing about you."

David didn't seem surprised. "We didn't much see eye to eye. Needless to say, we won't be collaborating on anything anytime soon."

"Hmm," Maxi mumbled, running her tongue across her teeth, contemplating. And then said, "How about *your* wife? Is she here?"

"No," David said, "she's also out of the country."

"I see," Maxi said, repeating his words from moments before.

"You know," he began, and then stopped and Maxi spied him steal a glance at his watch. No doubt a Rolex. "It's late, you're drunk. I think I should call you a car."

Maxi stood; staggered, noticed she came up to his chest. "It is late, I am drunk, but I think you are too."

"So?"

"So, I have a better idea. Instead of a car, let's get a room."

Thursday, September 17, 2009
1:10 PM

And that's how it had all started. A drunken night of lustrous, meaningless sex at the Beverly Hills Hotel, eventually spinning like a rapid top into a regular, weekly encounter, and that of course, turning into unexpected love. Maxi sighed to herself; a lot had gone down during the short time period of just six months.

The clicking again, reminded Maxi of where she was and her task at hand. David, still briskly walking in front of her, oblivious to her presence, seemed to have no destination in particular.

Maxi didn't see herself as a slut, a whore or her relationship with Mr. X an affair. It was fate. Two people in the midst of an awful marriage, finally finding each other, and making the absolute best they could from the situation. Maybe not exactly Cinderella, Maxi thought, and definitely not a fairy tale, her life, but she thought she still deserved to be happy. She wanted to be happy, and dammit, Mr. X made her so happy.

Maxi came to a sudden halt. Mr. X had ducked into a store, and after waiting a few beats, Maxi followed him in. Large, gold italic letters sparkling bright, the single title said it all—Cartier.

Maxi couldn't help but wonder if David was buying jewelry for the wife or the mistress. And then, swiftly, Maxi was launched back into a memory, the first time Mr. X had ever surprised her with a gift.

Wednesday, June 10, 2009
12:15 AM

"You don't like them, do you?"

"No, that's not it. I didn't say that." She tightly slammed down the navy velvet lid to the small box containing the biggest diamond earrings she had ever seen.

"You didn't say *anything*, Maxi. You look disappointed, and I want to know why." David was angry, and she didn't necessarily blame him.

He paced around their regular room at the Beverly Hills Hotel in a white robe, which was alluding to Maxi's headache. Or maybe it was the bubbly champagne that was causing the beige walls; queen sized bed, and modern décor to swirl around in her head, inflicting pain. Or maybe it wasn't a headache at all, Maxi contemplated. Maybe it was actually a heartache.

"David, our relationship has never been about gifts. That's not why I'm here."

"I know," he said. "But I wanted to surprise you, show you how much you really mean to me."

She closed her eyes, squeezed the bridge of her nose. "But you don't need jewelry to do that."

He threw up his hands in frustration, Maxi knew, and then stepped past the long, silk curtains and onto the balcony. She gave him a few minutes and then joined him. Across the soft carpet, onto the small, dark landing next to him. Also in a white robe, she reached for his hand, tried to guess what he was thinking about, where his mind was. When he didn't give her any clues, she turned, focused her attention on the view.

Beautiful. The city sparkled like her new earrings. Stars filling the dark and hazy sky, buildings lit up as if on holiday. Rough mountains trying to peek out in the distance, and the far off cry of bustling traffic and angry horns. Maxi always wondered why Los Angeles hadn't been nicknamed 'The City That Never Sleeps.'

"You want a ring, don't you?" His voice was practically a whisper, she had to strain to hear and even then she wasn't completely sure she had been correct.

"Excuse me?"

"I saw your expression, Maxi. First, excitement and then after you opened the box your face fell utterly flat. You expected me to propose."

"David, I—"

"Am I right?"

"David, please."

"Just tell me if I'm right."

After several long minutes passed, she finally answered, "Yes, okay. Yes. David, I love you and want to—"

"Maxi, I love you too. But this is the best I can do right now. My career is finally where I've always wanted it to be. A scandal right now would only ruin things." You understand, right?"

She nodded, fighting to hold back the stinging tears. Maxi hated that she really did understand, and expected nothing less from Mr. X.

Thursday, September 17, 2009
1:25 PM

The air was stuffy in the store, almost suffocating, as if a tight, thick fist was holding her firmly by the neck. Maxi couldn't fight the tears now, and again let them fall and take residence on her face. To prevent a scene, she braved the heat outside, and exited the shop.

Her lungs felt as if they might burst. She craved water, ached for it. Maxi pulled her bag off her shoulder, slightly remembering bringing a bottle from home. She placed her hand in the purse, began digging. Her fingers didn't brush against the round plastic bottle, but instead, against the cool, metal gun.

Maxi felt her knees buckle, heard the *snap*, and thought she might fall. She urgently reached out and took hold of the stucco building, catching herself.

A deep breath, and then another. Relax, she told herself. But how on Earth could she relax when she was getting closer to committing murder.

Maxi leaned against the side, considered letting herself slide down to the pavement. She bent at the waist, positioned her head down, sighed slowly.

Maybe this could have played out differently, she thought. If she would have refused more strongly, or perhaps bargained better, then she wouldn't be here, in this impossible predicament.

Dammit, her mind vibrated with would and could have's. And then her thoughts seemed to twist around unconsciously, all inevitably going back to that night. That night that sat at the awful core of this chain of events.

Thursday, September 10, 2009
10:30 PM

Who in the hell was at her door? Richard wasn't home, of course, and though deep down Maxi wanted it to be David, she regrettably knew it wasn't. Only at the hotel, never at each other's home—an agreed upon imperative.

Another knock and Maxi was trying to place its owner by the soft, subtle noise. Still no idea, and tired of playing the guessing game, she unbolted and gently pulled the door open.

"Hello, Maxi."

She tried to disguise her sudden shock, knew she hadn't succeeded. There was a reason she wasn't an actress. Maxi felt her eyes widen, probably from their normal kiwi size to that of ripe oranges. Her breathing stilled, and her mouth became painfully dry.

"Good," the woman said, entering the house through the small open space on her own accord. Maxi received an overwhelming scent of vanilla. "I can tell from your expression that you know who I am. At least now we won't have to go through *that* song and dance."

"W-w-we've never met," Maxi stuttered out, shutting the front door that now seemed to weigh a ton. She turned, faced the other woman. What was she going to say? Do? So quickly now, back to the guessing game and she didn't welcome it. Not knowing felt like dozens of tiny, sharp needles prickling deep into her soft skin.

"No, you're right," the woman agreed, "We haven't." Maxi watched as the woman walked from the poorly lit, tiled foyer and into the wide, carpeted living room. Without being asked, she took a seat on the large, leather couch.

Maxi held her position strongly at the door. "I'm not sure I understand as to why you are here."

"Oh," the woman started, then made a *tsk tsk* sound. The noise made Maxi see red in both anger and annoyance. "If you think about it real hard I'm sure you can come up with the answer."

"I-I-I—"

"You've been screwing my husband for the past several months."

Maxi lost her balance. Her small feet tangled in her silk slippers, and she tumbled to the hard floor. She stayed down for a moment, closed her eyes, and prayed that when she opened them again Ashland would be gone, and the encounter nothing more than a forgettable nightmare.

"Careful, dear." No such luck. "I need you well, and all of your two hundred and six bones intact."

Maxi found the strength to stand; walked into the living room and flipped a switch. A diluted yellow light spilled into the room. She couldn't take the suspense, no more beating around the bush. This was really happening. The possibility had always been there, in the back cobwebs of her mind. It was time to be a big girl.

"What are you doing here, Ashland? And what do you want."

"I like your change of attitude, respect it."

"You didn't answer my question."

"In short, I want you to kill my husband."

A huge fit of laughter rippled through Maxi and quickly burst out. After she collected herself, she said, "Seriously, what do you want."

Maxi saw the woman stand, saw the intensity and purpose in her eyes; watched as Ashland came to her, stopped by the small table Maxi stood behind. The swiftness and determination of the other woman's motions prevented Maxi from blinking. And abruptly there was a manila folder staring up at her.

"Go ahead, open it. I brought it especially for you."

Maxi had trouble finding her voice. But then, "I d-d-don't—"

"Open it now!" Ashland's livid voice rang out, echoing throughout the living room, causing Maxi to take a step backwards.

"Okay," she said. She reached out with shaking hands, picked up the feather light folder, and opened it.

Pictures, lots of them. All different sizes, all captured at different angles, some black and white, some in color, but all depicting the same graphic and incriminating evidence—Maxi and Mr. X at the Beverly Hills Hotel.

"Will you excuse me?" Maxi didn't wait for an answer. She ran from the living room, through the foyer, and took a hard left right into the bathroom. With more vigor than she had intended, she slammed the door shut.

"Dammit!" She said aloud, putting the lid down to the porcelain toilet and taking a seat. She avoided the mirror that was directly across from her. The last thing she wanted to see was herself. Lavender lay thick in the air from her earlier bubble bath. The smell was now nauseating.

Maxi noticed for the first time Richard's small black tape recorder on the marble counter top in front of her. It was usually attached to his hip, and his relentless motive of having it so he would never forget a good idea rang through her ears. Richard, she groaned. She contemplated picking up the device and smashing it.

She had to get herself together, line up her thoughts. And Maxi knew she couldn't very well do that while hiding out in the bathroom.

Goosebumps invaded her body, and she realized she was unexpectedly cold. She made it to the sink, patted warm water to the back of her neck, and before leaving the bathroom, grabbed her terrycloth robe from the back of the door, and wrapped herself comfortably in it.

"Nice robe." Ashland had resumed her seat on the couch. "Kind of bulky though, don't you think?"

Maxi ignored her, stopping again at the table. "Just tell me what you want, okay."

"I already did," Ashland said. "I want you to kill my husband."

"I don't understand. Kill? How?"

"Shoot him, stab him, choke him, screw him until he drops dead. I don't care about particulars, I just want him dead."

Maxi chose her next words carefully. "And just what exactly would my incentive be for killing David?"

It was Ashland's turn to laugh. High pitched, shrill—Maxi despised the sound. "I just showed you, the pictures. Surely you couldn't have erased them from your mind that easily."

Maxi swallowed the large, unsettling lump that had formed in her throat. "So, I either kill your husband or what? You're going to send these pictures to my husband?"

"You make it sound so simple, so monotonous. But I

think I can fix that little problem. Here's the deal; my husband cheated on me. He took our five year marriage and threw it down the drain as if it were some sort of disposable scrap of food."

"Ashland—"

"He betrayed me, and now I want him dead. Good, old fashion revenge. I can't think of anything more satisfying than that."

"Then hire a hit man," Maxi ordered, holding onto the table so she wouldn't fall down again.

"You know, I actually considered that. But then I thought that a professional would be too messy. Too many things could go wrong, lead back to me."

"Instead you're going to put it all on my shoulders."

"Precisely," she said, without the slightest bit of emotion, causing Maxi to break out in a panic induced sweat. She took off her robe, placed it on the table. "Two birds, one stone. You killing my husband takes care of punishing the both of you."

"You're insane. I'm not going to kill David."

"I think you'll change your mind about that. If you don't kill David, yes, I will send these pictures to Richard. I'm guessing he won't take too kindly to the affair and in turn will divorce you."

"So?" Maxi threw the word out with no hesitance.

"And since you married Richard after he made his millions, I'm guessing the prenup you undoubtedly signed says you get nothing for your infidelities."

"You know, David loves me. And I love him, and he won't—"

"Please, honey. David loves himself, his career. And if this got out he would be ruined in Tinsletown and therefore done with you. He's not going to leave me for you, he's not going to marry you. If you don't do this, you will be left broke and alone."

"And if I do this, what exactly is going to stop you from going to the police?"

"Well, you'll just have to trust that I won't. I mean, I trust that you won't go to the police and inform them of this conversation. Of course, you don't have proof, and there's the consequential fact that a picture is worth a thousand words. And

I've got over a hundred pictures."

"Ashland, I don't—" Maxi's voice came out barely audible, and then stiffly dropped off.

"I'll assume your answer's yes. You have one week. If it's not done by then, I'd suggest you start packing your bags, because I will be personally delivering a folder much like the one I gave you tonight to your husband."

Thursday, September 17, 2009
1:40 PM

This was it. As Mr. X briskly walked from the store, Maxi fell in line behind him. It seemed as if he was on mission, walking fast, intently heading to the exclusive parking garage where he had parked his Mercedes earlier.

Pedestrians with bags, parking meters, store logos—everything became a blur as Maxi rushed to keep up, increasing her pace severely.

She entered the garage behind him. The burning sun was no longer an obstacle, and Maxi relished in the small delight of darkness and shade.

He was parked close to the entrance. The silver emblem on the hood of the car stood out, as if it were standing up and waving. Mr. X had his keys out, deactivating the alarm, and she promptly made her move.

Hand in purse, she grasped the butt of the gun, brought it to the surface of her bag, and made adequately sure the safety was off. This was definitely it.

"David X, can I get an autograph?" She didn't recognize the sound of her own voice as the lie fell out.

He turned, smiling, always eager to greet a fan, she knew. But then he saw the gun, undeniably becoming all too aware of his surroundings, and Maxi didn't have to guess. Mr. X knew what was coming next.

"No, please," he began pleading. "I have money and my car. T-t-take it, it's yours. J-j-just please, don't shoot me."

Maxi couldn't breathe, and gulped helplessly for air. She raised the gun, pointed it, and tried to steady her jittery hand.

"Why are you doing this? Who are you?" Confusion and fear filled his voice, causing Maxi to loathe herself even more.

"I'm the girl who's in love with you." And then, gun aimed and loaded, she pulled the trigger.

Monday, September 14, 2009
9:30 AM

She had to talk to David. Had to explain, had to enlighten him of the most recent events. Maxi paced in the warm, colorful study, not really taking in her environment. She kept her attention focused on the rough, hardwood floor that she kept stepping across.

David was out of the country, she knew. Re-shooting some scenes for some movie. He hadn't returned any of her calls, was still oblivious to Ashland's threats. Maybe together they could come up with something, form a plan of some sort.

Finally, three rings and then a disgruntled, "Yes?"

"David, thank God."

"I'm shooting; I told you I would be extremely busy the last few days."

"I know, David and I'm sorry. But—"

"You shouldn't be calling me on my cell anyway. What if Ashland were to get hold of the phone bill?"

"That's what I have to talk to you about."

"Listen, the director's motioning for me, I have to go. Don't call me again. I will talk to you when I get back to LA in a couple of days."

"David—wait! Please!" But there was nothing on the other end of the line. Just dead silence. Mr. X was gone.

Thursday, September 17, 2009
1:42 PM

That had been the last time she had spoken with David, and now she was watching him slowly die. He didn't deserve this. Maxi couldn't let him die all alone, not knowing how much he was loved.

She knelt down beside him, scuffed her bare knee on the rough flooring, but didn't care. Reaching up, Maxi removed the wig and sunglasses. Wet streaks stained her face, and in response to David's expression, she swore her heart stopped beating.

"Maxi, I d-d-don't understand."

"No, baby. Don't talk." She lay next to him, took hold of his hand and squeezed. His breathing was shallow, almost not existent. Blood stained his white shirt, leaking from the tiny dime sized hole in his chest.

"I love you, Maxi." It was all over. Sprawled out on the ground by his luxury car, Mr. X spoke his last words.

She lifted his still, warm hand and placed it on his chest. For the first time she noticed the bulge in his upper left shirt pocket. Maxi peeled the pocket open, removed its contents. She acknowledged the box immediately—Cartier. She guardedly opened the lid and a pathetic groan erupted from deep inside of her.

Maxi had suspected the next part to be difficult, but now, she knew it was going to be pretty damn simple, rewarding almost. She was going off script.

First, she opened her purse wide and removed the small tape recorder. Documenting Ashland's blackmail had been the smartest thing she had ever done. Maxi placed the device next to Mr. X where it could effortlessly be seen. Ashland would be responsible for her own sins.

Next, Maxi opened the jewelry box again, carefully took out the diamond engagement ring and placed it on her left hand. David *was* going to propose.

Finally, Maxi reached out and grasped Mr. X's hand one last time. She held it so tight that her own began turning bone white. And then, raising the gun again, calmly and collectively this time, she put the barrel to her temple and pulled the trigger.

About the author: Cutter Slagle is a graduate of The Ohio State University. He has a bachelor's degree in English and a minor in creative writing. He's previously had five short stories and four poems published for online magazines. The magazines include: *The Cynic, Yellow Mama, The Hog Creek Review*

Literary Journal, Orchard Press Mysteries, Short Fiction & Poetry, and *Static Movement.* His latest psychological suspense story, "Examination," was recently chosen for the third annual print edition of *Static Movement.* He is currently seeking representation for his first novel, *Bad Actress.*

THE MISSING MUSE
Clara Waibel

In the blink of an eye, every news channel was mentioning Dawson in rather demeaning ways.

The tabloids were a bit kinder (to much of anyone's surprise) as they claimed 'Famous artist goes completely bananas'.

Dawson James, renowned painter and poet, was found by friends in his apartment, malnourished and apparently delusional. He had been cloistered for three weeks having no sort of social contact.

The only signs which showed he was alive were the soft, Celtic instrumental songs which came from his apartment everyday from four to six. The songs weren't loud or low, long or short. They were just the perfect daily dose of tranquillity and peace.

In later documentaries, Dawson's neighbors stated that during those hours children behaved, no one shouted; everyone smiled and felt better about their existence. It seemed they had fallen under some sort of spell.

Few people claimed that the enchanting music was of a special kind, supposed to please Muses. Specifically Arabella, Dawson's favourite.

After weeks of reclusion, it was hard to believe Dawson had even the slightest resemblance to a sane man, especially when his best friend broke through the door to find him shouting desperately that his Muse had been kidnapped.

Family and friends soon booked him to be taken to a mental facility, but Dawson James was faster and in less then four hours, he was gone.

***

Most people don't believe in Muses. But then again, who can blame them?

Muses are beings which bring inspiration to people, taking part on many stories of Greek mythology. In some of them there were only three Muses, in others, nine; they varied in shape and many times didn't have one at all.

Due to such inconsistencies regarding their origins as well as general lack of proof, people stopped hearing them in the wind or feeling them at the sea. Soon humanity forgot about Muses.

Yet Muses didn't forget about humanity.

Few know that right now there are billions of Muses inspiring billions of people without them noticing it. Just had an incredible idea or a sudden inspiration? That's because a Muse just passed by and kissed the tip of your nose.

They often operate like in the tales: Invisible, unnoticed and discredited. They can also choose freely their shape, and that's the main cause of the discrepancy from early stories.

Few humans reckon their existence and fewer had a direct encounter with a Muse, not to mention endless conversations. Dawson was one of these fewer. As time passed by, he and Arabella became great friends and he confided in her much more than in many humans.

***

Two days after his escape, Dawson found himself wondering around the Forest of Dean, an ancient woodland at the western part of Gloucestershire. He had a good notion on how to camp and survive outdoors, which was quite valuable to him during his journey.

Although camping facilities could be more comfortable, he had a famous face and the last thing he wanted was to call any sort of attention.

As he sat by the fire at night, he remembered all the clues that had led him from his big yet cosy apartment nearby London to that exact place.

The first hint came to him while he ran through the streets and bumped into a blind old beggar, who claimed he had seen someone take Arabella against her will.

Dawson knew Muses showed up to all people including the blind; they had no discrimination on whom to inspire.

"Poor thing!" cried the beggar. "I loved that little one; from all her sisters, she was meh favourite. So sweet and kind! I'm sure they headed towards the Queen's Alleys."

The second clue lied on a gnome who worked as an all-trades man under an old cement bridge in the Alleys.

The neighbourhood of the Alleys looked forgotten, messy and dirty; nothing alike Dawson's in the fancy and hip part of town. Varied shapes of ugly graffiti could be seen stamped everywhere, from around broken windows to decadent building façades.

The Alleys looked like anything but an honest place, which seemed to suit well a gnome since they carried a doubtful reputation and a gift for lying.

"We gotta blend in nowadays," explained the tiny creature as it noticed Dawson's confused stare at it. The gnome looked like an old man in a child's body: tiny and wrinkled. It had two giant ears badly hidden by a black woollen cap, and it dressed an larges jumpers. Its trousers dropped way below its waist line and its voice was as sly as its appearance proposed it to be.

"I saw ye Muse, bean. The bloke bought golden strings, and we all know what that's for." He lifted a brow towards Dawson, frowning his entire forehead. "I ain´t in the Muse likin´ business, but Arabella was a good one. She came from some woods in Gloucestershire and that's the only place she can be killed. The bloke is doin´ it, ye be sure."

"Did you see what he looked like?" he asked as blood rushed through his veins. The idea of someone killing his little treasure was unbearable.

"Ne, he had a balaclava just like ´em damn spies. But he was big. And I ain´t saying that ´cause ye ´ll look alike to me; this bloke was really big."

***

Dawson James first met Arabella, direct descendant of Calliope, one of the most famous Muses in Greek mythology, when he was sixteen years old.

"What are you?" he asked puzzled as he spotted tiny Arabella walking through the pages of an art book.

"I am a Muse." she answered as if it was the silliest question in the world. "Look!" she pointed to Bridge over a Pond of Water Lilies. "I inspired this one."

"You inspired Monet?"

She nodded. "And who are you?" asked her gentle voice in a large smile.

"I...I'm Dawson." he answered trying to hide his red face. Something in Arabella's soft and warm ways made him feel like giggling, but naturally, he would control such urges by clearing his throat and trying to look as manly as possible to impress her.

During their ten years of relationship Dawson came across many Muses but none like Arabella: smiley in her 6 inches, the little woman's brown curly threads flowed as if there was no gravity in the room. She dressed a long white roman dress and shone like a little star.

Dawson could spend hours admiring her, talking about so many different things. Then she would gently kiss the tip of his nose and he would start working for hours in a row, coming up with the masterpieces and poems that would make him world widely famous.

His nemesis, a frustrated artist called Troy, wined that Dawson had some sort of secret but everyone knew the man poured out jealousy. Yet, when he saw a little light floating towards Dawson's apartment, he knew he was right. He observed and stalked Arabella for one whole month, as he studied every known source about Muses.

Although they should be invisible most of the times, Arabella wasn't very careful on that aspect.

Lucky Troy.

When he approached her and asked if she could help him, Arabella promptly refused. She wasn't intimidated by his big height or strong muscles, which was a remarkable sign of courage.

What did scare her, however, was the man's nature. Muses usually know when people are bad and Troy, well, he was quite the evil chap.

Upon her refusal he took her, claiming she would never help Dawson again.

***

At the Forest of Dean, the second largest Crown forest in England, Dawson looked at the moon, thinking of his lovely Arabella.

He had followed river Wye's margins but hadn't seen his Muse so far, which meant her kidnapper was rather smart.

Dawson then took a pinch of dust from a small leather bag. It didn't have much left, which meant this was his last try. It had brought him that far and for that, he was grateful.

"Here. Ye 'as a big area to search. Muses leave traces ye guys can't see. This dust will help ye out." echoed the gnome's voice in his head.

He spread the dust all around him and a smoky bluish thin trace that floated in the air started to lead him to the depths of the woods. He walked for a long time until he finally spotted Troy on a small glade; a dim fire shaped fainted lights against the trees.

Poor Arabella was tied against a small rock by the weird golden strings, and although she tried, they didn't let her go anywhere. Dawson immediately reckoned they were one of the dark items that could trap Muses.

Arabella's shine was as faint as the fire's.

"Arabella!" he screamed, but Troy's big body stood in his way.

As she spotted Dawson, Arabella smiled and shone brighter.

Troy's wicked grin rejoiced as he set up his terms.

"Dawson, you should tell your little friend here that if she doesn't bless me with inspiration, I will kill her."

"Don't touch her!" he yelled, trying to free from Troy and reach for his Muse. "Arabella, do as he asks!"

"I can't. Inspiration comes from a Muse's heart. Mine can't inspire him." she replied, shivering.

"I can't loose you, please, do it!" he begged.

Arabella was about to reply when Troy, bored by the conversation, pushed Dawson back and approached her. The little Muse swallowed dry as she saw he had grabbed a big rock.

Before Dawson could jump over him, Troy smashed Arabella with no mercy.

Mad by hatred, a skinny and short Dawson punched tall and strong Troy until he was unconscious. Then, he grabbed the rock, thinking there was still time to save Arabella. Yet, Dawson hesitated for a few moments: Would he wish to see his beautiful Muse brutally smashed?

After a long pause, he decided not to lift the rock and laid it back, crying compulsively.

He even thought about taking his life, and just when he was about to jump from a cliff, Dawson felt a warmth in his heart that was very familiar to him.

He put one hand over his chest and closed his eyes.

A tear fell down his face and he murmured something as he tried not to giggle. "Arabella..."

About the author: Accountant by day, writer by night

THIS LITTLE PIGGY...

K.G. McAbee

Miss Harriet Timmons glanced around to make sure she hadn't forgotten to do everything she needed to do before she left for her Saturday morning run.

She hadn't, of course. She never forgot anything. But she always checked. Order and control; those were her watchwords.

She stepped out onto the front stoop and pulled the door shut behind her, then slipped her key into the zippered pocket of her running shorts.

"Mornin', Miz Timmons." Her gardener, Arnie Bagwell, offered her an uneasy, gap-toothed grin.

"Good morning, Arnold."

Harriet Timmons glared at Arnie. He had on his ragged old denim vest with not even a t-shirt beneath it, and cut-off jeans. His belly bulged over the waistband, and his legs, hairy as spider legs and nearly as crooked, were dirty where they weren't peeling from sunburn.

"Arnold, I thought we'd discussed—" She stopped abruptly as that annoying pain hit her again, right below her breastbone.

Indigestion. Had to be; she'd already made up her mind about that. Could not possibly be anything else. She was in excellent health for a woman of her age—even for a woman two decades younger than her forty-nine years.

Indigestion. Of course it was.

It was certainly nothing to keep her from her regular Saturday morning run.

Besides, she had to break in her new running shoes before next month's 5K. She fully intended on winning it again, as she had for the last seven years.

"You all right, Miz Timmons?" Arnie Bagwell had taken advantage of her distraction to draw closer than she liked to see him.

Harriet frowned and snapped, "Of course I am, Arnold! Did you take that twine off those new azaleas as I asked?"

"Yes'm." Arnie held out a handful of coarse brown string. Other bits hung out of the pockets of his vest. "They look swell. I got the trimmer out; thought I'd trim them bushes out back."

"Those bushes," Harriet corrected automatically.

"Yes'm." Arnie turned and began his slow waddle around the house.

Harriet Timmons strode down the stone path to the wooden bench at the edge of her yard. She grabbed the back of the bench for support and did her usual stretches and bends.

Never run without stretching first; she told all her students that. She had every intention of still running at seventy and beyond.

A buzz echoed from behind her house. Arnie had started up the trimmer, at the first pull, naturally. Everything Harriet owned was always in tip top condition.

She started down Pine Street at a slow lope. She'd pick up the pace after she turned the corner at Whitney, run flat out until Mill, then slow back down again, finishing her usual Saturday three miles coming back down Pine to her gate.

She'd been taking the same route for more than twenty years, never varying. It took her right past Piedmont Junior High School, where she'd taught English and Physical Education since she'd graduated college. She'd taught many of the people who lived on her street, and a few of them had children she'd taught. Even Arnold Bagwell was a former student—a disappointing one. She hadn't had many of those!

Neighbors waved; some in cars honked. Mr. Thompson was watering his petunias; he pointed to his watch as she passed—his usual joke, that he could set it by her.

Harriet smiled at him and nodded, but didn't slow down.

Just over thirty minutes later, Harriet slowed as she turned back onto Pine Street. Another half a block and she'd be home. The new shoes were performing well, as they darn better should! They'd certainly cost enough!

Arnie was sweeping the walkway, the last task of his usual Saturday morning chores.

Harriet stepped inside her gate and opened her mouth to tell him goodbye. At that very instant, a fierce pain hit her in the chest. It raced down her left arm, and though her mouth was still open, nothing came out but a soft sigh. It was almost as if there was no air, no air... and why was it getting dark at nine in the morning...

***

"Miz Timmons? Miz Timmons?"

Arnold's moon face, spotted thickly with pimples, swam into her view, solidifying from black mist.

"Miz Timmons?"

Harriet held out a hand, meaning to push him away—his breath smelled like a butcher's shop; she'd warned him about eating too much red meat. But a sharp pain made her gasp. She dropped her hand. This time the pain was even more intense, like some animal clawing at her. But the pain didn't seem to be in her chest this time, or even her arm.

Her legs?

Harriet blinked, willing her vision to clear. After a few seconds, it obeyed, and she could see that she was lying on her own couch, in her own living room. The hideous red-and-yellow afghan her sister Lynn had knitted her last Christmas covered her legs and was pulled up to her chest.

"Miz Timmons, you fell down! I done called 911 and they on their way. They said to keep you warm, so I covered you up. I know you wouldn't want no shoes on the furniture, so I took 'em off for you. They're right there on some newspaper, right by the door. See?"

"Arnold. Stop blathering," Harriet snapped. "You always did have a tendency to blather."

"Yes'm."

Harriet tried to push herself up, but that sharp pain came again. And her legs; she couldn't feel them.

"Miz Timmons?"

Harriet looked up at her gardener. "Yes?" She didn't like the way her voice sounded, weak and shaky, so she tried again. "Yes, Arnold?" There; that was much better.

"Miz Timmons, you remember when I was in your class

in seventh grade?"

What was the fool blathering on about now, at a time like this?

"Yes, of course I do, Arnold. I remember all my students." She tried again to push herself up with her arms. Not so much pain this time, but she still didn't have feeling in her legs.

"You remember that one time when you made me run around the football field three times as punishment cause I forgot to bring my gym shoes?"

Harriet perked up her head to listen; was that a siren?

"Miz Timmons, you remember that?" Arnie asked, insistent.

"Yes, yes, what about it?" she said absently. She was almost sure that was a siren.

"I forgot my gym shoes, like I done said. And you made me run in my boots, and I got awful blisters on my toes. They hurt me for days and days and days, Miz Timmons."

"Well, you should have been more organized, Arnold. Organization is critical in life."

"Yes'm. But don't you think it might have been, I dunno, kinder of you not to make me run that day? At least, not all that long way?" Arnie was standing beside the couch, looking down at her. His knees were filthy, and his hands were covered in something dark and nasty.

"Discipline, Arnold. Sometimes, one must be cruel to be kind. I never meant to hurt you. I did what I did because of love." It was her stock reply; she'd used it thousands of times. This time, though, it sounded wrong somehow. Must be the pain, making her doubt what she knew was true.

Was that a siren?

"Yes'm." Arnie nodded. "That's exactly right, exactly what you said. Cruel to be kind. You make me run to learn me a lesson, right?"

"*Teach* you a lesson, Arnold. Naturally; that's exactly why I did it." Harriet sniffed. Her vision had almost completely cleared, and she looked at the front door, willing it to open, conjuring up a pair of EMTs with a stretcher to appear.

Doctor Philips might possibly have been right. Perhaps

she did need to slow down just a bit. She'd tell the old fool when she saw him next. They'd both get a good laugh out of it.

The door stayed stubbornly shut. Wait, though; what was that beside it?

"Arnold?"

"Yes'm?" Arnie stepped back a bit, and in the process hid what she'd caught a glimpse of behind his dirty, flabby figure.

"No, no, move this way a bit." She pointed, then gasped as a frightful pain ran up both her legs. The feeling was coming back to them, and rather unfortunately, it seemed.

Arnie obediently shifted to his right.

Harriet pointed. "What is that, Arnold?"

Arnie turned slowly. "Oh, that? That's the hedge trimmer, Miz Timmons. You see, I was just getting ready to put it away, when you fell down in the path, and I didn't want to leave it out on the stoop cause the EMTs might trip over it, so I just set it down on some newspaper, next to where I put your shoes. I'll make sure it goes back in the shed when the ambulance gets here, okay?"

Harriet tried to raise herself up on her arms, and had to fight down nausea as the pain in her legs intensified.

To take her mind off the agony, she examined the trimmers. Just as Arnie had said, they sat beside her white running shoes. Their jagged teeth looked dark, as if Arnie had been trimming something he shouldn't, and something had drained from them onto the newspaper beneath them. It looked dark as well.

"Arnold, don't you put those trimmers up dirty, you hear me?"

"Yes'm. No'm. I won't."

"What in the world have you been cutting with them anyway?"

Arnold's head jerked up.

Harriet heard it too.

Sirens.

At last!

Arnie shuffled over to the trimmers. He picked them up, then grabbed the paper, crumpled it up and shoved it into his pocket.

Then he picked up Harriet's new running shoes.

"I'll just drop these here shoes in the trash on my way out back."

Arnie tucked her shoes—her extremely expensive new running shoes—under his arm.

Harriet winced; she could see the greasy hair of his underarms against the white leather.

Then she realized what he'd just said. "You will certainly do nothing of the sort, Arnold Bagwell! Whatever can you possibly be thinking—or are you thinking at all?"

Arnie turned to face her. Her shoes looked like small white butterflies trapped beneath his flabby arm.

"Oh, yes'm. I'm thinking all right. I'm thinking all the time." He grinned his gap-toothed grin, and Harriet suddenly felt cold. "Some folks don't believe I can think. You never did, and you didn't tell my classmates you thought a whole lot of me, did you? So nobody in town thinks too high of me, ever since I was in school."

"Too highly," Harriet corrected automatically.

"Yes'm. But you're wrong, you're all wrong. I think all right. And I remember. And I plan. Like today, when you collapsed right in front of your own door, cause you're too stubborn and hardheaded to listen to Dr. Philips, or much of anyone else."

"Plan? What do you mean, Arnold?" Harriet asked, and the words seemed to tear out of her. The pain came again, and it was positively no longer anywhere near her chest. This pain came from her legs. Her feet. She tried to wiggle her toes and gasped.

"Yes'm," Arnie replied, as if in answer to her gasp. "I can plan. That day you made me run, you wouldn't listen to me. You wouldn't let me wait to run the next day, when I had my gym shoes with me. No ma'am. You made me run anyway. My toes sure did hurt. It took seemed like forever for them blisters to heal. And everybody laughed at me when I limped around school. Hurt my feelings. Hurt my feelings real bad. I don't like to have my feelings hurt, you know? I don't forget when it happens either."

"Arnold," Harriet began. Then she heard doors slamming

and people talking, but they'd lost their importance somehow. "Arnold, what have you done? Put my shoes down and open the door, please. Those shoes; they're very expensive." That last word sounded almost like a whine, so she repeated it, making her voice firm: "Expensive."

"Yes'm. I sure am sorry you wasted your hard-earned money and all," Arnie said. "But Miz Timmons, ma'am—they ain't gonna fit you no more, are they? They gonna be too long. A good bit too long, what with your toes being gone and all."

Arnie Bagwell turned.

Harriet heard the newspaper in his pocket crackle.

Dark red liquid dripped from the teeth of the hedge trimmers and made rusty spots on her beige rug.

About the author: K.G. McAbee writes steampunk, fantasy, horror, science fiction, pulp, paranormal, gothic and YA, and has had more than a dozen books and nearly seventy short stories published. She lives in upstate South Carolina in a haunted log cabin with her gorgeous husband and two black Labs, all three of whom she lives to madly spoil. For more information, please visit her website at: kgmcabee.com.

Dark Heaven
Gwendolyn Joyce Mintz

I called 911.

"I need help for David," I told the woman who answered. "He's on the floor."

"Ma'am, what's wrong with David? Can you tell me?"

"He's dead," I said.

The woman took my address and said help would be on its way. I thanked her and hung up the phone.

I knelt by David, put his head on my lap. "It's okay, Baby. Somebody's coming to help you."

***

A flurry of questions.

Confusing.

An explanation wouldn't change anything— David was dead and knowing why I had killed him would not bring him back.

***

I asked for a cigarette.

"There's no smoking in the building."

I explained that I just wanted to hold one.

The detective pulled out a package, shook a cigarette free and placed it before me.

I picked it up, ran its slender form through my fingers.

"You were saying that he was your first love?" he asked.

"Only." I held the cigarette to my nose and breathed deep.

"So let's go through this again: You had a date tonight."

"Yes. A college production of 'Harvey.' It was okay," I said, placing the cigarette on the table and rolling it in the detective's direction. "After Jimmy Stewart, it's hard to imagine anyone else in that role."

The detective looked at me, a slight smile on his face. "And you didn't go with David?"

I shook my head. "I wanted to date others."

"And he didn't want you to."

"No. He didn't."

"Did he know you were going out tonight?"

"Yes."

"Did you see David before you went to the play?"

I said I hadn't

"Did you talk to him on the phone?"

I shook my head. "I stayed away from my apartment all day. I didn't want to argue anymore."

"But he was there when you came home?"

"Yes."

"And you argued then."

"Yes."

"Tell me what happened."

"He was inside the apartment. My date had walked me to the door, but he didn't come in. I knew David would be there. I knew.

"I went in and David was pacing. He was frantic, angry but then he seemed... relieved?"

"It's about fucking time."

I toss my jacket across the arm of the sofa. "It was just a play," I tell him.

"Where is he?" David demands.

"Home. I sent him home."

David walks to the window, lifts the curtain edge and looks down into the parking lot. "Did you hold his hand?" he asks.

I say nothing.

David turns to me. "Did you let him kiss you?"

"David, please." I start down the hall.

He is there, immediately beside me, my forearm locked in his palm. "You're not going to see him again."

I glare at his fingers squeezing my skin and then bring my angry eyes to meet his. "I'm tired of you telling me what to do!" I yank my arm free and step away from him.

"We continued to argue. I can't remember exactly what was

said... and then he tried to kiss me and I didn't want him to. I had kissed the man I'd gone to the play with and I didn't want..."

I reached for the cup of coffee cooling before me. I took a sip.

"Eva?"

I took a breath.

"He calmed down some... he sat on the couch, asked me to sit by him, but I didn't want to."

"Why?"

Why?

"I was afraid he'd try to kiss me or..."

"Try to have sex with you?"

"Yes."

"So you were angry. Angry because he might push you to have sex and you didn't want to?"

I shook my head. Even angry with David, I'd given myself to him.

***

It is my fifteenth birthday. David has snuck in my bedroom. When I warn him — parents sleeping in the next room — he simply smiles and strikes a match. He has brought chocolate brownies, stacked in a pyramid, a solitary blue candle stuck atop.

"A wish," he tells me, holding the plate before me.

I close my eyes. My heart expands with longing. I open my eyes and blow at the flame.

David sets the plate on the nightstand. "Did you wish for me?" he asks and I nod.

I feel his smile through the darkness. His hands tremble across my shoulders. One finger trails between my breasts. My chest rises and falls with panic and desire.

David leans forward and presses his lips against mine. It is gentle at first, and then it grows and moves him against me. I slide back down on the mattress and David is over me. We scramble against the other — the sheet, my nightgown, his pants.

David kisses me again and again: my forehead, my cheek, the curve of my neck...

He licks the place between my breasts and I squeeze the curls on his head between my fingers.

I feel him rubbery and firm against my thigh. I suck in my breath. David holds me tightly in his arms and whispers words of comfort.

He moves between my legs, moves us to another place. Some dark heaven because we have lost our way. David whispers to hold onto him and I do because I have no choice otherwise.

***

"He became angry again."

"I hate it when you don't listen to me!" David charges across the room.

"Kiss me," he says, leans toward me, lips pursed.

"Stop it!" I turn away, wipe at the wetness left by his lips as they passed across my cheek.

My shoulders gripped in his hands, David rattles my body. "Why? Have you already been kissed tonight?"

"He wouldn't stop." I looked up at the detective. "I... I didn't mean to..."

His hand falls to my arm, tightens around it. I pull away again. The sleeve of my shirt tears —

"He... he wouldn't stop," I murmured. "He just wouldn't."

"So you killed your brother because...?"

I took a breath. "I killed David because tonight he tried to rape me."

***

The detective had left the room. When he returned, he told me a public defender was on the way. Someone from the rape crisis center.

He was a kind man. He said that the circumstances were "unusual" and that bail might be possible. I might not spend too much time in jail.

I shook my head and laughed.

Whatever happened now would not change what I had always known: I could never be free. I would never be free.

Gwendolyn Joyce Mintz is a fiction writer, poet and aspiring photgrapher. Her work has appeared in various places, online and print. She blogs about life at gwenotes.blogspot.com and about writing at wwwonewriter.blogspot.com.

THE SPACE BETWEEN US

Sandra Crook

The space between us at this moment is just about six feet. That's a lot closer than we've been during the last couple of years, though on this occasion that six foot space is packed with cold, damp earth.

I miss you.

We were inseparable, you and I. Soul mates, that's what people called us.

But then the spaces started. At first it was just the spaces in our conversation, those few seconds during which you realised I'd spoken, and tried desperately to remember what I'd said.

Then came the space in your head; that absent gaze, seemingly looking right through me. You began to forget birthdays, anniversaries, meetings.

But I really hated the space in our bed. Oh, your body was there; well at first it was, but your soul could have been on the moon for all the union there was between us. I was so lonely then.

And finally there was the space in our home. After you'd gone. You needed space, you said.

To be with your new lover, your new soul mate. Sharing her space.

Divorce, you proposed. Leaving a space where our marriage used to be.

I thought not.

That was when I knew you would have to die. If I were to heal… if I were to pick up the threads of whatever life I could scavenge for myself, there had to be a space where you used to be. There was no way I could survive as long as you still did.

I spent weeks planning your murder. It had to be perfect, and I had to be certain that I could not be implicated. What good would derive, if I were to languish within the claustrophic confines of a prison cell for the rest of my life? No space to breathe.

93

Poison, I decided... for I couldn't bear to mark your perfect form in any way.

But things never go according to plan, do they?

Like the true soul mates we were, you too felt there should be a space where I used to exist.

So tonight, or maybe tomorrow, I expect you'll open that special bottle of Puligny Montrachet; the one I gave you that day, just before you pushed me off the bridge. You and your new soul mate will toast to my passing and your newly acquired space.

Your death shouldn't be too painful, my love, I did my research very carefully. I never wanted you to suffer. And you always loved a good Montrachet.

For the moment we are in different places, occupying difference spaces. But when I bought this plot I made sure to reserve a space beside me for you. The least I could do for a soul mate.

I'll see you soon, sweetheart.

About the author: : Sandra Crook has been published in Every Day Fiction, Every Day Poets, Backhand Stories, MicroHorror, The Pygmy Giant, The Shine Journal, Financial Times Weekend and various magazines. Her work can be found at http://castelsarrasin.wordpress.com/

HAPPY VALENTINE'S DAY
Thomas M. Malafarina

The sun was a burning ball of orange fire as it set slowly in the western sky. Its fiery light pierced through the small spaces between weathered planks of lumber nailed securely across the window frames; the setting sunlight being the all that was capable of entering the secure building.

Across the room from the window, a young man in his late twenties sat quietly in a large wooden rocking chair, a sawed-off shotgun lying across his lap at the ready. The slow rhythmic rocking of the chair had a soothing effect because of its continuous back and forth motion. The man sat staring at light filtering into the darkening room. The rocker moved, back and forth, back and forth, back and forth.

The man, Roger Washburn, shook his head as if to break the chair's hypnotic spell and cautiously got to his feet, listening, turning his head from side to side. He slowly twisted, set the shotgun down across the arms of the rocker and approached the boarded window, still listening, ever vigilant. With some trepidation he peeked through one of the cracks between the boards to try to get a better view of the beautiful sunset. There was very little beauty in the world anymore so Roger tried to make a point to enjoy the simple things the world still had to offer whenever possible, such as a beautiful sunset; especially since he never knew when it might be the last he would ever see.

Looking through one of the small cracks, Roger saw the sun in the distance, its stunning glow a sharp contrast to the horrible destruction which permeated the once beautiful cityscape illuminated under its light. The city lay in ruins, a charred and ravaged shell of the great metropolis that once was. As he had done a thousand times before and would probably do a thousand times again, Roger wondered how so much destruction could have happened so quickly. He rested his head and his hand against the wooden planking, releasing a cheerless, frustrated sigh.

Wham! A hand slammed savagely against the outside of

95

the planking rattling the boards against Rogers's head, causing him to jump back in surprise. Pain shot through the front of his skull where the board has struck him.

"Jesus!" Roger shouted.

Though he was startled, he was much more than that; he was angry with himself for letting his guard down. He knew better. Perhaps it was that human need for things to be back to normal. Whatever the cause, he knew he never should have gotten so close to the boarded window, since it allowed his scent to escape out into the world, out there to 'them', to where 'they' now ruled. They could smell his humanity. They could smell his living flesh, and that smell was intoxicating for them.

He stood quietly, trying to calm his heavy breathing. He waited for a few minutes to see if the thing outside the window would leave or if it would attempt to break in. He realized how foolish he was to even think it would give up. They never gave up; as they were mindless eating machines.

After a few moments he heard a familiar groaning sound these beasts all seemed to make and then heard the thing scraping its fleshless bone-exposed fingers along the outside of the boards, trying to find a way inside. Scratch, scratch, scratch went the sickening sound of bone against wood.

Roger knew he had to act quickly. For the moment, he was fairly sure there was only one of them out there. But he knew if he waited too much longer others would take notice to the commotion and drag themselves over to see what was happening. Then there would be several all moaning, groaning and scraping their claws against the wood. Some might bang their fists against the planking and some might even figure out how to devise pry bars and try to pull the boards apart. And then before too long, there would be hundreds of them and if that happened, then it would be all over. The fat lady would be singing. And Roger was not ready to hear that tune, at least not just yet, anyway.

Reaching down alongside of the window frame Roger grabbed a long thin iron rod, about a half-inch in diameter, complete with a handgrip he had fashioned himself by bending the rod to fit his grip perfectly. He had sharpened the business end of the bar to a sharp thin point. He had no idea what the rod was originally used for in its past life, but he understood what it was used for now; since he had altered it for this specific purpose. He positioned the point of the tool in a space between two boards and stood quietly waiting for just the right moment.

Outside, the scraping and moaning continued. After a few seconds the scraping stopped and he saw an eye peering through one of the spaces, its lens covered with a grey film of death. Without a moment's hesitation, Roger shoved the point of the shaft deep into the eye with all of his might, driving it through the intruder's brain and out the back of its skull. Then just as quickly, he pulled the shaft back through the crack, scraping blood and brain matter along the rough edges of the board. He heard the thump of the creature's face against the planking as its face bones were shattered, and he grimaced at the sickening sounds the rod made as it freed itself from the thing's skull and as the brain matter sloshed and slid down the outside of the barricade. The fowl stench coming from the horror made Roger's stomach lurch, as he held back his urge to vomit. He needed to keep what little he had inside of him, as he had not eaten for days.

He listened as the body thudded to the ground outside, then he backed away from the window silently waiting; paying attention to see if any others had heard the commotion. He felt weighed down with futility knowing all he could do was hope and wait. This is what his life had come down to; hoping and waiting.

After a few moments, satisfied all was clear he silently walked across the room to a tall dresser where he lit a match, placing it against the wick of lone candle. This technique seemed to work well to provide minimal lighting without attracting unwanted attention. The last thing he needed was unwanted attention.

A calendar hung on the wall above the dresser showing today's date in bold characters as February 14, Valentine's Day. Roger already knew it was Valentine's Day, but seeing the calendar just served to reinforce the importance of this day to him and to his sweet Amanda.

Roger crossed back to his rocker, sitting, thinking about how quickly everything he knew to be true had gone completely down the crapper in a matter of just a few weeks. Again he wondered, how could such a thing have been possible?

Only a month and a half ago, he and his wife Amanda were toasting in the New Year and looking forward to the next year with great hopes and aspirations. They had been married about three years and were still madly in love. Roger's favorite expression of affection for Amanda was the short and sweet; 'My heart is for you, alone.' And Amanda had never seemed to grow tired of hearing him say it.

They had decided this would be the year they would start a family. They had paid off both of their student loans had managed to scrape together enough money for a down payment on a starter home. Both of them were comfortably secure in their jobs, and had agreed now was the time to start having children. They both decided if they were to give their children all of the opportunities they possibly could, a two-income family was required. Therefore, they would have to find a good daycare or hire a nanny. They were already looking for the right match for their future needs even though Amanda was not yet even pregnant.

Both Roger and Amanda were natural born planners. Many of their friends called them anal retentive, but they felt they were simply good planners. They believed in making a detailed outline of what direction they wanted their lives to take and then following the plan to the letter, never deviating from their pathway, always heading forward with their final goals in mind.

Now sitting along in the near dark, in a world gone to hell, Roger was astonished at how quickly their clear-cut plans had fallen by the wayside practically overnight. Roger's Uncle Mike had always joked with him about Roger's obsession with planning. Mike would always say, "When things are going well and according to plan, start to worry. Because that means life is waiting in the wings to kick you right in the nuts." Uncle Mike was never one for pulling punches and as it turned out had never spoken truer words in his life. Roger supposed his jovial uncle was now one of 'them' as well.

Yes, the world Roger knew was gone. The life he had planned was over. Civilization was a thing of the past. He did not understand how or what happened, but he knew the results; he dealt with the results every day of his life.

One of Roger's major frustrations was he never actually found out exactly why the dead had decided to leave their graves, rise up and start walking the earth, feasting on the flesh of the living. He did, however comprehend the world he loved was gone, forever.

In addition to being an obsessive planner, Roger was the type of person who tended to categorize and list things. The present situation was no exception. In Roger's organized mind, it seemed like everyone in the world now could be placed into one of three categories; they were either dead, missing or zombies.

Since the trouble started, Roger had also learned some new things about himself. He had never considered himself a strong or heroic type of person, but he quickly learned he had some previously unrecognized inner strength which apparently made its presence known during times of crisis, such as the present one.

When the zombies started roaming the streets, Roger found survivors behaved in several different ways. (Again he found himself categorizing.) Some found inner strength and rose to the occasion to fight for as long as was possible. This is what he surprisingly found himself doing.

Others broke down, unable to cope. Many committed suicide, the most considerate being those who chose to blow their own heads off. This action alone guaranteed they would not return as zombies. The others who chose hanging, jumping off a bridge, or taking pills; in other words those who perhaps did not think things through, simply died, then came back with a hunger for living human flesh.

One television news station reported a story about a man who had given up an hung himself by tying a rope around his neck, throwing it over a beam in his garage then climbing on a chair which he subsequently kicked out from under him. Unfortunately, the man's neck did not break but he eventually choked to death. Shortly afterward he re-awoke as a zombie still dangling from his neck in the garage unable to escape. The TV camera had filmed the creature twitching and swinging from its rope shortly before local volunteers blasted its head right off.

Still others just shut down, went catatonic. Many of those people could be seen sitting in a stupor while the hordes of zombies surrounded them and devoured them. These were the strangest for Roger to comprehend. He saw one 'cat' as he called them sitting in the middle of the street, ripped apart and eaten alive without uttering a single cry or whimper. The man literally sat there and allowed himself to be a main course, strange indeed. But then again, these were strange days.

Unfortunately for Roger, Amanda had become one of the 'cats' as well. He never would have expected her to react in that manner as she had always seemed strong and forceful, but he supposed after what she had been through, he was not surprised.

It happened shortly after all the dead began dragging their rotting carcasses out of the ground. Up until a few weeks earlier the living dead had been in the minority, showing up in spotty locations around the city. The city police department with the help of some civilian volunteers and hunters out for a good time had been able to keep the zombies pretty much in check.

Once the news broke, most people never would go anywhere unarmed. Everyone watched the news reports and learned quickly how to take the creatures down. The head seemed to be the key, whether severing the head from the body with an ax or other sharp implement; or penetrating the brain with a sharp object such as a knife or a stick; or simply blowing the creatures' heads completely off with a 12 gauge, destroying the brain seemed to be just what the doctor ordered.

Another thing Roger noticed was the zombies were not of the rapid moving variety pictured in many of the modern zombie-style horror films he had seen, but seemed to be more in line with the slow, clumsy, spastically moving types depicted in the old George Romero flicks. This slowness proved to initially be a help allowing everyone to manage them for a while. But soon the sheer numbers of the walking dead would turn the tide.

Although Roger had been aware of what was going on,

up until a few weeks ago he and Amanda had continued to lead their lives as normally as possible, neither of them having ever seen an actual zombie, other than those the saw on the television news broadcasts. The creatures seemed to be in isolated areas of the city and countryside and the authorities insisted the problem was being properly controlled.

As a precaution, Roger had purchased shot guns for both he and Amanda, along with plenty of ammunition and had taken her to some farmland outside of the city to teach her how to shoot. She had proven to be a quick study and Roger felt sure she would be able to defend herself if the need ever arose.

One day, Roger came home from work and saw a note on the table from Amanda saying her cell phone was no longer getting service, but she had gotten a call on their land line from her mother who lived across town. She said her mother sounded hysterical and needed her help immediately. The note said she had headed right over to their house and would be home as soon as possible.

Roger took out his cell phone and saw he too had no service. He got a horrible feeling in the pit of his stomach; something was definitely wrong. Next he tried the land line and saw apparently all traditional phone service had gone down as well. Now he knew things had really started going bad.

Roger decided he had better head over to Amanda's parents' place and make sure she was alright. He worked on the east side of town and Amanda's parents lived on the west side. He had not encountered any problems on his way home from work and hoped this would be the case as he headed west.

He ran to his car, shotgun in hand and headed west to his in-laws' home. Unfortunately, as he drove, he noticed the west side of town painted a completely different picture than his daily commute. This side of town proved to be zombie central.

Rounding a corner just a few blocks from his and Amanda's home he witnessed several zombies being shot in the street by locals. It appeared three men dressed in hunting gear were standing on a street corner backs toward each other, one pointing in opposite directions firing away as a steady stream of zombies stumbled toward them. It was like watching a video game. Bang and the top of one zombie's head flew through the air. Bang and another zombie fell to the ground.

The men were all laughing and drinking beer between kills and having themselves a great old time. That was, until a group of about thirty zombies staggered spasmodically from a nearby building, overpowering the men by force of the numbers, falling upon the men and ripping them to shreds. Roger had to look away in order to keep control of his car, while again struggling not to vomit.

As he traveled further, things got progressively worse. In one neighborhood he saw several residents who were overpowered by zombies being eaten alive. The creatures were gnawing on limbs which had recently been ripped off of the victims. Some of the wounded lay bleeding to death on the street screaming in pain as more zombies approached to finish them off. Roger wanted to stop and help but realized it was futile. Also he knew if things had gotten this bad, this fast, he had better get to Amanda's parents' house as soon as possible.

A block away from his destination, Roger saw several zombies clumsily shambling down the middle of the street directly in the path of his car. He did the only thing he could think of to do and pressed the gas pedal to the floor. Roger plowed right into the pack, sending bodies flying in all directions. Looking in his rear-view mirror he saw them fall back to the ground breaking into pieces, with arms and legs flying in several directions. Even without arms or legs the reanimated corpses surviving still squirmed on the ground like worms driven by an insatiable need for human flesh.

A few moments later, Roger pulled in front of his in-law's home and saw Amanda's car parked in the driveway, with the driver's door standing open. He pulled in behind, grabbed his shotgun and headed for her car, fearing he might find her dead inside. She was not there but her shot gun was which told Roger she must have panicked and ran right for her parents' home leaving the gun behind.

As Roger approached the front door of the house he heard a groaning, moaning sound from his left and saw an old woman in a housecoat dragging her wounded right leg and lurching directly toward him, her arms outstretched. He recognized her as Mrs. Wilson, the old woman who lived next door, but he could tell immediately she was no longer the sweet old grandmother he had known but was now one of them. Without hesitation, he lifted the gun, pulled the trigger and blew poor Mrs. Wilson's head right off of her shoulders. Her decapitated body continued to take one more step forward before dropping to the ground with a thud.

Roger looked around to make sure there were no more former neighbors to deal with and for the moment there seemed to be no other threats. He turned and noticed the front door of his in-law's home was standing ajar. Roger knew this would not be good.

Slowly he entered the front hall of the large center-hall colonial style home, and heard a sound which sent chills down his spine. To his right, coming from the living room he heard moaning and a sickening slurping sound, like he imagined would be made by a group of wild pigs. Being careful not to make a sound, shotgun at the ready, Roger slowly entered the living room.

His stomach lurched at the sight awaiting him. His young brother-in-law, Jared, was kneeling on the floor over top of the prone body of Roger's mother-in-law, Celia, Jared's own mother. The boy was covered in blood from head to toe and was gorging on her entrails which he apparently had ripped from her stomach. The serpentine intestines flapped through the air spewing blood in all directions as the hideous thing feasted on her, playfully allowing the slimy tube-like organs to slide through his fingers.

As if that were not bad enough, Roger could see the woman was still alive and though unconscious, was twitching uncontrollably, as if moments away from death. Again, without hesitation, Roger lifted the shot-gun and separated Jared from his head as the blast sent the zombie flying across the living room and splattering against the far wall.

No sooner had Roger reloaded the gun then his mother-in-law, or what once had been his mother-in-law, started crawling toward him, staring at him with dead eyes, bloody drool oozing from her lips as her innards sloshed along the hardwood floor behind her. Roger was shocked to see how quickly she had become one of them, it was no wonder they were multiplying so quickly. With one more quick blast of the shotgun her head was obliterated, leaving a large hole in the living room floor as well.

Regaining his composure, Roger heard banging and scraping sounds coming from the second floor. Taking the stairs two at a time he entered the upstairs hall, gun at the ready, to find his father-in-law, Bob, now one of the living dead, banging ineptly on the door to what Roger knew was once Amanda's bedroom, back when she was a little girl.

Upon hearing Roger's approach, the zombie turned and headed right for him. Roger aimed the gun at the creature's head, pulled the trigger but the gun did not fire, probably because he had forgotten to reload it in his haste. He did the only thing he could think of and swung the gun barrel at the zombie's skull. Roger heard a cracking sound as the creature fell to the floor, down but not out, as it started slowly crawling in his direction. He realized he must have broken the thing's neck because its movements were jerky and its head dragged along the floor, jaws snapping instinctively in search for flesh.

As it got within a foot of Roger, he grabbed the stock of the shotgun and drove the both barrels downward through the top of the father-in-law thing's skull like a knife through a melon as blood and brain matter shot upward. With a grunting sound, the thing ceased its forward motion, twitched a few times then was dead, really dead this time, on the hall floor.

Roger went to the bedroom door banging frantically, calling out to his Amanda. At first she did not reply. Eventually he heard her sobs coming from just inside the door and then heard her unlocking the lock which had succeeded in keeping her alive. Roger opened the door and Amanda collapsed into his arms, breaking down hysterically screaming and crying.

Keeping her eyes shielded from the gory sight of her once father's skull crushed in the hall, Roger guided Amanda down the stairs. Once on the first floor he again protected her from the carnage in the living room, turning her away, though he was already certain she had seen much too much on this eventful day.

Cautiously looking out the front door to make sure the coast was clear, Roger picked up Amanda and carried her to his car placing her gently in the passenger's seat, strapping the seatbelt securely around her. Keeping himself covered with the shotgun, eyes scanning the street, he went back to her car and picked up her shotgun, tossing in the backseat of his car as he climbed inside and secured his seatbelt.

He knew he had to find somewhere safe for them to lay low. Judging by the way this plague seemed to be spreading and how close it was now to their own home he felt he might not be able to safely make it back there. Locking all the doors and securing the windows Roger sped away in search of a less vulnerable location.

As luck would have it, he found a two story warehouse turned loft apartment only a few blocks from his in-laws' home and there did not seem to be any zombies anywhere near it. He noticed the windows on both floors had already been boarded up to prevent any zombies from getting inside but the front door was standing open. He got out of the car; leaving Amanda locked safely inside and quickly entered the property, making sure the apartment was clear of any unwanted activity.

He went from room to room on the first floor making sure each was safe, and then headed up the stairs to check the second floor out as well. It had four bedrooms upstairs each of which was empty that was, until he got to the last one. Upon entering the last bedroom Roger found the body of a man, most likely the former resident of the apartment, headless in a pool of blood on the floor with a note next to the corpse.

The note was barely legible as if written in hast and with little motor control. The note read 'I been bittn... I near dead... I dont wana come back... as 1 of those things' Next to the corpse was a high powered rifle which the man obviously used to do the deed. Roger was grateful the man had chosen to remove his own head, saving him the trouble.

As Roger left the room, he closed and locked the door behind him. He had to get back to Amanda. He raced down the stairs and out the front door to find Amanda was still safe in the car sitting and staring into space. Looking around to make sure no other zombies had arrived; Roger opened the door and lifted Amanda out of the car. He carried her into the living room, placing her safely on a sofa, and then returned to close and secure the door from any other potential invaders.

Roger realized although the zombies were the major threat at the moment, from what he had witnessed today, the very fabric of civilization was breaking down around him and he would have to be wary of everyone, the living and the undead.

Now many weeks later, instead of getting better, Amanda seemed to get worse. She was becoming more uncommunicative and distant every day. She had stopped eating and drinking several days ago and he could not seem to be able to force food or water into her. It was as if she had given up and wanted to die. Her ill-fated behavior was affecting Roger as well, causing him to lose his resolve. He found himself falling into a depression, which worsened daily and from which he might not recover.

Amanda had been the love of his life and to watch her fading away right before his eyes, with him helpless to do anything about it, was more than he believed he could take. He found it strange, even though the world as he knew it had ended, as long as he had Amanda, he believed he could deal with anything. But now he seemed to be losing her as well. Without her, he doubted he would want to go on.

Roger sat in the rocker looking across the room at the calendar displaying February 14th. He recalled how this was going to be a special Valentine's Day for he and Amanda. He was going to buy a beautiful bracelet for her she had been admiring and then he planned they would go out for dinner, come home and make love and perhaps this would have been the night they made a baby. However, now Roger realized this was not to be, not this Valentine's Day, not ever again. There would be no baby for Roger and Amanda, no babies for anyone.

He decided he should check on Amanda and see how she was doing. He walked the stairs to her second floor bedroom and opened the door to find her curled up in the fetal position on the bed. Roger approached her and gently touched her cheek, which felt as cold as ice to him. A second later, her eyes flew open covered in a grey film. She sat up in bed, her emaciated form visible under the nightgown, which now hung from her bony shoulders. Long gone was the look of loving affection, also gone was the catatonic stare, both replaced by a savage look of hunger Roger knew was reserved for the warm-blooded walking lunch wagons formerly known as the human race. And he had just made it to the top of the menu.

Without taking time to think, Roger backed away slowly from the bed, turned and ran into an adjacent bathroom, slamming the door behind him. He stood in the bathroom slamming his fists against his head, not knowing what to do next. His once beloved wife Amanda was now scratching and clawing at the bathroom door. No, this was no longer his wife. Amanda was gone. All that remained was a lifeless reanimated corpse wanting nothing better than to eat him alive.

He sat down hard on the toilet lid, his head in his hands and cried like he had never done before. His mind was on the verge of breaking, he new it and he simply didn't care. Without his Amanda there was no life. Then he realized he had been kidding himself all this time because even if Amanda was alive and healthy, there was no more life for them, no more life for anyone. It was futile; it was over.

Roger stood and slowly walked to the bathroom door, took a deep breath, grabbed door handle, saying "Amanda, honey?" He slowly turned the knob and said, "I love you." Finally he pulled the door open and saw the thing which had once been Amanda standing outside the bathroom, its white night gown covered in filth.

He looked directly into the zombie's dead eyes and said, "My heart is for you, alone, Happy Valentine's Day." With that, the creature charged into the bathroom, sunk her claw-like fingers into Roger's chest, pulled out his still beating heart and began her feast.

About the author: Thomas M. Malafarina is an author of horror fiction from western Berks County PA. He has three novels published through Sunbury Press, "99 Souls", "Burn Phone" and "Eye Contact". He also has two short story collections; the first called "13 Nasty Endings" and the second called "Gallery Of

Horror", as well as a collection of single panel cartoons called "Yes I Smelled It Too: Cartoons For The Slightly Off Center". Thomas lives in South Heidelberg Township with his wife JoAnne. They have three grown children and three grandchildren.

THE VOICE WITHIN

Lorraine Horrell

Everyone has that annoying voice in their head. You know the one that won't go away. The one that constantly puts you down and reminds you of your flaws and abilities or non-abilities. The one that knows all your secrets and desires. Yes, the voice we dread.

Billy had managed to suppress his. He didn't like that voice, in fact he hated it.

Loathed it, would be a better description. The voice in his head didn't belong to Billy but belonged to his Mother, Doreen. Billy and Doreen had quite a complex relationship. There was a time when Billy was a kid that he idolized his mother; as all young boys do. It's only when they grow older and learn that 'Mummy Dearest' isn't always right, that things turn sour (particularly relationships between families).

Billy wasn't a bad kid! He was quiet and extremely shy, predominantly with the opposite sex. He was in fact, afraid of girls. His Mother had warned him of their powerful ways of ensnaring men into their web. Doreen knew from personal experience just how dangerous and powerful women were and how they would stop at nothing to get what they wanted.

They will manipulate you into thinking what they want you to think. They will poison your mind. Billy, you have to stay strong and dismiss their advances on you, they will only lead to trouble and heartache. I am the only woman in your life, son. The others will damage and disturb you.

Billy was young and naïve and it was only went he went to high school he started to talk to girls, well they started to talk to him. His blonde hair and brown eyes couldn't help attract attention. Girls swarmed around him like bees to nectar. They giggled when he passed by in the corridors. They passed him letters in class, which he read, turned scarlet and carefully discarded the notes in the bin. What if his Mother found them? She would surely blame him for attracting all this attention.

TWISTED LOVE

I warned you Billy, if you read those notes you will go straight to the burning pit of hell. A one way ticket. Don't look at them, don't read that note. Throw it away.
I know boys like you Billy, perverted young boys. Easily lead by those tramps. Yeah the ones with the blonde hair and big tits. The ones who throw themselves at guys like you. They will use you Billy. They don't care about you Billy, not like I do.

***

Sometimes Billy thought he was going crazy. The voice was driving him crazy. His Mother was driving him crazy, without even doing anything. Billy longed for the kiss or even a touch of those wild and exotic creatures. The more he was forbidden the more he craved the girls. He dreamed about them at night and fantasized during the day. Once Billy turned twenty he realized he wasn't a kid anymore, he was an adult. He had the body to prove it and the stubble. He was in good shape. He had an athletic body, bulging biceps and astounding abs. He worked out at home. It was his escape from Doreen. Once college finished he locked the door of his bedroom and instead of studying and tending to his assignments and projects, Billy took out his weights and lifted them up and down till his arms trembled and shook. After the weights came the sit-ups, he did these until he gagged. Billy would then look at himself in the mirror and study his face and body. He wasn't admiring it. No, Billy was looking for flaws, before Doreen could point them out. He rubbed his fingers off his stubbly chin tracing his fingers around his jaw line. His rich chocolate eyes surveyed the face in front of them. His eyes were once full of life and now had turned cold and calculating just like his Mothers. He remembered a time when he looked in the mirror and saw Billy the Kid; he never examined himself in any great detail. No sir, Billy the Kid, took what he saw at face value-a pretty handsome young boy. That was when he was happy with what he saw. Now all he saw was his Mothers reflection. Her gaunt expression shadowed his. He hated those eyes of hers. The two cesspit eyes that poked out of her face, bulging and observing everything through her black as soot eyes. He also hated her lips. Crinkled and pursed, unzipping only to allow the hatred spill out. He checked his lips to make sure they weren't pursing.

Not yet Billy boy, but in a few years they will and you will look just like your old lady. Won't that be fun? Then see how many girls are interested in you when you are old and feeble and have to eat through a straw and have someone sponge bath you. Wear diapers and shit into a bag that's attached to your stomach. The future is bright Billy.

Billy looked away in revulsion. He walked over to the stereo and turned the music on. Turning it up so loud that he could feel the beat of the drums pounding in his chest, as if he ate a small group of Samba Drummers for lunch. The vibrations of the *music* flowed through his shelf lifting it up and knocking off his CD's. They crashed to the floor almost smashing the plastic casing that held them in place. He hated that voice.

The crash made him jump.

Wimp, a little crash like that and you jump like a rabbit. It's no wonder the girls like you Billy, they feel sorry for you. They want to protect you Billy. Back off bitches- that's my job.

Billy cupped his hands over his ears and shook his head violently. It was official he was going insane.

That's right Billy Boy - you are insane just like your old pop. Maybe you should take that lemon squeezer and point it at your head. Go on Billy, blow your brains out. Live a little, die a lot!

From downstairs in the kitchen came a loud high pitched screech and then a clatter and finally a thud. The CD skipped when the thud hit the ground. Billy's first thought was Doreen had dropped one of the pots again, she had been busy preparing dinner downstairs. She was always dropping things, especially when she was smoking. Her two arms were weak and arthritis ridden, her fingers gnarled and curled at the tips. They were worn but she could still grip a cigarette and hold it firmly in her gnarly fingers, her purse lips clenched it in her mouth. He loved it when she smoked, this meant she couldn't talk, no talking meant no voice. So he thought, but lately he heard her rasping, hissing voice, like that of a snake (if it could talk), even when her arsehole like lips didn't move. He heard it in his head. Doreen noticed her boy going crazy a while before that. He would answer questions she hadn't asked. She was not surprised though, her husband Steve had been one crazy son of a bitch. He killed himself on a Friday evening when Billy was six. They had fried chicken, mash and corn kernels for dinner and afterwards, without saying a word, Steve headed upstairs to collect his pistol (a lemon squeezer), from the bedside locker. The one with the safety latch in case Billy should find it. If Doreen had known his intentions she could have stopped him, well could or would or two very different words, both with the same meanings. Billy looked like his Father, so he was told (he couldn't remember him clearly). Perhaps that's why his Mother resented him so.

***

Before Billy had placed his size elevens on the last step of the staircase, he could smell burning food, and hear the bubble and hissing noise of pots boiling over. The water had boiled onto the ceramic hob and smelt acrid. The burning fumes permeated from the kitchen. There on the floor lay his Mother, she was sprawled elegantly on the cold kitchen tiles, which Billy had laid down for her the previous year. Of course they were not laid correctly, so she informed him every day since. Doreen had complained of feeling dizzy and nauseous earlier, why didn't he listen? Simply because she always complained and if she hadn't recited one of a million ailments she had during the day he would tend to be more worried.

Now she lay helpless on the floor. The thought to leave her there and go into town on a date with one of his many swooning girls crossed his mind. He knew it was bad but he couldn't help his thoughts, or could he?

Don't you dare Billy. After everything I have done for you and you would have the audacity to leave me hear like some rat to die. Pick up that phone and dial 911 before it's too late. I promise to leave you alone then.

For a moment Billy contemplated his deal with the devil. It felt like he was selling his soul but he didn't care, it was worth it. If even just for the quiet life.

He picked up the phone and dialed 911 without even realizing it. He felt like he was watching the whole scene in slow motion. He was outside his body even, just observing everything. He felt calm and surprisingly serene, considering his Mother was lying there on the ground, with the air flow blocked to her brain. He could see her chest rise and fall. She was alive at least.

***

Doreen Tidwell had suffered a mild stroke; she was very lucky that Billy was there and got to her on time. If it had of happened an hour earlier she would be six feet under and be eaten by the worms. We spend our whole life being afraid of spiders and other creepy crawlies but really it's the worms and the maggots we ought to fear because after all, they are the ones that munch on our flesh and devour our bodies. Doreen had been saved from the worms and maggots for now. You would think she would be grateful, but not Doreen.

The stroke had affected her movement and speech. She was deprived of oxygen for so long (while Billy listened to the voice in head) that it was unlikely even with rehabilitation and speech therapy that she would fully recover. The Tidwell's insurance wouldn't cover a full time nurse to look after Doreen. Guess who was burdened with this laborious task? Yes, Billy. He left College to care for his Mother. Not by choice but by having no other choice. He tried not to resent her for it. She had so far kept her word about making the voice stop in his head or perhaps it was the fact that he was too busy to hear it anymore. He barely had time to look in the mirror, let alone be on his own long enough to hear his own thoughts. His mother's once bitter and twisted face had ironically become twisted and distorted like her fingers. The left side of her face was scrunched up in a knot and when she breathed or tried to talk, a god awful guttural sound rose from inside her belly. He couldn't help but sympathize with her. He could see how frustrated she got; trying to say something and all that came out was that awful sound. Even she looked amazed that the awful sound had come from her. The left side of her body was impaired leaving her in a wheelchair bound for the time being. He gave her a pen and a notepad, should she need anything but she flung it to the ground. She tried to talk through her pursed lips which now drooped to one side. He almost felt sorry for her especially as the voice had disappeared after she had the stroke. He still heard a voice in his head but it was his own voice. It was comforting to have it back after all these years. Billy, you see, said nice things, contrary to Doreen. Billy said things like, "Hey dude looking good today!" and "Hey gorgeous, I see you have been working out lately," as he studied himself in the mirror. This voice (his own voice) stroked his ego and comforted him. This voice made Billy Tidwell feel good about himself. Good things don't last, do they?

***

Billy soon tired of looking after his mother day and night. He felt suffocated and trapped by this poisonous wench whose features had become twisted and bitter just like her soul. And now that she didn't have a life, she felt she was entitled to take his, since she did in fact give birth to him. Therefore, giving her the right to take his life away too. She was welcome to it at the moment. What he realised was that his Mother had gotten her wish, to have him all to herself, to nurture and care for her. All she wanted was her sons undivided attention. Not much to ask from the woman who was in labor for fifteen hours so he could grace the earth with his presence. A small sacrifice. Billy had heard it all before and answered it the same Goddamn way he had for all those years.

'Well Ma, I didn't ask for you to spread your legs and nor did I ask to be born in the first place, and if I had of asked, I certainly wouldn't have chosen to be born to a purse lipped old hag like you."

Of course he didn't say that out loud, she would have killed him. He said the words clearly and slowly with resentment and ease in the privacy of his head. To Doreen he said,

"Yes, thank you Mother, I am eternally grateful!"

Billy's newfound voice (his alter ego) convinced him

to go out and leave the house. To get a life and maybe find a girlfriend along to way. His voice could be very persuasive(most minds are). After a few days of conversations with himself he eventually came around to the idea. Mother's sponge bath could wait until tomorrow. He felt a pang of guilt in his stomach that made him gag; the pang came and went like someone had stuck a needle in his stomach. He would have suspected his mother of practicing Voodoo on him only it was impossible for her to hold anything anymore- let alone a needle. It was nice to have a clear mind with no gravelly voice putting thoughts in his head. He was enjoying the peace. Billy splashed on some expensive aftershave, in the hopes it would attract the ladies like a moth to the light. He put on his best shirt and smartest jeans. He checked his firm ass in the mirror; he had to admit it looked good in those jeans. The music pounded in the background as he threw a few shapes in front of the mirror.

Look at you, dancing around like a flea infested monkey, scratching and throwing your hands around. What girl would be interested in you? Think about it-use your noggin Billy. Girls don't like monkeys, Billy; they like men. You aren't a man yet and you never will be. I don't think you would be able to satisfy a woman. You can't even satisfy me, your old Ma.

Billy turned suddenly towards the door, his head cocked upwards. He expected to see Doreen standing there. He knew it was impossible but where was the voice coming from? It was gone, and had been gone for months now. Doreen wasn't there; she was still lying in her bed, tired and helpless.

Thought you had gotten rid of me, did you? Fat chance Billy. Stay home and give me my sponge bath. I know you like it. I am the only woman you will ever see like that. I am the only woman who will appreciate you Billy. You like washing under my folds, don't you?

Billy covered his ears. He knew that wouldn't get rid of the voice but he couldn't help do it every time. It was some strange reflex he had no control over, just like his need to heave every time he saw his mother in the bath. Old, wrinkled and decaying. Her creased skin covering her brittle bones, he often thought about breaking each of her bones. Her thinning hair, sprouting in tufts from her flaking skull. She had bedsores all over her body and every time hot water soaked into them she screamed a distorted scream from her purse lips. Pursed and crooked lips. He hated even the sight of her. Now as he stood at the bottom of her bed looking up at her, it was obvious she wasn't capable of getting out of bed or talking yet. She could talk, a muffled sound, like someone gargling water whilst talking. Even her dentures sat crooked in her mouth. He hated everything about her but he had a moment of empathy and weakness for her. Billy couldn't help feeling sorry for his Mother, who looked tiny and helpless, hidden by the sheets of her bed.

Don't you dare feel sorry for me! Go have your fun, get your whole. I will still be here when you get back, here in the same sorry position you left me. Starving and covered in urine, ready for my bath- Billy boy. I will sit still this time, I promise...

Billy shuddered at the thoughts of it. It was ironic how our parents doted over us when were babies. Never complaining when we were sick or after a difficult bath time, but when the roles are reversed years later; the truth was, no one wants to, or should have to look after their parents. It was a further twist of the knife of faith, something else to look forward to when we are old, cantankerous and alone.

*** *

Billy gathered his sweater and pulled it over his broad shoulders; it fitted his body perfectly and hugged him in all the right places. He remembered the girls in his class talking about this bar they used to go to, 'The Thatch'. It was where they all hung out, all the cheerleaders. The easy ones.

"The cheerleaders are easy Billy. One tequila and they let you go first base, two tequila's and they blow the rocket, three tequila's and they are on their backs."

That's what his friend had told him anyway and tonight he was eager to find out if it was true. Was it possible to be so nervous and excited at the same time? He had never even touched a girl before. The only girl who ever touched him was Palm and her five friends. He had touched his Mother, but that turned his stomach. He could safely say it nearly turned him off women altogether. Tonight was going to be different. He couldn't wait to touch a girl and feel something towards her, attraction.

***

As the door opened a cloud of smoke expelled from inside. Loud singing and laughing erupted as Billy entered the bar. He wasn't used to being out let alone in a bar at night. This behavior would not be tolerated by his Mother. It's a good job she is at home lying in bed with a trail of saliva dripping from her lop sided mouth, he thought. A devious smile crossed his face at the thought of her alone and helpless. He felt empowered by his own authority and power.

They are laughing at you Billy. They know you are a virgin. The tramps sitting up at the bar can smell virgins. They could teach you a thing or two. That one with the bleached blonde hair and the cherry lipstick sitting alone, she can go all night. I doubt you could. I think you will only last seconds, like your Pop. He was useless in bed too.

Billy needed a drink, anything would do. Since he had tequila on his mind, a tequila he ordered and then another and another. He started to relax. His shoulders eased and he felt more comfortable. He noticed the girl at the bar with the cherry lipstick. Her sea blue eyes invited him over. Billy looked behind him; he thought she must be looking at somebody else. The bar was actually empty apart from him and sea eyes in the corner. She waved to him to come over. His heart sped up and knocked frantically at his chest. He felt tiny flutters in his stomach, like a butterflies wings tickling his tummy. *This is my lucky night. Act cool and stay calm!*

"Hey can I buy you a drink?"
The girl smiled, she revealed a glowing set of perfect teeth. Her eyes lit up as she smiled, so did Billy's insides but that could have been from all the tequila he devoured.

"I would let you but the bar is actually closed now."
She crossed her legs as she spoke and Billy couldn't help notice how toned they were especially her thighs. She wore a micro

mini skirt. His mother was right, she was a tramp but after a few tequila's Billy didn't care.

"No, it's too early yet. Hey can we get some service over here?" he slurred.

The barman wasn't impressed; he threw his eyes up to heaven and muttered,

"Jesus, there is always one."

The blonde grabbed his arm as it was just about to pound on the bar.

"Shush, you will get us kicked out, if you're not careful."

The thought had crossed his mind before and tonight he was in the mood for some fun, he felt like a new person. Billy the Kid was ready for some fun.

The barman went into the back to get some refills as he did Billy backed up and tried to jump over the bar. He jumped alright but missed the bar, his sight and judgment were severely impaired. He knocked his knee onto a bar stool and didn't even feel it. The blonde giggled as he tried to stand up straight. He looked like a new born calf, all feet as he swayed from foot to foot. His eyes firmly on the bar. Billy ran faster this time and cleared the wooden top with one swoop. The girl clapped but missed every second clap.

"Now ma'am, what can I get you?" he said, squinting to read to labels.

"Ah, here it is-the drink with the worm. Would you care for some lemon and salt with that?"

The blonde was in hysterics, and in his drunken stupor, Billy failed to notice she laughed like a hyena. Had he been sober he would have noticed she was about twenty years older than he. The barman reappeared just as Billy and the blonde downed the double tequila.

"Right, that's it Jerk. Get out. I have had enough shit tonight without you creating more. Get the fuck out!" He pushed Billy out the side entrance of the bar.

"Hey why didn't you tell me that was there? I wouldn't have to have jumped." Billy shouted. The blonde grabbed her cheap imitation bag and scuttled out the door after Billy. Once outside they fell to the floor laughing.

"That was the best fun I have had in ages," admitted Billy.

"Me too, it doesn't have to stop here though."

Billy agreed, he leaned over and his lips found her cherry stained lips. His stomach flipped as her tongue slipped between his lips. He could have died right there, he had been missing out on so much looking after his Mother. Her hot tongue moved in circular motions around his mouth and tipped off his tongue.

"You got a place near hear, honey?" She asked.

Billy nodded.

***

"The keys don't fit." Billy was trying to push his locker key through the lock in the front door. They were making so much noise, Doreen would surely hear. He hadn't thought about her all night. Eventually he figured out his mistake and opened the door.

"We have to be quiet, my Mom will be sleeping."

The blonde held him tight with her two arms firmly around his chest as she followed him through the house. The sound of Doreen's muffled snore could be heard drifting from her room. Billy led her to his bedroom. He swept all his clothes off his bed and began to take off his sweater. Her hands found his shirt and ripped it off. She then traced her finger tips all over his abs. Billy left the light off. He let his own hands roam over to her body. He could feel the heat off her body and smell her sweet cherry smell. His clammy hands hurried over her body to her chest. They quickly removed her bra and freed her ample breasts. His breath quickened as he fumbled his way around her body. She could tell he wasn't used to this. She didn't care.

The blonde took his hands and placed them on her breasts. Billy felt a hot flush rise from his neck, for a moment he thought he was going to puke, instead it was just excitement. She pushed him down onto the bed and forced herself on top of him. Billy didn't object. He liked a woman who took charge. Billy pulled his jeans off and his underpants. She took her panties off and left her skirt on. He liked the feel of her silky smooth legs rubbing against his bare skin. The blonde climbed further onto him until he could feel himself inside of her. She bounced up and down as Billy moaned and sighed. His head thrashing against his pillows as his hands dug into the sheets.

He felt ready to explode as beads of sweat dripped of his forehead.

Is that as good for you as it is for me? I knew you would like it rough Billy!

I also knew you couldn't hold it long enough to satisfy me.

Billy tried to push her off. She would not move. He felt the vomit rise from his stomach, an acidic belch gurgled out. His hands fumbled for the light. It wasn't there. Billy felt light headed. The blonde pushed him down again, this time with a force even he couldn't stop. Her hips gyrated on him again working up a rhythm.

"No, get off me." Billy tried to push her off.

It's no good. I will never leave you Billy. I love you too much; she doesn't love you, it's just lust. Stay still and don't move, you're spoiling it.

His fingers found the light switch and flipped it on. Billy stared opened mouthed into the blondes face. Her features were old and drawn. Her mouth was twisted to one side and carried a sinister smile. Billy would recognize those features anywhere, his Mothers. Billy heard a loud scream and realized it came from him. He tried to push the blonde wench off him but she held him tighter. Her purse lips moved as the voice he loathed so much escaped.

"What are you waiting for? Let's finish this, shall we? I was enjoying it until you stopped prematurely. Like father, like son.

Her dark callous eyes bore into Billy, taking in his exposed and vulnerable body.

Billy panicked as his hands tightened around her neck. Doreen's eyes looked back at him, they unnerved him but not enough to release his grip.

"Tighter, you wimp! I am enjoying this."

The whites of her eyes turned a pink color as her sea blue eyes bulged and the veins popped. Billy's eyes were firmly shut. He couldn't look at his Mother any longer. He heard a rattling sound emit from her throat as she released her last breath.

Billy forced his eyes open, he immediately wished he hadn't as he laid them on the sea blue eyes and the blonde hair he recognized from the bar. He leaned over the side of the bed as he wretched.

"No, no, I meant to kill my mother, not you," he said, kissing her cheek lightly. A necklace of purple finger bruises started to appear on her neck. Billy shuddered at the sight of what he had done.

Now you have done it, you dumb fuck. You have really done it this time Billy.

"Shut up already, I don't want to hear you, get out of my head."

Billy left his bedroom and ran towards his mother's room. She lay peacefully in bed.

Millions of thoughts swam through his head, all of them revolved around his hatred towards his Mother. There was only one way to stop the voice and that was to get rid of its source. With hesitation or thought, Billy grasped his murderer's hands around his Mothers throat. The old bag flinched at his touch, her eyes opened. She looked frightened as his hands gripped her neck. Her twisted mouth tried to scream but nothing came out only the awful gasping sound. Her tongue managed to poke out and reminded Billy of the one that had just been in his mouth. He wretched again, not letting go of his grip. Doreen's mangled fingers twitched as her limp body deflated. Suddenly there was silence. No voices, no gasping for breath, only the deafening silence. He was all alone with two dead bodies and his own voice.

What have you done Billy? You have done it now. We are going to jail, just you and me forever.

About the author: Lorraine has been writing for just over a year. She has had numerous short stories published with Pill Hill Press, Static Movement, Wicked East Press and Norgus Press. In the future, she plans to attempt to write a novel; watch this space…

WHEN WE ARE TOGETHER
Sandra Crook

Not long now... just another ten days and then we'll be together. But the days go so slowly. I can scarcely wait.

How sweet you looked this morning walking to the bus stop, that pink dress flaring prettily around your slender legs. You turn heads, you know. So much so that I knew no-one would ever notice me, strolling along behind you.

Sitting right behind you on the bus, inhaling your perfume (spicy, heady, but rather strong) I decided that when we're together you probably won't wear that. No. Something rather more fragrant, flowery... we can choose it together if you like.

I thought you might leave your office at lunchtime, as you normally do, but I was disappointed. I waited for a good hour, but you didn't show. As a rule, I don't like it when people don't keep to their routine. I find it upsetting. But we can work on that, no problem. We've got plenty of time.

When you called at the wine bar after you left work this evening, I was right behind you again. Those girls you were with seemed quite uncouth, noisy, completely lacking in grace. Not your type. I thought you seemed a little uncomfortable around them. I think it might be better if you don't see them any more once we're together.

And that lout who kept leering at you from across the room... touching your elbow at the bar... made me very angry. Couldn't he tell, just looking at you, that you were out of his league? I had to deal with him later on. Luckily he cut through the underpass to the bus station so I had a word or two with him there. Well, we didn't exactly speak... but I think he understood me. At the end.

It took a while, though. That's why I couldn't follow you home.

But I know you got home safely. I was watching from the shadows opposite your house, waiting for your bedroom light to go on. It was worth the wait, though it was midnight when you went to bed. I'm a bit of an "early to bed" person myself. You'll soon get used to that, though. And you'll feel better for it.

I caught a quick glimpse before you closed the curtains, your long hair swinging loosely across your shoulders. I prefer short hair myself–I hate all those messy hairs that gather round the plug hole in the shower. That's something we can talk about, though, when we're together.

Last night I lay awake thinking about the things we can do together, all that we can share over the years to come. I've been so lonely, you know. Since the last one left. Rather suddenly, I thought, and without explanation. That mustn't happen again.

Ever.

Are you nervous? I expect so, being away from home for the first time. But don't worry. I knew when you came to view the apartment that we would be perfect flat-mates, and I could see you knew it too. It was in your eyes.

I'll look after you. We girls need to stick together.

About the author: Sandra Crook has been published by Every Day Fiction, Every Day Poets, Backhand Stories, MicroHorror, The Pygmy Giant, Shine Journal, Eclectic Flash, Long Story Short, Horrorzine and the Financial Times Weekend Review. Her published work, waterway cruising reports and photographs can be found at castelsarrasin.wordpress.com

VERTICAL SCARS

Voicu Mihnea Simandan

"But forgetting's not something you do, it happens to you."
(John Fowles, *The Collector*)

The Freshies Party brought together not only the new students and their future professors, but also the senior students of the Institute. As usual, I arrived early. I had always thought that it was better to be ten minutes early than five minutes late. The room was almost empty. A few men in navy blue shirts were arranging the chairs in a semicircle, while others were testing the sound system. I found a place for myself in the back and sat quietly, waiting for the ceremony to start.

I had always been attracted to this part of the world. It fascinated me. I had read, seen and heard so much about it, but never really got my parents' permission to come here. Things changed after I graduated second in my class with a bachelor degree in Asian History. As a reward for my achievements my parents granted me the permission to enroll in a postgraduate program in Bangkok.

Soon the room was noisy with all sorts of nationalities. After everybody calmed down and found a chair to sit down, the director of the Institute opened the ceremony. While she was speaking I had the chance to have a better look at my future classmates. I was planning to have a great time here, far away from home and free of my parents' supervision. The girls were all dressed up, trying to look as good as possible.

"You both have to try and eat the apple suspended by the thread," the senior student in charge with entertainment explained.

I moved fast enough so as to be paired with the Chinese girl. She wasn't sitting too far from me. Dressed all in black, her tight skirt revealed interesting curves. A deep cleavage was automatically covered every two minutes with the long sleeve of

124

her costume jacket she was wearing. I had a better look at her face the moment we were in front of each other, with just an apple dangling between our noses. She had a round face with porcelain white skin. The scarlet lipstick on her small, thin lips made her so desirable.

As we tried to bite the apple at the same time she continuously closed her eyes.

"Open your eyes and bite the damn apple," I whispered as we gave it another try.

The other teams were doing a far better job. "You're not kissing me," I went on. "We have to win!" I didn't like to lose. We had to win. I had to win. I had always won. And from that moment on I wanted to win her.

Apart from the boring start, the party turned out to be great fun. As I was preparing to leave, I looked at her for the last time.

"I didn't get your name," I said when I was near the tinted glass exit door.

"It's Yin," she replied removing a strand of hair that had fallen over her face.

"I'm Mike. See you in class next week."

"Bye," she smiled back, waving her little hand in an exaggerated coquettish manner.

The building where we had our courses wasn't too far from the place where I lived. Although it was equipped with the latest technology and had a good resource center, it was painted in depressing shades of grey. Happy to once again be in an air-conditioned room, I took out my writing stuff and waited for the class to start. The first week I had the chance to meet all my classmates, but not all of my professors. Some of them were still on holiday, and one was attending a conference in Malaysia.

The Chinese girl used to sit opposite me. She seemed quite interested in what the lecturer was saying, but there was something strange in her demeanor. Her short skirt revealed her bare legs, while she absent-mindedly played with her toes and her high-heel sandals. This time she had arranged her hair in a big knot on top of her head. Her round ears revealed a multitude of earrings of different shapes and sizes.

As I was checking out her looks she suddenly faced me. I was caught. I smiled, raising my thick eyebrows twice. She grinned and said something mutely. While I was trying to read her lips saying, "Pay attention!" her hand pointed at the teacher. It was then when I saw the scars. They were ugly scars. Some were short, others were long and protuberant. When she put her hand back on her notebook I came back to the classroom reality.

A neat lounge was left aside excursively for the graduate students. A couch, a few armchairs and a long table with many chairs made the room a pleasant place to read *The Nation*, an English language newspaper provided by the Institute. It was in this lounge where we met one day.

She took out her laptop as soon as she sat down in an armchair on my left. We said nothing for quite a while. When I got bored with the newspaper, I turned my attention towards what she was doing.

"I'm reorganizing my files. I've just installed the English version of Microsoft and it feels strange," she said shifting the laptop at an angle so that we could both see the screen.

"What's this?" I asked pointing at a folder called "Model pics."

"Oh, it's me. Before coming to Thailand I used to be a motor show model," she said and clicked on the folder.

They were amazing. It was not only because the photos were taken by a professional photographer. She also knew how to pose and attract the viewers' attention. I ran my eyes over the photos again and again.

"These are the best ones," she confessed.

"I want this one," I said. She was on top of the hood of a Jeep. The long red dress she was wearing was blown by the wind, revealing two crossed legs. A strip had fallen down her arm, exposing one shoulder. The smile on her face was almost perverse. She was perfect.

"That was taken during my last performance in an outdoor exhibition in Peking."

"Could you e-mail it to me?" I asked while turning the laptop towards me to have a better look at the picture.

The next day I got up unusually early. I was so anxious to

get to the computer lab to check my e-mail as soon as possible. I realized how childish I was, so I tried to go back to sleep, but I couldn't. The breakfast wasn't as satisfying as the previous mornings. The lady selling noodles smiled when I paid and I rushed out of the restaurant, without even finishing the bowl I had ordered.

My mother's and a couple of friends' e-mails from back home were in my inbox. Then I saw hers. There was no other written message except "Enjoy" and her name. I set the attachment as the screen's wallpaper replacing the university's logo. I knew that it wouldn't last there for too long, but it made me feel good. I wished I had my own laptop so that I could admire her whenever I wanted to.

I used to meet her quite often, especially at lunchtime. One day I saw that she had a fresh scar on her wrist. I stared at it, feeling my appetite go away.

"What's that all about, Yin?" I asked pointing towards her scarred arms.

"Oh, it's nothing. Never mind."

"Why are you doing that?"

"It's a long story and you won't understand."

"Try me," I insisted.

"Come on, you don't want to know," she said.

"I do want but, anyway, why don't you do it properly? I mean, you've tried so many times, and you still couldn't finish what you've started."

"How do you know that?"

"Just look at your arms. They're too many of them. Some are too small to even cause any bleeding at all. You're just doing it because you want to attract people's attention."

"You're wrong!"

"Then prove it."

"No. It's personal."

"How personal can it be if you do it in such a way that anybody can see your scars? And there's a new one. When did you do it? Yesterday?"

"Leave me alone. You know nothing."

"I probably don't know the reasons behind all of your

scars, but there's one thing I do know for sure..."

"And what's that?"

"You don't want to die!" I looked at her and then at her arms, but she didn't say anything, so I went on. "All the cuts are made horizontally and you take good care of your wounds after you make the cuts. Believe me; you don't want to actually die."

"You don't know that," she said.

"If you really want to die, then the next time, you should cut yourself along the vein. Vertically."

"You're mean."

"I'm just right. That's all."

Soon after we finished our meals she opened up.

"My father used to beat me up," she started. "Whenever he was angry or drunk he would start beating me up. I still have his scars on my legs. He almost did it methodically every other day. He usually used a wooden clothes hanger, but sometimes he would beat me with his belt too. I wasn't even allowed to cry. If I cried, he would beat me harder."

She paused and stared outside for a while.

"What about your mother? Where was she all that time?"

"She was in the same situation. He would beat her too if she interfered. The best thing was to suffer in silence until his anger passed away. Then, after he put the hanger back into my own closet and banged the door behind him, I was free to cry. The older I got, the less I cried. Now, nobody can make me cry."

"But don't you think it's better sometimes to cry, than cut yourself?"

"I'm Chinese. I can take it. It's my *karma*."

"*Karma* has nothing to do with this. What you need now to do is try and heal your wounds."

"They will heal. Don't worry about this scar," she said pointing at the new one.

"I'm not talking about your scars. You need to heal on the inside."

"But I can't. The past will always haunt me."

"Why do you say that?"

"When I was eighteen I left my home, found a job and went to university. After I met him I thought that my life would finally turn out well, but I guess I wasn't that lucky." After a long pause, she went on. "He was in the same year at university, and I immediately fell in love with him. We moved in together, but soon afterwards, I realized that I had left my violent father to be abused by somebody else."

"Why didn't you leave him too?"

"Because I couldn't. I loved him. And he loved me, only that he lost his temper too often and I was always there to suffer the consequences."

"That's not love!"

"He helped me financially and with my studies throughout university."

"And where is he now?"

"He won a scholarship in England. I couldn't remain alone in China so I came here. He's the one who sponsors me for everything in Thailand, but he will be able to do it only for one year. After that, I'm on my own again. And I don't want to go back to China. There's nothing left for me there. Only sorrow."

"But don't you realize that you have brought that sorrow with you here. You have to stop hurting yourself. Let it all pass. Start a new life."

"I can't. I can't control myself."

From that point on I felt pity for her. Every time I saw her I remembered what a harsh life she had had, and tried to make her happy. But she didn't seem to appreciate it. Once I even tried to help her with the assignments, but she took it as an offense.

The truth was that there was a lot of work to be done. Books and articles had to be read, essays had to be written, and research had to be done every week. Dr. Giovanni pushed us to the limit, giving us more and more homework to do. He was quite a character. Most of the students enjoyed his classes. And, of course, his looks counted too. Every girl on the campus was after him. However, not only was Dr. Giovanni married, his wife was also a professor at the Institute. Nevertheless, for some that fact simply didn't matter.

It was during one of his courses that Yin sent me a message. I couldn't believe my eyes. It wasn't her style to mock or tease me, so I had to take the note literally. It read: "I have a

queen-size bed with no one to share it with tonight. Interested?"
I looked at her. She smiled and slowly started spreading her legs
in the most obscene manner.

It was the biggest disappointment of my life. The image
that I had about her in the red dress, totally vanished after that
night. The beautiful butterfly transformed into a vulgar and
noisy caterpillar with small and hairy breasts. And as if that
wasn't enough, while I was resting my head on the pillow she
said, "You don't have to spend the night here."

I was disgusted. I turned my head towards her and asked,
"Are you throwing me out?"

She took out a packet of cigarettes from the nightstand. "I
think you'd better go now," she said while lighting up.

The next day she acted as if nothing had happened. She
remained the same girl, always looking good and ready to make
new friends. We exchanged notes during classes on regular a
basis, and soon after that night we both knew what each of us
wanted.

One late afternoon after I'd finished the final draft of
an article, I decided to pay a visit to Dr. Dalin, Dr. Giovanni's
wife. She was the managing editor of the Institute's journal,
and I hoped that I might also see it published. On my way to
her office I passed Dr. Giovanni's office, so I thought of greeting
him. I could hear that there was someone laughing in his office,
but I didn't bother to knock on the door. He was famous for his
nonconformity. I opened the door, and then there was silence.
Wearing a short skirt, Yin was sitting on his desk dangling her
legs freely. Her sandals were thrown carelessly on the floor.

"Sorry," was the only thing I said, backed out and rushed
upstairs to Dr. Dalin's office.

In just a few weeks, the Institute no longer had that
peaceful atmosphere I was used to. There were rumors that
some of the teachers were planning to leave, while Dr. Giovanni
was no longer the students' favorite lecturer. And soon I found
out why.

Back into Dr. Dalin's office for feedback on my article, I
was surprised to see the mess inside. Boxes of every size were
scattered on the floor, while piles of papers waited to be sorted.

When she saw me enter, she tried to put on a smile. But I couldn't be fooled. In fact she couldn't fool herself either. Her eyes were red.

"I'm going back home," she answered my unasked question.

"To Malaysia? Why?"

"Yes. Well... I guess there's not much left for me here."

"But..." I said, "... don't you..." Then it hit me. The secret of Yin and Dr. Giovanni's affair had finally reached her ears.

It was pathetic. The way they flirted in class, the good grades she received and the obvious looks they exchanged made me sick.

As soon as the first trimester was over, Dr Dalin left to Malaysia, while Dr. Giovanni and Yin spent their holiday together somewhere in Europe.

When the lectures started again I was so happy not to have the Italian, as the students had taken to calling Dr. Giovanni, as a lecturer. Yin was absent almost all the time. By now she was a paria in everyone's eyes and she knew it.

Then, one evening, while I was closing the lounge door, the director of the Institute took me aside and whispered, "How does Yin feel? Is she going to be all right?"

"What are you talking about?" I asked.

"What do you mean? You don't know?"

"What happened?"

"Yin was hospitalized two days ago. She tried to commit suicide..."

That evening I visited her in the hospital. She was a wreck. Her hair wasn't brushed and was spread in all directions on the pillow. Her face was jaundiced and her lips were colorless. Her left wrist was bandaged up with white gauze. A thin line of blood had made it through the gauze, leaving a vertical red mark. As soon as I sat down on the bed she put her arms around my neck and started crying.

"He left me. He left me," she said sobbing. "He left me..."

About the author: Voicu Mihnea Simandan is a thirty-three years old Romanian writer, freelance journalist and educator who has lived in Thailand since 2002. He has published three books of nonfiction, one book for children, and several short stories in different magazines, journals and anthologies. He is now finalising his first novel, "The Buddha Head," a historical thriller set in Thailand. He can be contacted at www.simandan. com.

VERTE
Richard I. Prescott

He went by the name of Thorne. It was not his real name, but that did not matter. It was a name that he could hide behind, and mascaraed as a character. His image was the epitome of an emo stereotype: a romanticized embodiment of angst that was birthed from music. Music was his life, his nourishment, and blood. He was sure that if he were to slice into his wrist, (which he had no intention of doing), then musical notes would bleed out.

Thorne glanced around the bar - which was nearly empty. It was a Tuesday, and so the patrons of The Confines were mostly sober. He had no interest in being sober. He also had no interest in company, and was glad that there was no one that he knew. He was seventeen, and his fashion firmly asserted this, but he had drunk here many times. This bar was where the under-agers went to drink after stealing money from their mother's or father's wallet. If not, then they would simply take their parent's beer, wine, vodka, or anything alcoholic, and sit in one of the various car parks.

Absinthe was the drink of choice within The Confines. It was the drink of the bohemians. The bar was where the freaks, weirdoes, and outcasts congregated each evening. During the weekdays they would talk about music, literature, politics, and their individual subculture, while at the weekends they would be a dense mass of studded jackets, velvet, bondage straps, Doc Martins, and hair that has been stained impossible colours - all thrusting themselves into each other; dancing the night away, while avoiding a stray liberty spike, or moheaken that could possibly spear into their eyes. The music were local DIY bands, that would pulse incomprehensible screams through a microphone, while all the instruments would collide inside the speakers, merge, and lose their separate distinctions.

Thorne walked to the bar. A punk was leant over it. She looked at Thorne, or rather – looked around him, and he could see that she was on more than alcohol. She then returned to staring through the transparent glass of the fridge that contained the different bottles of beer, alcopops, and soft-drink cans.

"What can I get you, sweetie," said Maggie, materialising from behind the threads of beads that lead to the small kitchen.

"Absinthe," Thorne said. "Triple."

Maggie nodded, and picked up one of the many bottles that sat behind her on the shelves. She poured it into a long-stemmed glass, and passed it over. He paid, and carried his drink to an unoccupied corner.

Smashing Pumpkins was playing in the background, but Thorne did not know the title of the song. He had never been a huge fan, but most of his friends were, and they had played many of the Pumpkin's songs while on car journeys.

Thorne was on a mission to get as drunk as his body would allow. He looked at the bright green liquid within his glass, and wished it was as potent as classic absinthe. It was merely an urban legend that this beverage would make the drinker hallucinate. He knew this, but it still did not stop him and his friends attempting to drink enough for the Wormwood to take effect. Those nights had been sent into a swirl of alcoholic delirium, and resulted in much vomiting.

He fished into his pocket, and produced his phone. There were no messages, but this was no surprise. The most frequent texts that he had received were from Scott, but there would be no more texts from his ex. Thorne flicked through his contact list, and hovered over Scott's number. He considered texting him. At that moment, Thorne was not above begging Scott to take him back, but his pride stopped him. He knew that begging would somehow lead into an argument, and while this seemed like a perfectly good reason to text him, Thorne knew that it would not help matters. It would simply help him vent his emotion, his anger, frustration, and tears.

Scott had dumped Thorne earlier that day. It was over the phone, and while that was widely considered the disrespectful, and cowardice way out, Thorne was grateful that it had happened like that. "You are just too immature for me," Scott had said. "You seem dedicated to putting on an act, rather than just being yourself. I hate how you dedicate your life to being a stereotype. I wanted to date you, not your image, but you seem too dedicated to being something that you are not."

Thorne had stayed quiet while listening to this. He did not really know what to say back. Scott just could not understand how the image was a strong part of him. It acted as a safety blanket that barred people from penetrating in, and seeing the real Thorne. He detested the person beneath, and refused to let other suffer him. But he was sure that his image was enveloping him, suffocating him, and becoming a part of him. Soon it would not be an act, or, at least, that was what he wished for.

Thorne raised his glass, and took a long gulp. If he was not intent on getting drunk, then he would had requested a sugar-cube and melted it on a spoon. Tonight was not the night to drink Absinthe correctly, or even to taste it. In fact, Thorne was sure that he was only drinking it out of habit, or possibly because he felt that it was his true drink. Absinthe was the drink of artists, and Thorne considered himself to be a musical artist. He had read about how Edgar Allen Poe was constantly fucked on the stuff when he wrote his masterpieces. While Thorne strongly felt that intoxication was not a necessity to tap into a person's creativity – if a person was gifted, then they could simply bring out their talent whenever they wish – he still felt that it could not hurt. He had joked with his friends that Absinthe was his muse.

He took another sip, and basked in the familiar taste of the herbal liquorice that was wormwood – his sweet poison. Thorne then realised that he was no longer alone. There was someone sitting opposite. He looked up, hardly believing that he did not notice someone walk over, and sit down right in front of him.

"Hello," he said, in a tone of voice which really meant "What the fuck are you doing?"

The guy was not much older than him, possibly his own age. His clothes were basic – white top, dark blue jeans, green hair sat on his shoulders, and there were a pair of sunglasses on his face. He had no drink, but was looking in fascination at Thorne's absinthe.

"Ah, an Absinthe drinker, I see. A very good drink," he said, voice like cotton soaked in chlorine; soft but with a distinct edge.

"This is one of the few places that you can get the stuff," Thorne replied. He was not rude enough to tell the stranger to go away, but he kept a sharp tone in his voice which stated clearly that he was in no mood for company, least of all the type that just invites his self over.

"It is shockingly obscure these days," the guy said.

As though you were around to see how popular it used to be, thought Thorne, but he did not say this.

"You know the drink used to be banned?"

Thorne nodded. "Yeah, it was because people said that it made them hallucinate. It was all bullshit."

"Well, you never know. Wormwood can cause hallucinations; there could have easily been a select few bottles that had incorrect measurements of the ingredients."

Thorne shrugged.

There was a brief silence. Thorne took another sip, and then another deeper one. Before he knew it the glass was empty. He laid it back upon the table.

"Would you like another?" offered the stranger.

Thorne nodded. "Yes please."

The guy left and soon returned with two fresh glasses of the green stuff. He placed Thorne's before him, and Thorne stroked his fingers around the stem. He knew that people spiked drinks with rohypnol far too often in these places, but he did not care. Thorne never turned down a free drink and, besides, this guy was not the worst looking guy in the bar. He would have no problem waking up to find him looming over him, thrusting into Thorne. But this though could just be the alcohol talking. He realised just how tipsy that one drink had made him. No doubt it was because of how quickly he had consumed it.

"So, what name do you go by?" asked the man. "I am guessing by your appearance that you could be in a band. Do you have a stage name?"

"Thorne."

"Ah, I like it. Are you a prickly fellow, Thorne?"

"I can be," said Thorne, and wished he had not said that in a prickly tone. "And who are you?" he said, contorting his voice into something much softer.

"I am la fée verte,"

Thorne smiled. "You are The Green Fairy?"

"Indeed," said the stranger, matter-of-factly.

"Isn't the green fairy meant to be a woman? Have you had a sex change recently?"

The stranger laughed. "My gender is entirely up to the person who happens to hallucinate me."

"So you are saying that you are a figment of my imagination," said Thorne with a wry smile.

"Nope. As you saw earlier, I went up to the bar and purchased two drinks. I could not do that if I did not exist."

This was a point that Thorne was about to make, and he felt slightly disappointed that the man had beaten him to the punch.

"So, are you in my mind, or a real person," asked Thorne with pleasant sarcasm. He was quite enjoying the bizarre conversation.

"Oh, a bit of both."

Thorne nodded, humouring the man.

"You do not look all that green," said Thorne.

"I am quite green," said the apparent fairy, pointedly twirling his green hair around his finger.

Thorne went to take a sip of his drink, but was stopped when the man held up a hand. The hand then went into his pocket, and produced one of the most beautiful ornate spoons that Thorne had ever seen. It was incrusted with small diamonds around its edge, and was dotted with small holes. The man then plucked a sugar cube from thin air. Well, it looked like he did, but it was obviously a trick. He placed the cube on top the spoon, dipped it into Thorne's drink, and allowed it to absorb the liquid for a moment before raising it back up, and kept it hovered just above the bright green surface.

Thorne watched as the stranger set light to the cube, let it to burn for a few seconds, and dropped it into the drink, setting the drink ablaze. He wondered if the guy typically walked around with these items in his pockets, on the off-chance that he would come across some lonely boy drinking Absinthe.

"The Bohemian Method," said Thorne with a smile. He would have preferred the cube to be melted with water, rather than have much of the alcohol burned away, but he felt no reason to complain.

"A Flaming Green Fairy is the best way to serve the drink, in my opinion," the man replied.

Thorne took a sip of the warm drink. It was very pleasant, and the taste was notably less harsh.

"So, do you not have a name?" Thorne asked, after putting the glass back onto the table.

"What would you like to call me?" asked the stranger.

Thorn considered for a moment. "Verte," he decided.

Verte smiled widely. "I could not approve more."

***

It was warm out, but Thorne was sure that this was likely due to his drunkenness. The drink had led to confidence, and he had secured himself to Verte. Verte did not complain. He had wrapped his hands around Thorne, and kissed him. His lips tasted of wormwood, and never had a kiss tasted so familiar. He also had come to believe that Verte truly was The Green Fairy, and he rejected the sober part of his mind that insisted that this was just him wishing Verte was the embodiment of Absinthe.

"Where shall we go?" asked Thorne. "My flat is not too far, and I guess my roommate would be out by now."

Martin was Thorne's roommate. He was a geeky boy that worked in the local second-hand DVD store. Most of his life was spent sat at the desk, watching films on a shitty little TV, while being rudely interrupted by customers, or his boss reminding him that he still needed to price-up the new DVD's, and put them on the shelves.

"No," said Verte. "I like being outside. Is there a near-by field where we could... chat?" He chortled at this.

Thorne nodded, and directed Verte toward the local field.

***

The Downs was a bit of a misleading name. Most considered it to be far too small to be called The Downs, and Thorne was sure that the name was not its original title, but a sarcastic one that had caught on in the past. It was usually occupied by kids, desperately showing off how much they could drink, and smoking cigarettes that they had paid a drunken adult to buy for them. Thankfully The Downs was empty.

Thorne and Verte found a patch they approved off, and sat down – Thorne positively fell down, and found this incredibly hilarious. Verte smiled, and pulled him into an embrace.

"Scott was a fool to let you go," said Verte.

This roused Thorne. "How do you know about Scott? I did not talk about him."

"I am the Absinth Fairy, you have consumed me tonight. I can see into you," said Verte, as though speaking to a child.

In reply, Thorne leaned in, and kissed Verte once more. Verte rubbed Thorne's leg, pulled back, and Thorne then noticed that a guitar was clutched in the fairy's hand.

"I would like to hear you play," said Verte.

Thorne smiled. It did not matter how drunk he got, he could still handle a guitar. He received the instrument, and gave it an experimental strum. The strings broke the silence of The Downs, and Thorne could feel the subtle vibrations. It was perfect. There was no tuning necessary. He then unleashed a few more cords into the night.

Verte relaxed onto the grass, ready for the music.

Thorne did not feel the need to get acquainted with the new guitar, it felt like an old friend. He began to play one of his own tracks. A haunting number, but glimmer of hope, that he titled "Malicious Sedative." It was inspired by the music of Akira Yamaoka, a composer who he considered was an underappreciated musical genius.

He found himself becoming the music. He was plucking his heart strings, and the sounds were engulfing, the field, the town, the world. Then the music was the only thing in the world.

When he finished, he placed down the instrument. When he drew back, Verte pulled him back in, and gave him a deep and passionate kiss. His lips tasted of Thorne's beverage, and his tongue tasted of sugar; that, Thorne was sure, was melting, and dripping down his throat.

When the kiss ended, Verte's grip on him grew stronger, and he felt like he was sinking into him. Thorne caressed Verte's back, submitted himself to the drunken delirium, and to Verte's embrace.

"Your music is an expression of your soul. You are an innocent child, terrified of this world. I can tell this in the pauses between your cords. You seek someone to protect you."

Thorne simply nodded.

"I can rectify this," said Verte. The cotton in his voice became softer.

Thorne felt Verte's hands smooth over him. His penis steadily grew hard inside his skinny jeans. He knew he wanted Verte to take him, and not only sexually. He wanted this stranger to claim him.

Verte's hand had snaked beneath Thorne's shirt now, and was caressing his waist. The flesh was warm against his own, like recently flamed Absinthe, and Thorne could feel his hairs stick out with the stimulation. Thorne raised his head to kiss Verte once more, and he noticed that Verte's skin was a dark green. He was sure that it would be bright with light. Verte kissed him, and then lowered him over the grass, no, not grass, it was a quilt.

Thorne was on top his bed, and Verte was there with him.

"I am hallucinating," said Thorne, confused.

"Are you really?" said Verte, a wry smile on his face.

Verte began to unbutton Thorne's shirt, but then they were both naked. At first Thorne attempted to make sense of how time suddenly had a mind of its own, but then he just did not care.

They made love. Their bodies merged, twisted, and undulated against each other. Verte's flesh tasted of Wormwood and sugar, and did not feel fully solid. It was intoxicating, and Thorne had never felt more at home. Verte's body was familiar, like they had been previous lovers. Thorne gasped and writhed in pleasure as Verte tasted him, and when Thorne tasted Verte, he was drinking.

Absinthe, Verte was Absinthe. He was a lover and a drink.

He was an intoxicant, and a man. Thorne drank Verte's body, and Verte stimulated Thorne's. When Verte came, Thorne was drenched in the taste of Wormwood. He then realised that he was drowning.

***

He was no longer in his bedroom, no longer in The Downs, he was somewhere new. He was also wrong. Thorne was not drowning, but he was in a liquid, and he knew that he was now alone.

He looked around, and soon realised that he had no body. The world was now tinted a bright green, and he soon realised that he was on a desk. He was inside a bottle. Verte was towering above him. His skin was bright green, as were his eyes, and his hair. His wings were also green.

Thorne realised that they were back at The Confines. It was empty. He was on top the bar, and Verte was sat opposite on a stool. Verte stroked the glass barrier.

"Now you have been taken away from your life," Verte said, with evil in his voice. "You shall no longer suffer the trials of the world, you will no longer be a victim. Is this what you wanted?"

Thorne knew that he could not reply.

Verte continued. "Do not worry, you shall be back before you know it. Absinthe is the drink of the bohemian. You could be the hallucination of a great artist: Maybe a painter, a writer, a musician, who knows. They all need their green muse."

Verte smiled then, but it was not a wicked smile. "We all have our place in the world, Thorne. I have given you the gift of purpose."

He then got up, and put his sunglasses back on, covering up his luminous green eyes. He looked toward the door, and then back again at Thorne.

"Good luck, my little green fairy. May it be the next Francis Bacon that you intoxicate."

Verte nodded at Thorne, and walked out the door.

TWISTED LOVE

About the author: Richard I. Prescott is a young author from England. Dark Fantasy, horror, and gothic tales drip from his pen. This was one of his more fun stories.

A Thousand Injuries
Michael Giorgio

Angie figured that one more really good whine ought to do it. She breathed in deeply and let it go. "But, Mom, I have *got* to go to the mall *tonight!* I heard Brad Isherwood tell Josh he was gonna be hangin' with some buds there. I have *got* to see Brad before Heather Penscott does!" She willed a small tear to come to her eye and roll gently down her cheek, but none came.

"Angelica Lange, quit trying to change the subject." Her mother sighed. "We were talking about you doing your school work. Now, what homework do you have tonight?"

"None." Angie could feel the glare from her mother's eyes burning into the pit of her stomach.

"Angie, I called your teachers today. *All* of them. Now, I'm asking you again, as patiently as I can, what homework do you have?"

"I don't know," Angie answered without looking at her.

"Well, I do. I know that you have a math test on Friday and a quiz tomorrow in English Lit on *A Cask of Amontillado.* Have you even read the story yet?"

Angie hadn't even been in English class for the last two days. "I can read it again on the bus tomorrow," she bluffed. "Besides, it's not that long a story."

"Good! If it's not that long, then you'll have no problem reading and thoroughly understanding it tonight, will you?"

"But Mom—"

"No more discussion." Angie's mother sighed and wiped a strand of hair from her lined forehead. "Angie," she said, soothingly this time, "you'll like the story. I read it when I was your age and I loved it. Edgar Allan Poe is my fav—"

"Mom, I'll read it tomorrow. I promise."

"Angelica." Her mother's voice dropped to that too calm level that always frightened Angie as a child. "I am tired, sick and tired, of having teachers call me about your school work. It hurts when they tell me that my intelligent daughter doesn't try, or doesn't care. It hurts, Angie, hurts me deeply, and it seems like there's been a thousand of those calls this year. I don't know. Maybe if your father were still around, things would be different. You're like him in so many ways."

Why did she have to mention her father? Dad was the one who ran away and left Angie with this witch of a mother. "Mom," she tried again, "I've got a seventy-one average in English. That's almost a 'C'. What's the big deal if I go to the mall or not?"

"Angie, you are trying my patience. I've been working all day, trying to make ends meet so that we'll have a roof over our heads. I don't need to come home to problems with you. You *will* go downstairs and read that story. Now!"

It was hopeless. "Yes, Mom," she choked out, unable to control the real tears welling in her eyes. "Can I go tomorrow?" She tried unsuccessfully to erase the mental picture of Heather and Brad sitting in the corner of the food court, sharing chicken nuggets and curly fries.

"I don't know, Angie Baby. We'll see, okay?"

Angie hated it when her mother called her that. It was her father's nickname for her, not Mom's. "Mom—"

"I know. You don't want me calling you that. Sorry, sweetie." Her mother got a far-away look in her eyes. "It's from a song that your dad liked. One that we heard when we—um, never mind about that now. I'll try not to call you Angie Baby and you go do your homework. Deal?" Her mother's smile looked more tired than cheerful. "Though you'll always be my sweet baby. Always."

"I am *not* your baby! I am fifteen, almost. Practically a legal adult!" Practically. Two long years, two months, and fifteen days until legitimate freedom.

"You'll always be my perfect little angel, no matter what. I love you, Angie."

"Yeah, right."

"I'm your mother. And as much as it hurts me sometimes, I have to do what I think is best for you—"

"As if. One day, I'm gonna be out of here and far, far away from you!" She wheeled around and headed toward the basement stairs. "I'll go do my homework and miss out on seeing Brad, but I'll never forgive you! Never!"

"Angie, I try—"

"Oh, sure. You try—not!" Angie slammed the cellar door and stomped down the wooden steps. She knew from past experience that her mother could feel each and every step vibrating through the floorboards to the kitchen. Good. Her mother wanted a nice, peaceful night after working oh, so hard? Well, too bad. If Angie couldn't do what she wanted, why should she let her mother have her way?

She stopped at the entrance to her bedroom. Angie hated this room, and the entire basement for that matter. Sleeping down here had been her mother's big idea, shortly before her father left. The cellar was the big play area for the three of them when Angie was little. It was Mom's bright idea to divide it up into separate rooms—laundry, storage, a den for Dad, and a 'private' bedroom for Angie. Divvying up the space made the entire downstairs seem so much smaller than it did before, even though the den was left unfinished when her father went away during the construction. Unused cement blocks and old bags of mortar from the incomplete remodeling were left where the den was to be, contributing to the nauseatingly musty smell. Besides which, the dryer hose had never been reconnected, so the cinder block walls were always covered with moisture from the humid heat of the drying clothes. There were no windows in her room to relieve the dampness, making it impossible to paint or tape up posters to brighten things a bit. Angie couldn't wait to escape.

Angie reached for her doorknob and pushed hard. The warped wood slipped a week earlier, making it difficult to open. "Mom," she hollered. "My door's still stuck and you promised you'd fix it!"

"I'll do it in a bit," came the muffled reply. "After I start the laundry. Make sure your dirty clothes are in the hall for me to do."

"Whatever." Angie entered her room and went to the closet, pulling out the dirty clothes. In one swoop, she tossed the whole bunch into the hall, purposely avoiding having them land in a neat pile. She slammed the warped door as best she could then crossed the room and flipped on her CD player. She scanned her collection, looking for the Satanic Booger Launchers disc that caused last night's argument with her mother. Remembering that she never took it out of the boom box, she switched the power button to 'on' and twisted the volume knob up a few notches. A year of living in this room taught Angie exactly what sound level would make the upstairs vibrate. When the first guitar riffs filled the air, Angie smiled. Try to enjoy your nice, quiet evening with your darling Angie Baby now, she wanted to scream.

Angie threw her backpack onto the bed and flopped down beside it. Pulling her literature book out, she flipped to the story she was to read. 1846! The stupid story was written in 1846! What was she going to get out of this? May as well read it and get it over with, she decided. She started reading.

The thousand injuries of Fortunato I had borne as best I could, but when he ventured upon insult I vowed revenge.

Revenge! What a great idea, Angie thought, giggling a little. Revenge for the insults her mother always heaped on her. Insults were like injuries, the story said. And it felt like she did it a thousand times a week, if not a thousand times a day. "Revenge," she whispered, grinning. "I vow revenge upon my mother, Joann Lange, for venturing upon insult." The nineteenth century language threw her into a fit of laughter.

She jumped at a scratching noise outside her door that was loud enough to be heard over the stereo. Great. "Mother!" Angie yelled. "How *do* you expect me to read this *wonderful* story if you *insist* on fixing the stupid door frame right now!?"

"Sorry, Angie," her mother shouted. "I'll try not to make it so noisy."

"Whatever," Angie huffed as she crossed the room and turned the music to the loudest level. As she fell back into her bed, Angie asked herself how she would do it. How does a fifteen-year-old get revenge against her cow of a mother? What would it take to show Mom who the superior one really was? Revenge would be too cool. She read on, hoping for a good idea for getting back at her mother.

You, who so well know the nature of my soul, will not suppose, however, that I gave utterance to a threat.

That was the secret! No threats, like her mother always used against her. Mom could have the threats; Angie would be more subtle. The secret to revenge was not to let the victim know just what was going on until it was too late. Who said school wasn't educational? She just had to decide what to do.

I had scarcely laid the first tier of the masonry when I discovered that the intoxication of Fortunato had in a great measure worn off.

Well, Angie wouldn't be able to wall her mother up in a catacomb, whatever the hell that was, but she'd come up with something. She put the book down and pictured her mother, in the windowless laundry room, surrounded by wet walls and mounds of dirty gym socks and old underwear. "Angie Baby," she'd whine, "let me out of here! I've always tried to be a good mother."

But Angie wouldn't let her out. She'd continue sealing up the doorway, ignoring her mother's panicked cries. "You drove Dad away," she would sneer. "You deserve to die!" Angie laughed at the idea of telling her mother this. It would be so great— her mother, slowly gasping for breath. Lying face down in the piles of moldy laundry trying to suck in whatever oxygen they might hold. Coughing, choking on her last gulps, panic-stricken. Wondering until the last why this was happening. Knowing her darling daughter was laughing at her from the other side of the door.

It was now midnight, and my task was drawing to a close. I had completed the eighth, the ninth, and the tenth tier. I had finished a portion of the last and the eleventh; there remained but a single stone to be fitted and plastered in. I—"

Sighing, Angie put the book down again. She couldn't concentrate on the story. The image of her desperate mother's pleading to be let free kept interfering. She could always finish it on the bus tomorrow morning. Closing the book with a loud thump and shoving it into her backpack, she yawned. Homework always made her tired. An early bedtime tonight. That would confuse Mom and be the first step in the revenge plan. She'd be the daughter Mom wanted, until it was time for her to put the idea, whatever it was going to be, into action. She crossed the room, idly wondering if Brad Isherwood was any good at bricklaying.

She flipped off the stereo and looked at the clock. Twelve o'clock already! She'd been fantasizing about killing her mother for over five hours! So much for going to bed early. Oh well, the sweet-daughter's revenge could just as easily begin tomorrow when she aced that test. For now, Angie would brush her teeth, climb into bed, and dream of doing away with Mom.

She went to the door, wishing for the thousandth time that there was a bathroom down here. She knew she couldn't see her mother's face right now without laughing, and that would spoil everything. Angie reached for the doorknob and pulled. She found herself face-to-face with a new brick wall, completely finished except for one last block. In that space, she saw her mother's face, beaming with triumph.

About the author: Michael Giorgio lives in Wisconsin with his wife, fellow author Kathie Giorgio, daughter/aspiring author Olivia, and two dogs, cats, and fish. His short stories have appeared in many anthologies and magazines including *The Strand, The Mammoth Book of Tales from the Road,* and Static Movement's *Literary Foray, Pot Luck* and *Comes the Night.* He teaches creative writing online and in studio at AllWriters' Workplace and Workshop in Waukesha, Wisconsin, and online for Writer's Digest University.

THE BROTHER

Voicu Mihnea Simandan

"That is the worst thing of all, to discover that all these wondrous things
you thought were yours alone are special to someone else."

- (S.P. Somtow, *Jasmine Nights*)

She was never alone. The day I met her, after my evening class
at the Language School from Si Racha, she introduced him as
her brother.

She was the one who was supposed to close up the school
that night. "Can you please help me bring down the retractable
metal door?" I was asked by the girl behind the counter after I
said good-bye to the maid.

Although I knew it was the maid's job, I thought it was
nice to see that in a country with such a profound consciousness
of class structure, someone in a higher position would give a
helping hand to a subordinate. So, I replied, "Yes, sure."

She was wearing the usual navy blue uniform all staff
members had to wear every day except on the weekend, when
they were allowed a more relaxed dress code. Being a front desk
clerk, the length of her skirt was above the knees, revealing two
long, very slender legs. It appeared that she wasn't one of those
Thai girls who are seemingly obsessed with their cleavage, who
always try to cover their neckline whenever they lean forward.
She squatted in front of the biggest metal door that I brought
down for her, and while I was holding it down she slipped
through the orifice a huge padlock. Her hair was tied in a neat
ponytail which covered her nape, but the cyan blouse with the
school's emblem printed all over it creased in such a way that I
could clearly see the lace margins of her brassiere.

We left the last retractable metal door that secured the
main entrance half way down and went back inside to get my
shoulder bag.

"Have you eaten dinner yet?" she asked me while stuffing

her belongings into a tiny purse.

"Have you?" I asked back.

"I'm starving," she said as she turned to pick something from the shelves behind the counter.

She wasn't a beautiful woman, but her half turned face hid the two bulging eyes and revealed the smooth skin on the back of her neck. As I had no one to be expecting me to return to my room, I urged her, "Then hurry up."

She turned back staring at me in surprise. "I'm hungry too," I lied. "Let's go."

"Just a moment. We have to wait for my..." she stopped in the middle of the sentence, and after hesitating for a couple of seconds, she went on, "... my brother. He's already late."

Both of them shared the same lack of beautiful facial features. The brother was much older than the sister. He was tall and thin, and his eyes twitched every other second. I *waied* in the typical palms-together Thai greeting and after that shook hands with this strange looking man and had the weird sensation that he didn't like me. But the criteria I judged people with might not be plausible eight thousand kilometers away from my own country, where I was never wrong when it came to judging people.

He drove us to a nice restaurant where both of them ordered too much for just the three of us. During dinner she bombarded me with the usual let's-get-to-know-each-other questions, but all I wanted to do was leave. I didn't want to go home early. What I really wanted was to get back into that car, which back seats were filled with boxes and tables. The brother had his own spot in the Chatuchack Night Market from Chonburi, and the car was full of merchandise. The only place for both me and Yui to sit was on the seat on the driver's left. When we first got into the car I was puzzled by the fact that the brother wanted me to share the only free seat in the car with his own sister. It was awkward to be so close to Yui in her brother's car, only half an hour after we had made acquaintance. Not that I didn't like it. Pressed between the door and her warm body, with our thighs and shoulders visibly touching, I felt like I would never want the ride to end.

On the way to my room, which was not far from the Language School where I was working, I was crammed even closer to Yui's body and felt her hand reaching for mine, right there, in front of her brother. She was the first woman that I had met in Thailand who didn't seem shy to express her feelings in public. I wondered what she would be like in a more intimate environment.

What unrolled in the following days was exactly what two people who liked each other would do. We visited temples, went to the movies, strolled along the pier, went sightseeing, and got to know each other pretty well. The only strange thing was that she was never alone. Her brother's shadow was always behind us, driving us wherever we wanted to go, and paying for whatever we wanted to buy. I couldn't complain that I didn't like being taken care of, but as every day passed by I wanted to have our moments of privacy, without feeling the brother's blinking stare on us.

When she finally met me one hot Sunday afternoon all by herself, I was more than pleased. I immediately thought of canceling the trip to the zoo that we had planned the previous day, and take her instead to a more romantic place.

"Oh, I'm so sorry I can't go anywhere today," she said after she listened to my new plans. She didn't wait for me to ask what the problem was, "I have to go to the hospital because my son is sick."

"What? Your son?"

"Yes, my brother's son has a really bad sore throat. It might be tonsillitis," she replied visibly worried and distressed.

"Wait, wait..." I said trying to make sense of what she had just told me. "Is the boy yours or your brother's?"

"What do you mean?"

"No," I said. "What do *you* mean? You never told me you have a son!"

"Oh, no. He's my brother's son," she said taking my hand into hers.

Her touch was warm. "Then why did you... Oh, forget it. Go if you have to go."

"No, please don't be angry. I thought you were happy to

see me."

"Yes, I'm happy to see *you*, but I kind of had enough of your brother following us."

"He means no harm."

"I don't doubt it. But he should give us more space. We're not kids."

"I know, he's a bit too protective. But he cares a lot about me."

"And you seem to care a lot about him. Why do you have to go to the hospital? I'm sure that the boy's mom is there too."

"You don't understand. I really have to go. I'll call you in the evening."

She hailed a motorbike taxi that passed by, got on one side of the motorbike and as the driver shifted the motorbike in the first gear she waved and sent me a flying kiss. For the first time since I had met her I felt that something was not right. I felt that both of them were hiding something from me. But I didn't let my doubts ruin my only day off in the week, so I decided against canceling the zoo trip.

That evening I didn't answer her calls. I didn't feel like complicating even more the situation I was in but, instead, I thought of cooling down our relationship for a while.

"There's something wrong with your mobile phone," she said as I opened the door later that evening after two barely audible knocks on my door.

I was surprised to see her all alone in front of my room. I didn't know what to expect, so I just stood in the door, staring at her.

"Aren't you going to invite me in?"

"Where's your brother?"

"Don't worry about him. He's at the hospital."

Then I remembered about the sick son, "How's the boy feeling?"

"He's all right. But let's not talk about them," she said as I moved out of her way and showed her in.

"You've arranged your place neatly. I didn't know you were so tidy."

I was still not sure what to make of her sudden visit, but I could definitely not ignore the provocative way she was dressed.

"Do you want to go out and grab something to eat?" I asked, still not knowing what to do with her.

"Let's stay in tonight. I mean only if you're all right with that."

"That's cool," I said.

She left the next morning, and promised to take me somewhere special that day. During the lunch break we jumped on a *songthaew*, a pick-up truck taxi, and rode for just a couple of minutes to a street not too far from *Thanon* Sukhumvit, the main road. She wouldn't tell me where we were heading, and after a while I gave up trying to find out. After all, it was supposed to be a surprise. We stopped at the corner of a narrow lane flanked on both sides by three-story townhouses. Then we walked to a house that had the ground floor transformed into a shop that sold all kinds of steel bars.

One hour after I had given my students an individual activity to complete I wondered why she took me to her house, where probably all of her family, with the exception of the brother, was waiting for us to have a huge lunch. The food was excellent, but I had a funny taste of bile deep down my throat, which foreshadowed something that I certainly wasn't prepared for. Not a single member of her family could speak English, so there wasn't too much conversation to make. And then the unexpected happened.

"Can you take care of my daughter forever?" Yui translated the exact words that her mother had addressed to me in Thai.

I looked at Yui for help, but she just assumed the interpreter's role and stared at me with her bulging eyes, that now seemed monstrously big, waiting for my answer. "I don't think I understand what you mean."

Yui translated what I said, her mother repeated the question, and Yui asked me again the same question. A dead silence followed. I looked at my Swatch. It was almost time to go. I avoided answering the question by explaining that I couldn't promise such a thing. The mother seemed happy with the translation, and then someone brought some *canom*, Thai desert. We didn't say a word on the way back, and that afternoon

I left the Language School using the back door without saying good-bye to anyone.

Three hard knocks on my door woke me up in the middle of the night. I sat up in my bed and waited to see if it was just a dream, but I didn't have to wait long. Two more loud knocks on the door assured me that it was very real. This time, not the sister, but the brother was sitting in front of my room. He was visibly disturbed.

"You want to take her away from me!" he shouted, hearing for the first time a complete sentence coming from his alcohol-reeking mouth.

"What time is it?" I asked, ignoring his nonsense. "Go home."

"I know what's going on here," he said pushing his way through the door.

As he entered my room, I heard Yui calling my name from the corridor. Breathing heavily she burst in and positioned herself between me and her brother.

"Leave him alone!" she screamed on top of her lungs, and then she turned to face me. Her eyes were red and hideously swollen from probably too much crying.

"You can't take her!" shouted her brother.

"Take her where?" I asked, aware of the mess I had got into.

"To your home country."

"What?"

"Tell him you love me and you will take care of me."

"What?"

"Please," she begged falling down on her knees, grabbing my legs, while her head was arched on her back.

Seeing the skin of her long neck and the sobbing ups and downs of her chest I remembered our previous night together, the touch of her body, the feel of her smooth hair. And there, with a woman at my feet, and a so-called brother staring down at both of us I realized that it wasn't worth the trouble.

"Leave me alone. Both of you," I said trying to free my legs.

I looked at the man who seemed to have lost his speech,

hypnotized by the scene unfolding before him. Then I felt a wave of hatred exploding from those two blinking eyes and knew that something bad would happen. He grabbed Yui by the hair and pulled her away from me. She was now at his feet, crying hysterically, trying to brake free from his grip. I saw his hand raise and then fall with a thunderous thud on her face. My heart ceased beating for just a fraction of a second, and when it restarted its rapid beat, Yui stopped crying.

About the Author: Voicu Mihnea Simandan is a thirty-three years old Romanian writer, freelance journalist and educator who has lived in Thailand since 2002. He has published three books of nonfiction, one book for children, and several short stories in different magazines, journals and anthologies. He is now finalising his first novel, "The Buddha Head," a historical thriller set in Thailand. He can be contacted at www.simandan. com.

THE RED HAT
Bellakentuky

Alex Smith looked pale, and lifeless, as he stared through the grimy window Of The 74th Street Coffee Shoppe.

He clutched a fresh brewed cup of thick, black, coffee. Tiny splatters of the dark liquid had spilled from the shaking mug and reflected the red and white speckled linoleum counter in front of him. They were the only indication of the rage that boiled deep inside.

An earlier downpour had slowed to a drizzle. Alex fixated on a puddle, and flinched ever so slightly, as each passerby splashed through the water.

Steam wafted up, and warmed the underside of his chin, and tickled his nose. The stimulation proved that he was still alive, when in fact he felt like he was dead, or last least wished he was.

This was the worst day of his life.

This morning, when Alex opened his eyes, he found Zoe standing over the bed with a suitcase in each hand. With one fell swoop, like the swift cut of a knife, she announced that she'd met somebody else. One sentence, she turned, and left.

Twelve fucking years he'd invested in her; and she gave him one sentence.

A black fly landed on the window in front of him. The fly rub it's legs together as it searched for food. Alex watched it and felt bile burn his throat. He hated flies.

Alex slowly turned his head and observed a fat guy at the other end of the counter. The man wore a ridiculously bright, blue, polyester, jacket; and was elbow deep into a huge jelly donut. Red filling dripped from his chin. Next to him sat a cup of coffee, three empty sugar packets, and a second donut waiting for its demise.

Alex returned to the fly.

An entire coffee shop filled with possibility, and you pick me. You bastard.

156

Someone had left a Saturday morning paper on the counter. He reached over, picked it up, and rolled it into a tight baton. While normally a mild mannered man, the circumstances of the day, made him want to kill.

He raised his arm and savagely swung at the insect. But the pesky fly saw the blow coming. It took off, got caught in the tailwind of the passing newspaper, did two small barrel rolls, and flew straight into his coffee.

The veins in Alex's eyes flexed with stress as he watched the fly struggle in the hot liquid.

He turned away from the window and searched for the skinny waitress with the Harley tattoo. But she'd disappeared. *Probably outside smoking weed.* Alex sneered at no one in particular.

The owner of the shop stood behind the main counter and chatted with several old men that looked like they had one foot in the grave.

"Hey! There's a fucking fly in my coffee!" Alex shouted.

The owner was a big guy, with broad shoulders, bulging biceps, and a beer gut that hung like a sack of potatoes.

"So buy another!" he yelled back.

Alex felt adrenaline surge through his skinny body. This was a fight he knew he couldn't win. But perhaps a good pummeling on the outside; might relieve some of the pain he felt on the inside.

He rose from his stool, fists balled, when his cell phone rang. He quickly yanked it from his pocket and flipped it open.

"What?" he asked.

"You want to get this deal done or not?" the other person responded.

Alex looked at the phone. The caller ID read *BLOCKED*.

"Who is this?" Alex asked.

"I'm done screwing around," the caller replied. "Today, Central Park, by the water fountain, at noon; and don't forget to wear the red hat, so we know who you are." The caller hung up.

Alex closed the phone. He looked over at the owner, who had gone back to his conversation, and gave him the finger.

He opened the door to the tinkle of small bells and stepped

outside. A cold mist hung in the air like a wet blanket. He pulled the collar of his jacket tight around his neck and headed down 74th Street.

Eight blocks away, Alex stood in front of *Bob's Sporting Goods*. Inside the display window was a *Cincinnati Reds* baseball cap. He looked at his watch.

At 11:45 a.m., Alex entered Central Park with the red cap pulled tight to his small head. *Why he was doing this?* He thought. *Idle curiousity?* He figured whoever the caller was had misdialed. Any other day, he wouldn't have given it a second thought. But today... *What did he have to lose? If something happened to him, Zoe would suffer when she read about it in the paper! Or maybe... maybe- he'd kill somebody! Then she'd have to live with the fact that she drove him over the edge. What a bitch! One way, or another, she'll pay.*

Alex stood near the fountain and stomped his feet to keep warm. He didn't know what to expect and looked questioningly at every person who wandered by. It was unusually quiet in the park. The cold, wet, day kept most people in the safety of their homes. But Alex watched, and waited.

From a distance Alex spotted an unusual looking man. The man was tall, lanky, and dressed all in black. He wore a wide brimmed hat pulled low across his face. His stride was long and determined. He carried a white Macy's shopping bag that hung heavy at his side. It contrasted brightly against the dull landscape.

The man approached Alex with the bag slightly extended. He passed by so closely, that Alex smelled *Old Spice* aftershave. The handoff between them occurred smoothly. So smoothly, that Alex never felt the thin rope handles slip into his fingers. The stranger vanished behind him, into the trees, like dissipating smoke.

Alex stood bewildered. He looked around, and was all alone, so he peeled open the bag, and looked inside. It was filled with cash. Dozens, and dozens, of tightly bound bills filled the sack. The only number he saw was- one hundred. He snapped the bag shut and glanced around again. It was more money than he'd ever seen in one spot in his life.

Alex took off in the opposite direction of the man. He walked swiftly but tried to appear casual. He couldn't believe his good fortune. He'd use this money for a fresh start. *Screw Zoe! Screw the coffee shop guy,* he thought happily. *Maybe, he'd move to Seattle, or San Diego, or maybe he'd even leave the country! Move to Paris. Maybe... this was in fact, the best day of his life.*

He turned down a narrow path, and stopped, then looked behind him. Nobody was following, and he smiled. It was the biggest, happiest smile to shine from Alex's sad face in a long time.

He turned to resume walking, and the last thing Alex saw clearly, was a bright red beret before a knife plunged deep into his chest.

Alex crumpled to the ground. His dying eyes, watched Zoe's beautiful face follow him, as he fell. She crouched down next to him and went through his pockets. She never looked him in the face, or said a word.

She pulled her cell phone from his pocket, and picked up the bag, and left him. He strained to watch her walk away, but couldn't turn his head, while blood bubbled from his lips.

As Alex Smith died, all alone, on his back, on a rainy day, in Central Park, he thought, *I knew, the two matching cell phones, for the price of one plan, was a mistake...*

About the author: Bellakentuky is an expat from the United States living in the far reaches of Argentina. She spends her days holed up in her small apartment writing stories that have a touch of humor and always explore the sad side of life. When she's not writing, you can find her taking pictures, painting, or hugging one of her loved ones; Clarisa, Bella, Lolita and Emmit.

JUST ANOTHER DAY
Bellakentuky

I leaned over my cart, and guided it down *Aisle One,* to the thump of a wheel waiting to die.

The scent of cinnamon bread teased me, pulling at my love handles without even the benefit of a taste, and the highly polished floor caught my eye; filling me with fantasies.

I imagined myself nude, with the exception of cotton socks that had holes in the toes. I saw myself run fast and spin into a pirouette of circles; before finally falling to the floor in a heap of ridiculous laughter. I'm not a young man anymore, but adolescence hangs on.

My wife picked up a loaf of wheat bread, and placed it into our cart, then mused over the bagel rack.

Dutifully, I followed her like all the other husbands. The grocery store was crowded, and I reveled in our anonymity. Families hurried about, gathering their food, ready to move on to whatever this Saturday had to offer. But we strolled.

Clarisa decided on blueberry bagels and tossed them into the cart. She winked at me.

She hates blueberry bagels, but I love them.

I wrapped an arm around her as we turned into the dairy section.

She looked hot today, and I felt myself become aroused. Her long black hair was pulled into a ponytail. She wore tight gray jeans that hugged the curves of her Latin body. Her long, dangly, earrings danced about as she moved.

I've always had a thing for fine cars and beautiful women; and Clarisa was a Porsche in a sea of Chevys.

We paused at the yogurt display, and she turned to say something. But I cut her off and pulled her close. She caressed my neck and my belly burned at her touch-

Then a hostile voice rang out from behind us, "He's too old for you!"

I looked up and saw an elderly woman standing several

feet away. She had that thin, blue-gray, hair that old women sometimes have. Her make-up was bright and grossly overdone. A pair of thick rimmed glasses hung from a beaded chain around her neck. She had her hands planted on her hips and vile disgust lingered in the air around her like a toxic cloud. Her proclamation sounded the alarm to everyone within earshot. We were now on display to those who hadn't bothered to notice.

Clarisa, and I, experience our own form of racism. We can relate to being the only black person in an office full of whites, or the overweight friend that gets invited to a pool party. We're in that special category that doesn't quite fit the mold.

In fact, it pleases me how different we are from everyone else.

But we stand together; and confront the plastic smiles that toss out gossip like chum to sharks.

Clarisa has weathered countless attacks of being a no-good golddigger, and I must accept the idea of being categorized as a dirty old man.

We are in love.

"You should be ashamed of yourself," the old woman sniped. She shook her head in a strange manner, and I thought she was going to spit on me.

"This is my husband," Clarisa responded with a dry smile. The words drifted past the woman as if she'd left her hearing aid in the backseat of her car.

"What are you a wetback? This old husband of your's, a ticket to the good old U.S.A? You black-skinned slut."

No one, but me, would ever know how much those words hurt my wife. Despite the fact that we're different... we really do try to fit in.

"I'm Argentine," Clarisa replied quietly. "I love my country. The United States isn't better; only different."

The woman barked a haughty laugh.

"You pathetic old man. It's sex isn't it? I'll bet you purchased this chippy- Pervert! The two of you should go back to Argentine where you belong with the rest of the savages."

Well, that was enough for me.

I reached into my pocket, pulled out a snub-nosed .38,

and put a hole about the size of a pinky finger right in the middle of the woman's forehead.

She dropped to the ground in beautiful silence.

In moments like this, I feel like I've just had sex. I know there is always a bit of commotion around me, but I don't hear it; all I want to do is sit down and have a cigarette.

Clarisa is more grounded in these situations than I am.

My wife looked at me, "Jesus, Honey, did you have to go and do that?"

"Well, you heard what she said!"

"I know, but couldn't you have just punched her in her fucking face, or something."

I stared at my shoes. I hate it when we have a disagreement.

"It's okay, Baby...," she added. "Let me sign it, and we'll be on our way."

Clarisa walked over to the woman and placed the tip of her four inch stiletto heel on top of the woman's lifeless left eye. She then shoved her foot down hard, crushing the eyeball into the skull.

I don't really remember exactly when we decided to make this our signature. But we both really enjoy it. It makes a popping sound; kind of like opening a bottle of champagne.

We headed for the door through the candy section and I grabbed a handful of Twizzlers on our way out. It's always good to have some snacks in the car when hitting the road.

Customers, and employees, watched from various hiding spots as we left. But it didn't matter. Experience has taught us that we have about two minutes to disappear, and we were gone with thirty seconds to spare.

I've always wondered what happens when the cops arrive. I'm sure they ask for a description, and people probably respond; Ahhh... old guy, you know, kinda balding... and a Mexican lady... you know... they all look the same.

People are so stupid. So caught up in their own shit.

I wheeled our Lexus onto the freeway, and we rode in silence for a while.

Clarisa said, "That woman didn't even know the country was Argentina; not Argentine."

I looked at her, and mimicked the old woman's twisted, angry, face, "I know! You savage!"

We exploded in laughter; a hearty belly laugh that lasted longer than it probably should have.

When our laughter subsided, I said, "I hear Tampa's nice."

"Go for it, Baby," she replied.

"Twizzler?" I asked.

"Sure."

Bellakentuky is an expat from the United States living in the far reaches of Argentina. She spends her days holed up in her small apartment writing stories that have a touch of humor and always explore the sad side of life. When she's not writing, you can find her taking pictures, painting, or hugging one of her loved ones; Clarisa, Bella, Lolita and Emmit.

Home Improvements

Brigitte Branson

Henry Carveth was the archetypal undertaker. Tall in stature, slim of frame, a long ribbon of a man; he cut a fitting figure in his expensively tailored mourning suit. His expression always one of submissive deference, his long sad face with the impossibly heavy lower jaw, never breaking into a smile.

An intensely private man, he lived with his wife and young son in an imposing house on the outskirts of the village, a few hundred yards from the funeral parlor that was his life's work.

Humming softly under his breath he strolled with gargantuan strides along the quiet lane on his way to work. Stopping when he reached the front door, he frowned with displeasure, then leaned forward to buff up the brass letterbox with a rag he always kept in his pocket. He inhaled the faint smell of formaldehyde and antiseptic on opening the door, and gave a satisfied sigh. Henry felt happier and more at ease in his work environment than he did at home. Everything meticulously clean and in order, everything in its rightful place. His work place was his refuge, his retreat, the only place he felt he could think straight.

The fluorescent light hummed then flickered as he switched it on revealing the body draped in a sheet lying on the gurney. He walked across the room then stood and stared for a long time, rubbing his hands together. The expression on his face one of barely repressed excitement as if he were looking at a present about to be unwrapped. His pale, long fingered hands trembled slightly in anticipation as he folded back the slightly stained sheet to waist level revealing the head and torso of the corpse.

Henry lifted the limp hand and tenderly stroked the flesh, still with a trace of last summer's tan, then rotated the arm as he examined the tracery of veins under the paper-thin skin. The blood was static, with no living, beating heart to drive it now, and beginning to pool and blacken leaving patches of discoloration.

Tiny blooms of death.

He gently placed her arm next to her body and checked the toe tag, reading the details written in the usual almost indecipherable scrawl; Annie Gardiner, age twenty-three, cause of death, road traffic accident. But of course, he knew who she was, no man in the village had ever failed to notice Annie Gardiner, she had always made sure of that.

He placed the tag back between the toes, sneering with disgust at the shell like nails daubed with garish, red nail varnish then rubbed his hands together as he looked at the mess in front of him. He liked a challenge.

It was time for him to work his magic.

***

He knew Annie, had known her since she was a young girl. He would get to know every single person in the village... one day.

No one ever crossed Henry Carveth. He was always treated with the utmost respect. They were only too aware that ultimately the day would come when each would have their own private and extremely intimate assignation with him. Whether they liked it or not. Familiarity provided no obstacle for Henry; it was perfectly feasible in a small village that you would encounter people you knew.

They were all the same when horizontal and without a heartbeat... in the end, all equal.

Her clothes neatly folded in a pile on the table; he looked disdainfully at the cheap, laddered nylon stockings and the flimsy summer dress that spoke of happier times. There was still a trace of tacky perfume clinging to the sordid looking little pile of clothes. Annie had loved her perfume. It probably drowned out the whiff of her deceit and treachery. He picked up each of her limbs in turn, smiling softly as he stretched, crunched and manipulated the joints in order to break the rigor mortis.

Poor, poor Annie; she had been due to get married the following weekend. But a speeding car and a fickle mind had been the silly woman's downfall; if she'd kept that silly butterfly mind of hers on the here and now and been a little more diligent in crossing the road she would still be here now. Still a young woman, still in her prime, some would say. Though rather common looking for his taste. If his heart hadn't been gradually coated in stone these last two decades he was sure it would have broken in two at the sheer waste of such youth and beauty.

Women traded on their looks their whole lives through, with their painted and powdered faces, the coy innocent glances. Ah yes, they knew exactly what they were doing. Secure in the knowledge that the promise of a lust-filled night would be sufficient to achieve their goal, be it a new dress or a lifelong pledge of marriage.

All women were the same, he thought. Never satisfied, always wanting that little bit more, pushing and pushing until they got what they wanted.

His wife, Alice was exactly the same, but thankfully, her desires only stretched to improvements to their home. First the conservatory, then new curtains, new carpet, the list went on and on. Anything she could think of to make their home better. He didn't mind, anything that made her happy was okay with him. Thankfully, her passion now stopped with the house.

There had been a small incident a few years ago when he had heard rumors about Alice's close attachment to one of the neighbors. But the man in question had moved away and everything had been sorted out. Now they couldn't have been happier. It was as if she'd realized what she could have lost and she barely left the house now. She had threatened to leave at the time and take little Josh with her as well but thankfully after a long talk she had come to her senses. A child Josh's age needed a father figure.

Henry's eyes were glazed, unseeing as the bad memories filled his head. He gave a small twitch, banishing them from his mind. Those days were gone, everything was all right now. He looked down at Annie and then ran his elegant hands up and down her lifeless body, enjoying the icy coolness of her flesh. His eyes roamed from the tip of her toes to her once pretty face, smashed on one side to beyond recognition; the same face he had seen laughing and flirting with almost every man in town.

Beauty... Pleasure, it's all so fleeting, so transient, he thought. There to hide the evil underneath, a pretty face could mask the blackest of souls.

It was time to get started. He worked quietly and diligently. First, the aspiration of the stomach, pancreas and small intestine, who would have thought such a beautiful veneer, could be harboring these vile fluids. Then the drawing of the ligature through her jaw to keep that pretty, yet dangerous mouth safely shut for eternity. He pulled the ligature as tight as he could, forever putting a stop to the filthy lies that had dripped from her cruel, vindictive little mouth. He peeled back the eyelids exposing the dull iris and put the eye pads securely in place before folding back the lids. Henry walked across to the other side of the room, filled a bowl with warm soapy water, and grabbed a cloth to wash that perfect little body for the last time.

No man would want to look at her now, that was for sure. One less temptress in the world to ruin a man's life. Smiling he arranged her arms into a suitable position and then pumped the embalming fluid into her body watching in childish pleasure and delight as the fluid flushed through her body bringing the pink blush of life back to her skin. He manipulated and smoothed the serum along each limb, pleased with the dramatic effect, the once grey tinged flesh now filling with warmth and color, like a soft fruit ripening.

He walked across to the door and picked up the bag containing the clothes she was to wear. She had been due to get married the following weekend and lifting out the wedding gown she had planned to wear, he held it at a distance and admired the prim, virginal style of the design. Quite unsuitable for Annie Gardiner, he thought, who was she trying to kid. He hadn't failed to notice her coquettish manner while she was alive; in fact, she'd been the talk of the village. No man had been immune to her advances, including her poor husband to be. Yet he seemed to be the only one oblivious to her track record, her long trail of conquests in the village.

He shook the dress free of any creases and hung it on the back of the door. Henry then set to work on the reconstruction of her ruined face; using wood pulp and morticians wax, he put into use his years of expertise and rebuilt the jaw and eye socket until she looked almost human again.

Taking the dress he slipped it carefully over her head, forcing her, now rigid arms, into the long sleeves. He took the shower hose and sluiced water over her blood-matted hair, the water running crimson then fading to a pastel pink into the sluice tray. She would have to make do with plain old medicated shampoo this time, he thought as he massaged the lather into her hair. Toweling her hair dry, he then combed it back from her pretty face. She really looked a lot better than she ever had alive. Her face stripped bare, looking almost virginal, he applied a modicum of make up; she had always overdone it with the face paint when she was alive, he thought. His job was to improve, not cheapen. The world was full enough of garishly painted whores selfishly intent on only their own desires.

He carefully lifted her, she only felt about the same weight as his son, and placed her in the coffin, her body now stiff and unyielding from the effects of the embalming. He plumped the satin lining around her now seemingly perfect face, stood back, and sighed in satisfaction admiring his handiwork. She looked like a porcelain doll, a picture of innocence. Leaning down he planted a gentle kiss on her waxy, unyielding forehead., then looked at the time; her fiancé was due any moment now for a last viewing. The young man should be counting his blessings, he was safe now, safe from whatever heartbreak this capricious young woman would have caused him. They would have had a few months, no longer, of what was loosely referred to as wedded bliss and then the suspicions would arise, her not being at home when he returned from work, the mysterious phone calls that all turned out to be wrong numbers.

Safer in a box, Henry thought, the only time they can be trusted.

Where was he, he should have been here by now?

He looked at the clock on the wall. Alice would be worried with him running so late. She had been pleading with him to put up some shelves in the kitchen and he'd promised he'd be back before dark. She'd said she'd let Josh stay up until he returned, but he would be getting tired and fractious now, eager for bed.

His wife had insisted on living a respectable distance away, stressing to him that it was no place to bring up their only son. Henry was so pleased they had managed to sort out their little problem. Josh was turning out to be a fine young man, so well behaved. And Alice, well she never wanted for a thing. He spoilt her really. That was what marriage was all about, compromise and learning to put up with each other's faults. People gave up too easily nowadays, the first tiff and they were discussing divorce proceedings. They had discussed a separation at first, but instead had reached a compromise conducive to both of them and they had never been happier.

He felt nothing but sympathy for the young couples hurtling head long into marriage only to find it was actually the hardest task they would ever be set.

Henry washed his hands at the sink, scrubbing away the traces of blood from under his perfectly manicured fingernails, unable to keep himself from looking over and admiring his handiwork.

He heard footsteps crunching on the gravel driveway followed by a timid knock on the door. He walked across to open it.

"Mr. Carveth, I've come to see Annie."

"Ah, yes come in, William isn't it?" he muttered impatiently. "I've been expecting you." He stood to one side holding open the door and ushered him into the room.

Hesitating before he walked in, he said, "Is she... Is she in there?" Pointing towards the open coffin.

"Yes, please come in. Would you like me to leave you for a while?"

He nodded, his eyes growing wide and filling with unshed tears as he neared the coffin and started to shake.

Henry used to this reaction quietly said, "Call if you need Me." Pulling the door closed, he shook his head in despair, finding it incomprehensible the fear people associated with death.

Impatient to get home, he paced up and down in the hall of the funeral parlor as he listened to the loud sobs and frantic mutterings of undying love. Henry sighed in exasperation; he'd heard it all before. When would they realize that women just could not be trusted.

For God's sake, Alice and Josh would be wondering where he had got to, he told them he wouldn't be longer than a few hours. Back before bedtime, he'd told Josh and now the sky was beginning to darken and he was forced to stand and listen to this man exonerating his grief.

The sobs diminished, then died out completely and the door opened. Henry gave the cursory forms of platitude, then ushered the still sniveling man as quickly as possible out of the door.

He walked over to the coffin, gave one last admiring look at his handiwork, and then closed the lid on Annie Gardiner before switching out the lights and locking up.

***

It was almost pitch black now and he wondered whether Alice had grown fed up with waiting and sent Josh to bed. He could usually see the houselights from here, shining like a beacon to guide him home. But there was nothing, just the velvety blackness of the night sky.

His heart started thumping wildly, ricocheting inside his chest like a drum out of tempo. What had happened, surely, she wouldn't leave, she couldn't leave him now? He fumbled as he put the key in the door and walked into the silence and blackness of the house calling, 'Alice, Josh?' Scrabbling in the dark along the wall for the light switch, he flicked it up and down... nothing. He groped along the wall towards the fuse box in the kitchen, and then gave a sigh of relief as he found the trip switch had blown. Pushing it firmly down the house was instantly flooded with light and sound and life.

Alice, Josh, sorry I'm late again,' he called as he walked down the hall. 'What on earth were you doing sitting in the dark?'

The sound of some inane quiz show on the TV blared out from behind the closed door of the living room. He sniffed in distaste at some unpleasant odor that filtered through the hallway. Housework had never been Alice's forte.

He took off his overcoat, hung it on the coat stand and

braced himself for the expected nagging. "I know, I know," he said, as he walked into the living room. "I just couldn't get away any quicker." Alice sat on the easy chair, her gaze fixed on the TV.

Mmm, the silent treatment again, he thought. Josh lay on the floor at her feet, his head cupped in his hands as he looked at the television.

Henry sighed as he stood looking at them, then walked over to Alice and planted a kiss on her cheek. Her head lolled to one side and a fat bluebottle crawled lazily from her slightly open mouth. He leant down and ruffled Josh's hair, a clump coming off in his hand and settling on the carpet. "Well, my dears. I'm home at last. Did you miss me?" He said, looking from one to the other. "Alice, my love, you're looking a little peaky." He walked across to her chair and held the back of his hand against her cold forehead. Staring at her face, he noticed a blue tinge to her complexion. The odor was stronger in here, much stronger. He pulled his handkerchief from his pocket, held it over his mouth and nose then went to get his briefcase that he'd left in the hall.

He took out the syringe containing the formaldehyde and walked back into the room and injected Alice, her eyes shrunken and immobile but still riveted to the silly game show she'd always loved on the TV. He kneeled on the floor and had to roll Josh over to inject him. His body stiff, hands still cupped under his chin, he looked as if he were a puppy playing. He emptied the syringe into his abdomen where the rot had set in, then looked into his face and smiled before rubbing him on his tummy. "There you are my son, all better now," he said as he rolled him back to his original position. "Right I'll get the dinner on shall I?"

As he walked into the kitchen, he thought back to the time when Alice had nearly left him, taking Josh with her as well. He couldn't allow that. So he had taken the only measure known to him. The perfect compromise. Things had quieted down since then and he could honestly say they were the happiest family in the whole town.

About the author: Brigitte Branson has been writing for many years but has only recently started submitting to various markets.

Drawn to the darker side of life she has had stories published in Suspense Magazine where she came 2nd in their annual writing contest. In August she has a story to be published in 'Mon Coeur Mort', an Anthology published by Post Mortem Press.

Dark Lake Ritual

Chris Bartholomew

Devona was so tired of the noises, the voices. She had welcomed the news that Franklin wanted to take her on one of his business trips. They had, after all, been seeing one another for six months; maybe he was ready for more of a commitment than their usual dinner and movie every few weeks. It could be a summer vacation, her on the beach showing him her wonderful tan in a skimpy bikini.

Their conversations had been a little strange, but everyone was entitled to their beliefs, and the paranormal was his job, so naturally the theme of most of his conversations would be what he knew best. Who was to say he was wrong in his beliefs; certainly not her, not now, when she was having so many strange experiences of the unexplained kind in her life.

Maybe Franklin would even let her go to the 'ritual' he was exploring on this trip. Not that she needed to be frightened any more than she already was, but maybe it would be entertaining.

Last night, when she was in her closet choosing what to wear to the movie, she heard Franklin ask her what she was doing, and as she answered, she turned around, and he was gone. She walked downstairs and found him knocking on the door.

"Why did you suddenly leave without waiting for my answer?" She had asked.

Franklin had said, "What? I just got here, what are you talking about?"

She was sure it was his voice, but he was not there. So many of these oddities happening in the last few weeks, she felt so spooked that he had to come up while she finished getting ready to go out. The conversation at dinner was about the trip they were about to go on.

"Franklin, do you suppose that there will be the odd dancing and singing of chants, and sacrifices?" Devona asked, only half joking.

"No, more likely it'll be along the lines of normal stuff, you know, a ritual doesn't have to be scary, blowing out candles at a birthday party is a ritual," he said with a smirk.

"Well, surely this one will have something to do with your job in the paranormal, but you are making fun of me. The very name, 'Dark Lake Ritual' has a sinister ring to it. Might be dangerous for you to go, but I'd love to tag along." Devona was not kidding this time.

At least he had said he would think about it. She would hate to think he would leave her in the hotel room while he was out lollygagging with exotic dancers. Oh, she had better stop thinking like this, finally invited to go away and she was feeling a tad jealous, she thought.

Since Franklin was going to be busy until they were to fly to Salem next week, she was trying to get up with her old friends for a time of gossip and fun, besides, with everything going so strange lately; she did not want to be alone.

Devona had tried to get her friends to like Franklin, but after a brief time of knowing him, they had all passed on that. They said he was nice enough, and yes, handsome but just too strange the way he was always talking about weird scary stuff.

She had just about every night filled with going places or having friends over, and Saturday night, six of them would be spending the night together in her house.

She spent the week with each friend, knowing that they were all still seeing each other, so she talked about herself and Franklin; she knew that they would talk; she was hopeful that they would begin to see that there was nothing wrong with Franklin and then she could feel comfortable being part of the group again.

Saturday she ran to the store at the last minute for things to munch on, but was home before her friends started arriving. She had taken a long nap earlier, she was exhausted from talking to her friends all week, and being woke up all night with strange voices and noises all over the house. She had decided to tell her friends of the things that had been 'haunting' her for so long. That might not help her but it sure might make the night interesting if they were afraid, she smiled to herself.

Devona invited Saundra and Cathy in and saw that the other three were just parking their cars, so she waited for them at the door. After they were all in, she had them come into the dining room where she had fixed a light dinner of sandwiches, soda and beer. Katie, Shannon, and Julia had beer and pretzels, but no sandwiches; she figured they ate somewhere else before coming.

After they ate, the settled into the living room and each started to fill the others in on what they had been up to, though Devona was certain that this was all for her benefit, as she was sure they all talked every day.

When it was her turn to speak, Devona started with how stressed out she had been over the last two months. She didn't explain why, and of course, there was no reason except for the noises and voices. She told them about things that moved from where she knew they should be, and lost mail.

"I mean, when you put your drink down on the counter next to the fridge, turn around, and the drink is now on the dining room table, and this happens over and over, you begin to let it make you nervous." she told them.

She told them of hearing something at night that sounds like bones clacking together, as if someone with no skin is moving around downstairs. She knew it sounded silly in a room full of her friends, but alone at night it was a terrifying noise. A voice coming out of the fireplace, screams when she is in the shower, strange images on her television, and it turning itself off and on. The constant ringing of the phone – even when it was off.

Shannon spoke up when Devona finished, "So, are you going to try to go to this 'ritual' Franklin is going to?" she wanted to know.

"I think it will be fun. I doubt he thinks it would be a bad thing for me to go, or he would not have said he would think about it. Besides, it will give me something different to do," she told them.

They each took turns telling her why they thought she should not go with him on this trip, let alone to the ritual. It seems they did a little research and found out some things about this Dark Lake Ritual and they were not happy with Franklin for suggesting she might go.

Saundra was adamant, "This is a yearly thing, this ritual, what they are doing is bringing all the negative energy that they can get to this same place, and they believe that in the spirit world, a demon will be born from the energy they bring to the table. I think it is a dangerous mindset. And no, I don't believe there are any "demons" being born, but this is a thing of you not going around a bunch of people, whom you don't even know, who think such strange things."

Devona smiled, "Oh please girls. Franklin probably won't even let me go, but even if he does, he is investigating this ritual, he is not part of the group, and he would not put me in any kind of danger, we really do like each other."

With the shaking of heads, and shrugs all around, the rest of the evening was spent on other topics. They had seemingly decided that they were not going to change her mind and so went on to other things.

They retired at a few minutes before midnight. Devona had thought they might talk all night, but was glad for the chance to collect her thoughts, call Franklin as she promised she would, and get some sleep before the flight tomorrow afternoon.

"Franklin, I hope your day was a good one and that you are fast asleep, I'm sorry I didn't call earlier, but with all the girls' here, I just forgot. Please call me and tell me whether I'll be going to the ritual, so that I can pack accordingly... as soon as you tell me what I should wear to such an event," she said to the answering machine. She had decided to believe he was sleeping, and not out on the town.

Sleeping, Devona dreamt of a different world than hers, of elves and fairies and good things. She slept so well that she felt better than she had in months. Getting up, she fixed her friends an easy breakfast, and by nine, they were gone.

While packing a few things she knew she would need, the phone rang.

"Hello?" she said.

"Do not go on this trip you are planning. There is danger, I cannot tell you why, but trust me; it will be a big mistake on your part. Do not trust Franklin, he has other motives for taking you with him," then click and they were gone.

Franticly, she dialed Franklin's number. No answer, but she knew he was at work.

As time makes trouble seem less burdensome, after two hours of waiting for Franklin to call her, she didn't think the phone call as menacing as before, in fact, she thought it good that she hadn't been able to call and franticly tell him of what the caller said. Obviously, someone, probably one of her friends was playing some sick joke. She should be mad, not afraid.

She put her two suitcases by the front door so she would be ready when he came to get her for the ride to the airport. An hour before they were supposed to fly away, he arrived.

Letting him in she said, "Are we going to be late? I thought you would call me."

"No, I made the flight an hour later, I was tied up with clients all day, I'm sorry I didn't call, but I did hear your message on my machine, you forgot about me last night huh?" he said with a light tone and a smile.

"True, you were busy but at least you didn't forget about me like I did you, I'm sorry, it's just that it's been so long since all the girls and I were together, I completely lost track of time." she decided not to mention the other call she received about the trip.

Her phone rang just as they were going out the door, and she decided to let the machine pick up. No sense letting the prankster have another chance to upset her she reasoned, she was on her way out of town with a man she was dating and serious about, nothing would ruin this.

At the airport after checking in, they went to the lounge for a drink to wait until they could board. The talk was light and nice, and she was happy to be in his company.

When they finally boarded and settled in, she asked about the ritual, and Franklin told her a wonderful, fantastic story of the whole thing.

"I don't know if you will believe this or not, heck, I don't even know if I do, but you will see at the end that it doesn't really matter if we believe in it or not. If true, it is a wonderful opportunity to help some other beings, if not true, the people who do believe will feel that they've done something to help other beings, so no one is hurt, and you and I have some special time on this trip together, and an experience to add to our relationship." Franklin took her hand and began the story.

"I started investigating the paranormal ten years ago. My first clients were a Mr. and Mrs. Smith," he smiled at Devona, "yes, that was the first thing I checked out, and it was their real name. Nicest people I have ever met, an elderly couple with quite a story. I couldn't prove what they said, nor could I disprove it either."

He ordered a drink from the flight attendant and continued after he sipped. "Here goes, there are other worlds, other beings right here on earth; things that we rarely, if ever see. The Smiths are kind of caretakers of a people we have come to call Darklings. These creatures are black in color, and very small. In a world of theirs, this spirit world, children are not born as they are here. Others of their kind are born of energy, energy that they get from people here in our world."

Franklin let her digest this, "Well, on with the story, the Dark Lake is where the birth place is. I know it sounds mysterious, but actually, it's a beautiful place where there are so many trees, the place looks deep purple because no light gets through, and there the water is purple, hence, 'Dark' Lake Ritual."

Devona asked, "Okay, what is the ritual part then?"

He continued, "All during the year, the Darklings try to communicate with as many people as possible, to create energy. I hope you won't be upset, but the haunting of you has actually been the Darklings. Every time they tried to communicate with you though, you turned it into something scary. I tried to tell them to quit, but they were so sure that the energy, even though it was terrifying you was strong, and they said they needed that strong energy at the ritual."

"Are you really expecting me to believe this?" she said as she sipped some of her drink.

"No, I'm just telling you the story, believing is up to you. The ritual part of it is that each year, the same people get together at the same spot, adding some new ones and we get in a circle around an old big table. We sit around and talk of what has happened over the last year, if you come along, talk about your haunted house, and the energy of us all will go out into the center of the table."

In a low voice, Devona asked, "Then what will happen?"

"Then my dear Devona, you will see the most wonderful, fantastic, beautiful thing you have ever seen, if you allow yourself the sight."

They decided to wait until they landed in a few minutes to talk further, but she was very curious, and maybe a little enchanted. It seemed too much and too strange to believe, but Franklin had a way with words, and she was beginning to think it was all true.

Later, after arriving at the hotel, Franklin told her he would rather that she sees it all for herself. He told her there was no danger involved, but that she had to come only if she wanted to, and that he would still like her and continue to see her no matter what she decided to do. She didn't even hesitate; she told him she wanted to go.

The next night, they went to the Smiths and the ritual began. Everyone there except for the new ones were just eager to get down to business. Told to concentrate on the center of the table, that if the Darklings decided to let her see, it was there that the vision would be.

She didn't know how to concentrate on something, but relaxed and hoped that maybe it would take care of itself. They hadn't been silently concentrating more than ten minutes before a vision came. A scene of purple and green appeared; she could see the prettiest pond she had ever seen, shimmering purple, completely calm.

Out of the sides of the vision, tiny little black beings came floating out, they had no mouth, but the biggest red eyes, she could hardly contain her excitement. Out of the pond came a little black dot. The dot plopped itself down in front of these two Darklings, and color spilled all over the place. The two beings scooped up the color, and put it back down all together and stood there waiting. Soon, the dark began to move into a pile that looked like a lump of play dough.

Devona felt as if they zapped her spirit into the table. She was still sitting there, but felt her skin pulling toward the center. It was all she could do to keep her seat. Fear and terror permeated every fiber of her being and she thought she was going to die. The new Darkling made itself right before their eyes.

After this ritual was finished, there were tears, shouts, and drinks all around. As Devona sat there wondering about what she had just witnessed, one of the elder Darklings smiled at her from the center of the table where the vision was, and she saw his long yellow fangs, in fact, all of the teeth were jaggedly sharp.

About the author: Chris Bartholomew has over three hundred stories in print. She is owner/editor of the online magazine Static Movement, as well as publisher of these print books.

CURTAIN-LESS WINDOWS

Chris Bartholomew

It was a cold February day and ten year old Frank Cigens was sitting at his school desk waiting for the time they would be putting the Valentine's Day cards in the bags of the students, and he couldn't wait. His sister told him this would be the last year in school that they traded cards, so this one was very special to him. This valentine card was in the form of an invitation to the school dance, the first one ever for them. He had loved Jenny White since kindergarten, and he planned on marrying her one day.

The children took turns walking around the room dropping the cards into the bags, and when Frank got to Jenny's, he hesitated, and then went ahead and dropped it in, giving her a wink and a smile.

Frank's sister told him Jenny had told her not even if he was the last boy on earth would she go to the dance with him. He was devastated.

***

He kept his eye on the water cooler all through the day, wanting to be there when Cindy Jones walked over. He just wanted a conversation, just a bit of her time. He had more than a simple crush on the girl, it was love and since his second year with the company was upon him, he wanted her to celebrate with him; soon he got his chance to ask her out.

"Cindy,"

"Oh, hello Frank, I hear congratulations are in order. Two years here, wow, that is quite an accomplishment. I've only been working on the hotline for about nine months."

"Well, would you consider celebrating with me over dinner this weekend?"

"Oh, well, thanks for asking, but I already have something else to do, but really, congratulations on a job well done! See you around."

Though he knew he shouldn't care what anyone thought, he looked around the room before going to his own cubicle. On the advice of Chuck he'd asked her out, and he was devastated at her denial of his request, but determined not to give up.

"Hold the elevator," he hollered upon leaving work for home. Getting out of the building wasn't hard, but timing his leave so that he'd be right behind her was not easy and he'd almost failed by walking down the hallway too slowly and almost missing the elevator, but it stopped, the doors remained open, and he stepped inside.

As they all got out of the elevator on the bottom floor, he noticed that Cindy grabbed the hand of a co-worker and began a mad dash outside giggling like two school girls. He quickened his pace and was within earshot when he heard Cindy tell her friend, "Not even if he was the last man on earth, can you imagine? I'd have to be dead first."

***

He was beyond distraught now, he was livid. What had he done to warrant this disparagement, he just wanted to have a relationship and twice now in his life he'd heard this saying about going out with him, he fought to keep himself under control and get into his car, and then he let loose and began hitting the steering wheel all the while saying, "I'll show you, I'll show them all."

***

"No, you did the right thing by calling the hotline. Holidays are the toughest, and if we can be of assistance to you, if I can help you in any way to get through this bumpy spot, then next time you might feel a smidgen less panicked. I know you don't usually tell strangers where you live, but I would feel remiss if something happened and I couldn't find you, so please give me your address, just in case."

Valentine's Day, a day of love, romance, and blood read hearts. Frank got her address, and her name, which happened to be Jenny. He stopped at the corner department store and bought the most ludicrously huge Valentine Day card, and went home to prepare himself for a night of savage love. He decided maybe dead wouldn't be such a bad idea, and this one wanted to be dead anyway so that made him feel almost like an angel of death, doing the right thing.

He parked his car three blocks away, and felt a bit comical carrying the dozen roses and bottle of wine, but not so humorous as to go back home unfilled, no he had his plan and he would arrive at Jenny's house and everything would be perfect.

He stopped across the street from the address he memorized and thought of what he would say, what she would do, how the evening would escalate, and finally how it would end. By the time he was finished thinking about the evening, he couldn't cross the street fast enough to get into her house, into her heart.

For another half an hour, he would play the peeping tom. He needed the courage to ring the bell, knock on the door. He watched her prepare her meal, eat, wash the dishes. He was right in her face at the kitchen window. People never look outside a curtain-less window at night. He fantasized about her, he sought after her and he was ready.

When she answered the door, she looked a tad startled, but nothing he couldn't handle. "I am Frank. I didn't want you to have a Valentine's Day without the fixings. You don't have to let me inside; I just brought you flowers, roses, and a bottle of my favorite wine."

Miraculously, she stepped aside and let him in her house. She scarcely made it into the kitchen talking about a vase for the flowers and he was all over her and in a few minutes, had her on the floor making frenzied love, and then he grabbed her kitchen butcher knife out of the knife holder on the counter and stabbed her repeatedly in the heart.

Completely happy with the way the whole thing went, he took great care in the ultimate touch of this, the best Valentine's Day he'd ever known, this was what he'd dreamt about his entire life. He prepared the card he'd brought with him, and inserted it in an slit he made right above where her heart would have been had he not taken it out just moments ago.

He sat next to her for a few hours, just reliving the moments of love, lust and want. He thought about doing it again, but he wouldn't think of having this one again, he needed another. He got up to leave, looking one last time at the panorama of his transgression, his infatuation, his life's conquest.

Walking out into the night was exhilarating for Frank. He felt as if he'd tamed a wild animal, and in a way he had done something, he had let the wild animal out of himself and he had no desire to control it any longer.

**

Frank was barely able to contain himself when the police showed up at the call center the next day. They were asking questions about one of their callers, one who was murdered the night before. Frank wondered which one they'd found, for there were two murders that night, and they were both regular callers of his.

He already vowed that not until Valentine's Day a year from then would he endeavor this murder again, but he was very thrilled to hear that the police believed there was a serial killer loose in the city, and they would be cautioning the citizens about it at the next town meeting a week from now.

The police never released information about the Valentine card that was tucked nicely inside an incision of the body, as a placeholder for the absent heart. This was something the police would use to filter out the crack-pots that wanted fame and gave false confessions. No one was caught within the year, and soon everyone forgot about being wary of strangers.

**

His second Valentine's Day was prepared by Frank to be a feast of unprecedented pain for three someone's who'd called in earlier on in the month of February. He bought his wine and roses early on in the month and froze them to keep them fresh. He had gotten them from a town miles and hours away, where no one would ever think to go.

With everything in his car and the three addresses committed to memory, he went to the first house and peeped into the windows until he found his prey. She was sitting at her computer, back to the door that he assumed would be unlocked. He turned the knob, and as he surmised, it turned until the door popped silently open, and he slipped in. She finally heard a noise and turned around, but it was too late, he had his lariat ready, and strangled her so well that her head almost came completely off of her neck.

She was dead before she hit the floor, yet Frank sat there and helped her to sip wine, while he played with her using the flowers. When he was finished, there were roses in all orifices, and the Valentine Day card was in its place where he heart should have been.

Frank slunk out of the house and went to the second place, a girl of only eighteen live there, and he killed her with a knife as she was lying in the bath tub, completely surprised to see a man standing over her in her own sanctuary.

He was tempted to stop at two, but since he had the plan, the roses, and the wine, he went ahead to the next house on his mental list, that of an elderly woman who had recently lost her husband. Frank didn't bother with the usual peeping here, he wanted to get this one over with and send her to her missed husband where she kept saying into the phone at the call center that she wanted to go. In peace he left her, heart intact, with the card in the slit he cut in her chest.

When he arrived home, he put the two hearts into the freezer and had a good night's sleep. The next day he was his old self in his little cubicle at the crisis call center.

***

Everyone knew the police were keeping close tabs on the call center, and its employees, and the fact that no more murders occurred made the police once again slacken their grasp on the situate and the next Valentine's Day Frank had the run of the city's women once again.

***

Three days before Valentine Day number three, Cindy met Frank at the water cooler. "Are you coming to the picnic? If so, I'm on the food committee and need to know what you want to bring so I can keep track and fill in anything we might be missing."

"Cindy, I will be glad to come. I'll bring chili; I have an award winning family recipe." And Frank cooked the hearts that he kept in the fridge and served it to his co-workers who had not, until that day, included him in anything they did as a group. Watching his coworkers eat the hearts in the chili made him feel vindicated in a way, superhuman, and he was happy.

***

On this Valentine Day, Frank decided it would be his last kill. He was getting worried that he'd been too lucky, so this would be the most extraordinary last fling he would ever have, he made up his mind. He would execute Cindy, and as he found his childhood sweetheart, he'd kill her too, and then be done and happy with the reminiscences on the chaos he'd reeked on women for the rest of his life. He could taste the blood of Cindy and Jenny, and it was almost enough to make him go home contented, but of course he had to finish out his fantasy, it was the only thing keeping him alive, the desire and want of vengeance for all the botched attempts at a relationship would stop with these two who'd started the ordeal of his unsatisfactory life.

He had to lure Jenny away from her family, by calling on the phone pretending her boss was at the hospital after an industrial accident. He captured her when she was running around the corner of her house, headed for the car. He dragged her, unconscious, to his car and together they showed up at Cindy's house for a little one on two. Stabbing them both and leaving them with Valentine Cards in the right places, he felt so alive that he knew this would not be the last of his scavenges into the death of women. He would do it until he was caught, and being as careful as he was, he knew it wouldn't be for a very long time.

***

Many nights were filled with terror as he thought the women he watched through windows saw him, he thought sure some of them knew they were being watched, just by the way they looked oddly through the glass, but he was never caught. People don't look up; neither do they look out on a dark night of curtain-less windows.

About the author: Chris Bartholomew is a writer of dark fiction and has over 300 stories in print publications, anthologies, and some online venues. She is head writer for the international print Serial Killer Magazine with over 70 articles in 8 issues. She also has an ezine where she publishes speculative fiction of other writers, entitled; Static Movement, and the print Static Movement imprint.

THE BRIDE

Jason D. Brawn

What was supposed to be a long drive to York only took the Hendersons a two and a half hour drive, from their wedding reception in St. Albans, Hertfordshire, England. The weather was sunny throughout the build-up to their wedding. The groom, Eric, drove casually in his brand new Jag. The bride, Katie, was beaming with excitement for being with the man of her dreams. He was tall, dark, handsome - and most importantly - rich. Oh yeah, he was the youngest millionaire - at the age of 18 - and today he's worth an estimated £125 million. Not bad for someone who was brought up in a council flat by his single mother. Aged 42, Eric used to be a playboy, but now wanted to share his wealth with someone and raise a family as heirs for his business.

Eric knew the way, as travelling in his motor had always been part of running his own enterprise. Been to York many times and its striking and historical importance had always attracted him to the place. Katie did suggest having their honeymoon in Barbados, but Eric's always busy taking phone calls from his clients and staff. So four days in York was perfect for him, but disappointing for Katie.

As they arrived in York, they passed the main station and cruised over the bridge, overlooking this unspoilt city - formerly a Roman fort - and the River Ouse underneath. A place of culture: The Theatre Royal; York Minister; museums and York Castle. Plenty to do for four days. Already it was Tuesday noon and the Henderson's were feeling peckish.

"How long is it for the hotel?" asked Katie.

"Nearly there," answered Eric, and he was right. The Coach House Hotel was behind the main art gallery and Yorkshire Museum.

Located in a quiet side road, there were a few inns along this road, but The Coach House was five star.

"Here we are," he said, as his Jag crept cautiously along

the driveway at the side of the place, parking in front of the side doorway. He clutched the handbrake and turned off the engine.

Katie's response was, "Very oldi worldi," which it was. A family-run hotel, close to all the major attractions and 300 yards from the Minister - the largest gothic cathedral in Northern Europe. The hotel was established over three hundred years ago, containing lots of history. Maybe haunted?

"Let's go." He was the first to climb out and reach for the boot, despatching their luggage cases.

The inn was small but cosy and looked welcoming. Almost like a lounge with a nice log fireplace, a few leather sofas and dining tables - in the restaurant area. The newlyweds waited by the bar. Katie had her eye on the dancing flames, crackling and spitting sparks. The fireplace sent a comfortable heat in here. Eric palmed the reception bell and waited patiently.

"How do you'll like it here?" he asked.

Katie was happy to say, "Looks stunning. Very period," she was referring to the overhead beams adorned across and gorgeous paintings of Vikings and Roman soldiers in this room. Mahogany antique bookcases attracted her too.

Approaching footsteps attended their call. A greeting middle-aged lady, in her sixties, came to the bar. Eric did find her attractive and would have considered bedding her - back in his womanising day.

"Good afternoon," said the lady.

"Good afternoon," they both said.

"We have booked a room, for Mr and Mrs Henderson," said Eric.

"Oh yes, we do," the lady was pleased to remember. "Congratulations, both of you."

"Thank you," responded Katie. Eric smiled too.

"I'm Mrs Flowers, the landlady," she introduced herself to them, without mentioning her first name, and explained the hotel facilities, their finest suite and their meal times. When she finished, "I'll show you to your room." Mrs Flowers ushered them to the back and up the carpeted stairs to their room - first on their right. A mahogany polished door stood before them and their suite. "Any problem, please give me or any member of staff a shout."

"Thank you so much," said the Hendersons. Mrs Flowers retreated downstairs, leaving them to open the door and enter a luxurious suite.

It was perfect for the kind of money Eric paid. It was booked eight months prior and the most expensive. A king-sized bed, a combo DVD/television set bracketed on the wall, an alarm clock and a chest of drawers in mahogany finish.

"They do like their mahogany," observed Eric. He paced about, examining the room, ensuring it matched the price. Katie plopped on the bed, expressing her tiredness. Her arms and legs were spread out. She closed her eyes, hearing Eric checking the bathroom and emptying out his case, placing the clothes in the wardrobe and drawers. She wanted to fall asleep, but something made her get up and look out of the window. The room was on the first floor of this small building and saw a girl, roughly the same age, standing across the road looking directly at her. Her clothes dated back to the nineties and her hairstyle was red and reaching her back. Skin was pale and her look seemed very creepy, as if warning her. The girl kept a close eye on Katie, still standing behind the grand wall, forming a perimeter behind the ruins of St. Mary's Abbey. Marygate was the name of the road.

Eric appeared beside her, watching too. "Katie," he interrupted her thought. Katie was still gazing at the girl. He followed her gaze and saw nothing. She too shared his vision and turned to him. "What's wrong? Been calling you. Been staring into space," he vocalised his thoughts.

But Katie seemed affected by what she saw. She rushed past him, out of the room, bolting down the stairs and exiting the hotel, where Eric watched her cross over to the same spot. She looked lost and strange to him.

***

Later in the afternoon, they explored most part of the town, visiting antiquarian bookshops and a few attractions, like Haunted - York's most haunted house, on 35 Stonegate. It's supposed to be a 700-year-old house, now open to the public.

Katie and Eric thoroughly enjoyed it, erasing the ghostly visage of what she'd seen earlier.

Afterwards, they stopped at a tearoom in the Shambles - one of the oldest streets in England, dating back to the fourteenth century with its timber-framed buildings overhanging the cobbled and snaky road by several feet. It's the most visited part of York, with gift shops, bakeries, taverns and an alehouse. A place that has also had a shared inspiration for the Harry Potter films.

The Earl Grey Tea Rooms was sandwiched between a pizzeria and a fishmonger. Katie and Eric sat by the window, indulging in the finest cream tea and scones.

Eric was still hungry, eating greedily and showing that he had a sweet tooth. "I may order cakes too," he declared.

Katie was sipping her tea in a delicate manner. Someone with perfect table manners. "Eric, what do you say we visit the Minister after this?" she suggested.

He was still eating his scones. "Yeah, I'm up for that. But we got to do York Dungeons and the ghost walk tonight."

"What time's the ghost walk?"

"Eight pm outside the Minister," he answered. "Should be good." He was eating with his mouth full. Then, without looking, she didn't say more.

Katie stared out the window, at the same flame-haired girl, standing far across noticing her.

"Katie." Her eyes transfixed on the same girl. Eric's hand dropped down, intruding her eyesight. Girl's gone. Katie immediately looked at him.

"Eric, you're going to think I'm going mad, but it's the second time today that I've seen this girl watching me."

"And?" He didn't get it.

Katie said this quietly, for no one to hear her, "I think I've seen a *ghost*."

His instant response was a long and thoughtful silence, followed by a burst of sceptical laughter, embarrassing her.

"I mean it," she gritted her teeth, still lowering her voice.

"Really?" he continued patronising her.

"Yes, it's true. She's a solid figure, as if she's trying to tell me something."

"Maybe she wants to take us on the ghost walk," he joked.

Katie ignored his fun and said this, "She is medium height, possibly five-ten, and has ginger hair."

The joke was over now. Eric's face became twisted with rage and shouted, "What clothes was she wearing?"

"She had a yellow jumper on and stonewash jeans. Very dated clothes," explained Kate.

"Oh dear," the pitch of his voice lowered. She recognised his odd change -

"What's wrong?"

"That's Rachael. My ex," the words slipped from his mouth.

The bombshell dropped on her. Been together for two years now and never had he mentioned anything about his ex.

"When did this happen?"

"It was a long time ago." He wanted to change the subject and already lost his appetite.

"When?!" She slammed the table, demanding answers.

"Twenty years ago, exactly," he reluctantly said.

She looked away, horrified with this dreaded thought. When she returned her curious gaze towards him, "What happened to her?"

Eric swallowed and said, "She killed herself."

The sentence arrested her thoughts, as she sunk down in her chair, with the rest of her world. Darkness soon caved in, forming a blackout.

***

"Katie," whispered her husband's voice, in the fading dark. She began to regain her full sight, capturing Eric sitting - very close - in front with concern. He continued repeating her name.

A few people offered their worries, too, bunched around the Hendersons.

She had no idea she had fainted for longer than ten minutes, having no recollection. But hadn't forgotten her ghostly

192

encounter.

"Ambulance should be on its way," said the manager.

"That's OK, she's alright," Eric spoke for her and said to Katie, "Let's head back to the hotel."

Katie, still dazed, allowed him to guide her out of the tearoom, as sightseers formed a passage for them.

They arrived in one piece, but Katie wouldn't sleep. Her mind was now clear and she wanted answers. Answers about his previous relationship with Rachael.

Eric helped himself to a glass of mineral water, swallowing it nervously and being too scared to tell her what really happened.

"I must know!" she insisted.

Eric was still standing. He looked into her eyes, gulping.

"Rachael and I met at polytechnic, and immediately we hit it off. We lived together and later she fell deeply in love with me. But I couldn't commit myself to her. I was all about sex, drugs and rock n roll." She's listening. "Then, once we got our degrees, I made the boldest decision to end it. But she wouldn't accept it and continued following me and badgering me, assuming there was somebody else. But there wasn't. She was too clingy and always getting jealous. To cut the story short, me and my buddies went here for a weekend break, but somehow she found out and showed up, when I was by myself, with some news..." He paused and looked away in shame.

"Go on," she knew what he was going to say.

Eric turned to her, shamefaced, "She was pregnant with my baby." His eyes widened with extended shame. "I told her to have an abortion, but she refused. Then, when I told her that I wish I never knew her, she cried watching me walk away. And that was the last time I ever saw her."

"Where was her body found?"

"It was fished out from the nearby River Ouse. I am so, so sorry," he pleaded and rushed to her side, begging for forgiveness and cried for the first time in front of her.

Katie considered him, "I need some time to myself." She got off their bed, putting her hooded jacket on and walked to the door.

Eric watched her. "Where're you going?"

"I need some time to think." She opened the door and left.

He stared at his reflection beside the door and burst out in tears of regret.

***

Daylight still remained, as it neared six o'clock. The town was getting emptier and the shops were closing for the day, leaving Katie plenty of solitude and time to think. She wandered, passing many more shops and sightings like the Jorvik Viking Centre, Clifford's Tower, York Castle Museum, the Memorial Gardens, Micklegate Bar - an ancient gateway - and the Treasurer's House, hidden behind the Minister.

By now she had covered every square inch of this small town. She even paced along the Roman city walls - used to defend the city from intruders - overlooking the entire city and passing a war memorial. Katie could see the crimson sun giving its final appearance. But there was something important she had to do. Something she'd been keeping to herself shortly before the wedding, and felt now it was time he knew.

Half-six, she saw on her watch, and headed straight back to her room.

Eric was lying on the bed watching the regional news, waiting for her. He was still worried about her response and feared for their future. But Katie was worried about what she was about to tell him.

"You alright?" asked Eric, who sat up watching her.

She nodded and sat on the chair, facing him. "There's something I need to tell you."

"Sure," he nervously replied.

"I haven't been quite straight with you." Eric didn't respond. "I'm expecting a baby."

She looked at him, expecting a yell or cold response. Instead, Eric's frightened face broke into a joyful expression, laughing and:

"Love you so much, baby," he was pleased to call out.

This too added a smile to her face and before she could

get up and rejoice, he leaped at her and kissed her lovingly.

"We're going to have a baby," he bragged. Then again raised his voice, "Oh baby, this is the best news I heard all day."

He kissed her again and again, unbuttoning her top, and later they both made passionate love.

***

Katie and Eric celebrated in the dining area downstairs, over a bottle of the finest red wine. The guests, consisting of middle-aged people, sat nearer. They had a beautiful roast, with Katie opting for the vegetarian choice. Now Eric's hungry appetite was back.

But Katie had something else to say.

"Would you mind if it's a girl?"

He stopped eating to answer, "Of course not. Have you any idea how much I wanted to have little Erics running around?"

"And little Katies," she corrected him.

"Well, of course. This is fantastic. Our children are our future. Here's to us." He raised his glass for a toast. Both glasses clinked.

That night, they made an exploration of this town, despite the chilling wind and visited an alehouse called The Golden Fleece, York's most haunted pub. But the strangest thing about this place was that no one was talking. No music and it looked as if the locals knew each other very well. When Eric and Katie spoke, they listened. This caused them to leave the pub and wander further. Only the distant shouts of the ghost walk tour echoed the streets, seeing a large group of tourists clustered around a man in a Victorian suit and top hat - like Jack the Ripper.

It was time they headed back to their room. On their way, they stopped at a mini Sainsbury's store, for some snacks to sneak back to their room for a cosy night, watching a couple of horror films - like The Company of Wolves and Robert Wise's The Haunting.

So far, no ghostly appearance from Rachael.

***

Three days had passed, and the golden couple were enjoying their honeymoon. Everything was going incredibly great: the tour bus ride; York Art Gallery; York Museum and its neighbouring Museum Gardens. Things were beyond perfect and Katie was now looking forward to being a mother. As for Eric, he found a great woman.

The next day - their final day - was a little gloomy for Katie. She - by now - loved York. Could see why Eric wanted to take her there.

When Eric got up, Katie was already looking out the window, fully clothed.

"Darling, it's half-seven," he yawned.

She turned and replied, "I know," and flashed a grin. "Going to miss this place."

Eric smiled. "We can always come back here."

"I know." She set off, calling, "Breakfast should be ready."

While having their breakfast, Katie wasn't eating much. Just playing with her bowl of cornflakes with a spoon. *She will miss this place.*

***

Afterwards, they headed back to their room and packed.

"Need to go for a walk," said Katie.

"I'll come with you."

"I prefer going on my own."

He looked at her, bothered. "Alright. Don't be too long, the car will be ready soon," he said, while zipping his case.

She went astray, seeing this quaint city for the very last time. She even shed a tear. That's how she always felt whenever her fun was coming to an end.

Finally, she had a potter about York Museum Gardens, a botanic gardens, with plenty of greens and several historical buildings (the Hospitium, an octagonal observatory, the remains of St. Leonard's Hospital chapel/undercroft, a surviving precinct wall, a lodge, St. Mary's Abbey and the ruins of the abbey church). She was all alone. No one jogging. No one sitting on the bench. Only her and the birds.

A place I can die, her famous last words here. Then she felt a strong chill and folded her arms. More wind approaching, this time attacking her. *Time I head back.* But, as she did, there loomed the spectral figure of Rachael. She appeared before the entranceway, next to the abbey. Katie's only path to the hotel.

The wind got stronger and stronger, getting more and more angry.

Katie didn't flinch. She wanted to confront her and speak to her, to apologise. Katie quickly paced towards her. Getting closer and closer. Then, she walked through her and, like the wind, she was gone. Never to be seen again and suddenly the visitors appeared in the gardens.

***

"Darling, we ready," was the first thing he said to her when she arrived. Katie stared straight into his eyes. "What's wrong?"

Her look was still narrow. Then she charged towards him, kissing him - like there was no tomorrow, dying to make love.

"Hey, hey, hey." He struggled to push her back. "We got to check out," he scanned his watch, "at ten."

She shed a tear and said, "I missed you," making him feel taken aback. "Hey, you were only out for nearly an hour."

She kissed him again and again.

When she was ready to go, she looked at herself in the mirror - following her Eric out - and saw *Rachael.*

About the Author: Jason D. Brawn lives in London and his short fiction and poetry have appeared in anthologies, magazines and ezines from Static Movement, Wicked East Press, Pill Hill Press, Living Dead Press, House of Horror, The Horror Zine and many more. Jason's also completed his first ever novella, *Refuge,* a Hammer Horror inspired tale. His blogspot is jasonbrawn. blogspot.com

PRINCESS
Danica Green

The air of the basement was still and warm, as always, and the single light bulb was fading slightly, casting shadows across the floor. The room didn't hold much of interest, a single bed with a pink duvet cover, a rickety set of shelves with a few second-hand books, a bucket and a large bowl of water in the corner at the back. There was no carpet to speak of, just dirty bare planks and a threadbare, circular rug by the bed that may at one time have been green but was now undecided as to its color. A small wardrobe by the door was the last thing in the room, with the exception of the filth-streaked child that sat cross-legged on the floor, flipping through a book she had read many times before.

"They, hand in hand, with wandering steps and slow, through Eden took their solitary way." Her finger passed under the rows as she read, tongue curling awkwardly around the world 'solitary' that was still foreign in her eight year old mind. She closed the book and placed it back on the shelf, the creases on its old cover fanning the book out at angles. She pushed a fingertip to the book's spine and spoke aloud.

"Paradise Lost." Looking around at her surroundings, a combination of ironic laugh and desperate wail escaped from her rosebud lips. She flopped back, greasy hair fanned out on the rug and for the thousandth time she wished for a clock or a calendar. One of the worst things about this place was the timeless, windowless monotony, never knowing if it was day or night, no cool breezes or warm sunlight. She often missed the rain and despite the fact that she used to hide under trees or wrap up in a waterproof when a storm hit, her skin somehow felt parched without it. Sometimes she'd throw handfuls of water from her wash bowl up in the air and smile as it fell down in heavy blobs on her face. She didn't flinch as the key rattled in the lock and the short, squat man entered with his plastic tray. She didn't acknowledge him as he set it down next to her and stroked her hair, her eyes remaining fixed to the ceiling.

198

"You're up early princess," he said with a smile. His round glasses dipped with his eyes as she lay in silence and he started to scowl. "Say good morning Annabelle." My name isn't Annabelle you freak, she screamed inside her head, though she'd learned not to voice such thoughts. He never hurt her, his little princess, but he did withhold food, or sometimes refuse to clean the bucket that served as her toilet. That punishment was definitely the worst. Once, early into her captivity when she was still overly defiant, the bucket had stood unclean for three weeks. He finally relented and took it out when he found her hiding from the smell in the wardrobe with vomit on her dress. He was still crouched beside her and the girl whose name was not Annabelle knew that he wouldn't leave until she said it. She allowed herself the comfort of a barely audible sigh.

"Good morning daddy." The man grinned broadly, lips straining the excess of fat on both his cheeks.

"That's my girl." He ruffled her hair and stood, reminding her to eat all her breakfast before walking out and locking the door behind him. The girl, real name Louise, looked bleakly at the tray of food that sat unappetizingly beside her and laughed slightly at the plastic spoon that sat next to the porridge. Her captor was cautious, and ever since she had tried to maim him with a fork he had replaced all her cutlery with plastic, though Louise found it amusing that he thought she might be able to hurt him with a spoon, even a real one. Amusement was one of the things that kept her going. For the first few months it had been nothing but tears and terror but when she came round to the fact that her captor didn't have any ill-intentions towards her, aside from keeping her locked up, she began to relax a little and formulate what now constituted her failed plans of escape. The fork had been first, another had been hiding until he came in and running for the stairs but he caught her before her foot touched the first step. Recently she had bitten a hole in her mattress to get at the springs, thinking that a sharp piece of metal would be a good tool but the springs had proven impossible to uncoil so she'd covered over the hole and set her mind to something else. Her other shining beacon was her books. She didn't want to associate anything in the room with home, it was the bed, the wardrobe, the clothes, not *hers,* but she saw the books as prisoners too, lying miserable and unread until the day she arrived to appreciate them. She'd read each cover to cover numerous times by now but she still enjoyed them in every way she could, sometimes reading them out loud and doing funny voices for the characters, sometimes pretending she was reading to a room full of people, often staring and staring until the book blocked out the room and she could pretend she was in those worlds, invisible. Her favourite two were *Alice in Wonderland* and *Paradise Lost,* though she understood little of the latter, she just found many of the words interesting, some of the sentences sounded beautiful and each time she read it it made a little more sense. Some of the books were even harder than that, while some were for children much younger than her and she didn't often touch. She had seventeen books, up from fourteen, the man she called daddy having brought her a new one on both the Christmases and one birthday she had spent with him. Louise began to eat her porridge and toast, trying to mentally calculate how long it had been since last Christmas. She was sure it was her birthday again soon and that meant an eighteenth book to add to her collection, a prospect which pleased her immensely. It wasn't her birthday of course, not really, it belonged to the other, the one who really was Annabelle, the one whose brown hair and green eyes were a mirror of Louise's, the shape of their faces, right down to a crescent-shaped scar on one side of the chin. A photo of her sat on top of the bookshelf and, beyond anything but freedom, she desired to know who the girl really was. She had asked on occasion but the conversation always went the same way.

"Who's the girl in that picture?"

"It's you, silly princess."

"Is it Annabelle?"

"Annabelle, stop playing games."

It was impossible to get a straight answer out of him, twisted and broken as his mind appeared to be but the final question, the one she woke up every morning fearing she would learn the answer to, was what would happen to her as she got older? The girl Annabelle looked about six in her picture and

Louise was seven when he had taken her. She knew that at some point this year she would be nine and already her face was starting to lose the chubbiness of early childhood, the scar on her chin stretching out as she grew and turning from a crescent into a line. What would happen to her when she no longer looked like Annabelle? She shook her head and shoved the last spoonful of food into her mouth, just as the door started to rattle again.

"All done princess?"

"Yes daddy."

"There's my girl."

"Daddy?" Louise blurted the question out as the man turned to leave the room with her empty bowl and tray. She hadn't really meant to, not entirely knowing what it was she was going to ask.

"Yes princess?" She chewed the inside of her cheek for a second.

"Is it my birthday soon?" The man grinned and shifted his bulk from one foot to the other.

"Two weeks today. Is my Annabelle excited?"

"Yes daddy." Then, he asked her something she didn't expect.

"Well, what present would you like?" Louise looked up at him in surprise and and said nothing, her mind throwing her a thousand different choices at once.

"I'm not sure," she finally replied. "May I think about it?"

"Of course princess. Let me know at dinnertime." He grinned again and walked out of the door. The key clicked in the lock. Louise was starting to worry. She desperately wanted another book but she knew that she needed to ask for something that might be of use to her, something innocuous that she could use to her advantage. She almost thought to ask him for two presents, but wasn't sure if she could push her luck. The whole time she had been here she had toed the line, saying what he wanted her to say and doing what he wanted her to do, slipping into the role of Annabelle. It was the safest way. He kept a knife at his belt in plain sight, and although he had never referred to it, or taken it out, she was sure he kept it there to intimidate her. Lunch and dinner came and each time she had no answer for him about what she wanted for her birthday, making promises that she would sleep on it and tell him in the morning. The rest of the evening she lay across the floor, mind whirring through the possibilities but everything she came up with was too obvious, or not useful enough. She still didn't have a decision when he came down to tell her to sleep.

"Get ready for bed Annabelle." She opened the wardrobe and picked her nightdress out of the pile, removing her dress and slipping it on over her head. The man went to say something but Louise answered him first.

"I'll tell you what I want in the morning daddy. Promise." She smiled sweetly and he ruffled her hair.

"Sleep well princess." He watched Louise climb under the covers and close her eyes, then flicked off the light and locked the door as he left. Louise lay in the dark and felt herself start to cry. It was in the loneliness of the night that she always found herself really thinking about where she was and how long it had been since she last saw sunlight. She missed the simple things, grass, dogs, cars, even feeling a twinge for the dreary days stuck in school. The most painful thing to think about was home. By now, everyone would think she was dead. She could see her mother, crying, sitting day and night by the phone as she waited for news even though it had been so long. She could see her father trying to convince her to give up and move on, because as much as he loved Louise he was sensible, a practical man who would insist they keep going for Jimmy. She missed Jimmy the most, the way he teased her, the way he mocked her, the way he would sneak into her bedroom at midnight if she had a nightmare and tell her stories to make her laugh, filling them with curse words that they would never dare utter around their parents. People always said that when you were faced with a tough situation you should think of the people you love to keep you going but for Louise it just drained every last ounce of the fight out of her, filling her mind with Christmas morning they would have spent staring at her empty place by the tree. She was ruining their lives by not being there. No, she corrected herself, *he* is the one ruining their lives, that stupid, fat, pig of a man upstairs who's too damn insane to realise that no matter how much he wants it, I will never be Annabelle. Louise wiped away her tears and focused on her anger, a much more useful emotion on nights when she couldn't stop dwelling. The memory flashed into her mind spectacularly. She had walked into her bedroom one day to find Jimmy with her favourite doll, the poor thing dangling off the edge of her bed, Jimmy laughing. She'd cried, she'd been angry, she'd cried more and then Jimmy had apologised and shown her how to do it. That trick with the rope. She stopped herself from smiling, not entirely sure that there was any merit in the plan that was forming in her mind but either way, the comfort of having something to focus on let her drift off to sleep.

Louise awoke in darkness, though her internal body clock had developed sufficiently that she knew it was almost time for breakfast. Normally she would turn on the light, get dressed and pick out a book to read but today she was going to wait. He loved to wake her in the mornings. An hour or so passed before the door opened and the light from the stairwell illuminated her face as she feigned sleep. She heard him walk over and place the tray on the floor, then gently shake her shoulder.

"Wakey wakey Annabelle." Louise yawned and blinked, pretended to rub the sleep from her eyes and rolled over to face him.

"Good morning daddy," she said, smiling broadly. He was always so pleased when she played her role well that his glasses nearly fell off with the depth of emotion on his face. He reached out and hugged her tightly, Louise trying not to gag on the unwashed stench of him, the greasy feeling of his skin, the folds of fat pressed up against her face and restricting her breathing. She kept her smile in place and swung her legs over the bed. The man handed her the tray and then sat down on the floor as she started to eat, staring at her every mouthful, watching each sip of orange juice go down. When she had finished, he took the tray.

"Thank you daddy, that was lovely. Say, I've been thinking about what I want for my birthday. Would you like to know?"

"Yes please." He sounded disgustingly eager.

"Well actually, there are two things I want, but I can't choose between them."

"Just let me know sweetheart, maybe I can get both."

"Okay. Well I would like a new book, but I also really want a piece of material or a drape or something, to separate the toilet from the rest of the room. I just think it would be nice." She smiled her prettiest smile as the man thought about it, before nodding.

"Yes, I think we could manage that." He ruffled her hair and gave her another quick hug, then picked up her tray and walked towards the stairs.

"I love you princess."

"I love you too daddy." The words tasted foul in her mouth but she kept the smile going until the door closed on her. This was her last chance.

The next two weeks passed dully, a blur of books and meals and false congeniality. When the day of Annabelle's birthday arrived, the door swung open and Louise's breakfast tray held a rectangular object wrapped in newspaper and a cupcake with seven candles on it. He placed it next to her bed and she sat up, trying hard to radiate excitement from every pore of her body.

"Happy birthday Annabelle." He handed her the gift and she tore off the newspaper to reveal a fairly good quality copy of *The Wind in the Willows*.

"Thank you daddy," she beamed, offering him a hug and twisting her mouth into a grimace as she did so. He took a lighter out of his jeans and started to sing 'Happy Birthday' as he lit the candles. She was nearly nine, but there had been seven candles the last time she'd had to celebrate Annabelle's birthday so whoever she was, she must have been seven years old. Louise liked to think she was a daughter, killed in some tragic accident at the age of seven and this poor wretch couldn't face that harsh truth. She felt a small stir of pity and pushed it away, replacing the image of him mourning at a grave with the image of a young girl beaten, bruised and finally killed by an abusive father. This evil creature did not deserve her sympathy. He held the lighted cupcake to her lips and she blew out the candles, following it up with a little clap of her hands. He told her to eat her breakfast and ran out of the room, then quickly back in, holding a length of pink material, a hammer and two nails sticking out of his mouth.

"Your other present," he smiled, beginning to nail the material across the corner of the room with the waste bucket. Louise's heart fluttered in relief as she'd worried that he might have forgotten. She stared at him as he worked, visualising the results of her plan that the pink fabric was so integral to. When he had finished he stood back to admire it and Louise thanked him profusely, then handed him her tray. He leaned down and kissed her on the forehead before leaving.

"Happy birthday again princess." When he had gone, Louise ran over and passed a hand along the pink drape. She almost went to tear it down before realising that she only had a few hours before he returned to give her lunch, but a much longer interval came between lunch and dinner. She left it be and returned to the bed, opening her new book and beginning to read.

When he came down at lunch she was still absorbed and she could feel the contentment arise from him. She finished the book as she ate, him sitting and staring at her in that creepy way of his.

"Wow daddy, that book was great, I loved it." He smiled and gave a laugh.

"I'm glad." He took the tray. "Love you princess."

"Love you too daddy." She waited patiently for the sound of the door locking, waited until she heard his foot hit the final step at the top of the stairs, then she walked over to the corner of the room and ripped the pink material off the nails, dragging it over to the bed. She assessed it from every side, then ran a finger through the dirt on the floor and started to mark lines along its length. When she was done, she pushed the mattress up against the wall to expose the spring that she had failed to utilize in her last plan. It didn't uncoil or come out of the mattress like she had needed then, but it still had a sharp corner and that was all she needed now. Placing a marked piece of the fabric up to the point of the spring, she tore a hole, then repeated the process all along it. Replacing the mattress, she sat on the floor and began to rip it into thin strips, using teeth and fingernails in her haste, terrified that the man might return before she was ready. When the strips were prepared she laid them out in front of herself and closed her eyes. She thought back to that day in her bedroom, her doll, Jimmy laughing, the tears in her eyes. She pictured Jimmy comforting her and rescuing the doll. She remembered picking up the tiny rope and asking Jimmy how he did it and then, hardest of all, she pictured every tiny moment sat on her bed, as Jimmy showed her how to make a noose. She opened her eyes and started to plait the material together, making it as strong as she could while keeping it thin. Several times she did it wrong and the material tangled, so she unlaced it and laced it again and again, until it was right. She couldn't afford a mistake. She wound it all together, over and under, round and round and secured it, grabbed the slipknot and slipped it up and down the length, then stood and held it out in front of her. It was perfect. She knew several hours had passed since she started the task, clumsy as she was and working off a years old memory but a small spark of hope was welling up in her. It was a couple of hours until he would be down to give her dinner but she didn't want to risk losing the adrenaline that was flooding her. The fact that she was planning to kill someone kept pushing at the sides of her mind and she tried her hardest to nudge it away. Sitting down behind the door in wait, she closed her eyes and thought about her imprisonment, the withheld meals when she didn't cooperate, the stench of the bucket, the stale air without sunshine or rain. She thought of her family crying over her loss, her friends playing at school without her. Lastly, she thought of the man whom she called daddy, the one who had forced her here and taken away her life. By the time she heard the key rattling in the lock, murder didn't seem like such a big deal any more.

The door opened and the man looked around at what seemed to be an empty room. He walked across the floor and looked at the small scraps of fabric that hung from the nails where the drape used to be. Louise crept out from behind the door and flung the noose, watching joyfully as it fell over his head. He dropped the tray in shock as she yanked it as tight as her thin arms could. He clawed furiously at his neck and tried to pull it loose, choking and gasping for air. Louise gave a tug and he fell to the floor, now desperately reaching out and trying to hit her. She sat down hard on the floor with the rope coiled around her hands, then placed her feet on his shoulders, pushing down to give herself extra leverage. His face turned red, the purple as he alternated between tugging at the rope and gouging holes in Louise's legs with his fingernails. The knife at his belt shone, reflecting the scene in its mirrored surface and, one hand still pulling, Louise reached out and grabbed it. The man's eyes went wide and he rolled over and stood, ripping the rope from her grasp and finally pulling it free of his throat. He sucked the air fiercely with his eyes pinned to Louise.

"Princess," he croaked. "Please stop." Louise looked at his pleading eyes, then at the knife, then at the open door behind him. She ran forward, ducking under his arms as they came up to protect him and pushed the knife under his ribs and up into his heart. Blood poured over her pale hands and the man fell again to his knees.

"Princess..." Louise threw the knife across the room, sneering, then spat onto his dying face.

"I'm not your fucking princess." The man hit the ground without protest, blood pooling out onto the rug at Louise's feet. She looked to the door and began to walk, paused and turned towards the bookshelf, placing the picture of Annabelle face down, then picking up *Paradise Lost* and running a hand across the cover. She clutched the book to her chest, briefly looking back at the corpse that lay sprawled out across the floor of her dungeon and, with a small smile on her lips, disappeared up the stairs, shutting the door behind her.

About the author: Danica Green is a UK-based writer who has been published in 3:AM Magazine, PANK magazine and was a finalist in the Tenth Annual Wergle Flomp Humor Poetry Contest. Her work is forthcoming in Eclectic Flash Magazine and anthologies by Silverland Press and Static Movement.

Mother's Ruin

Catherine Hoyle

Today was a very special day for Cassie. Her Nan had told her there was a surprise for her after school today and to hurry home. She wasn't sure what it was going to be, but Nan told her it was an adventure!

Imagine that!

Maybe she was going to see the hippos and the elephants in Africa like Nan did when she was younger!

Nan was her most favourite person in the whole world, well, since Mummy and Daddy got sick anyway. That's what Nan called it. They used to be brilliant, especially Mummy. She gave the best cuddles in the whole world. She didn't want to cuddle anymore and was always angry or being sick or had a headache. Yucky.

Cassie had to leave her alone when she was really sick because she shouted at her for making loud noises. Nan said it wasn't Cassie's fault though and that Jin did horrible things to people. Cassie didn't know Jin but thought if she ever met her she would tell her to stay away from her mummy and stop making her so sick!

Cassie missed the way Mummy smelled, warm and safe... After they had started getting sick, she had stolen her mum's perfume from the bathroom. Covering her teddy bear, George, in it, she would hold him close and breathe in the familiar scent. If she closed her eyes and thought REAL hard, it was almost like having Mummy back, just for a moment.... almost. But Cassie couldn't think about that now, she had to get ready for her adventure!

When Cassie got home, Daddy was there. He looked like he'd been crying. Daddy never cried though, so maybe it was hay fever. A boy in her class had hay fever. Around her birthday in April his eyes were always red and he sniffed a lot too! But her birthday wasn't for ages. Christmas was first! Cassie asked if he was okay and tried to give him a hug but he just turned and made a choking sound before pointing towards her room. She hoped he was okay but you didn't argue with daddy.

Curling up in a ball on her bed, she drew George near and thought about Mummy and Daddy and how Nan had said she was going to make everything better. Maybe they were all going to join the circus? Cassie decided that would be brilliant. Daddy could be a clown with his big feet! And Mummy could be the ringmaster and wear a top hat and everything! Of course Cassie The Great would be holding lions and tigers back with chairs, just to make sure they didn't eat anybody! And maybe they could all be happy again, away from horrible Jin. That was the best part, Cassie decided. She fell asleep with a smile on her face and was whisked away to a Big Top with her name in twinkling lights outside.

It was dark by the time Cassie woke up, but Nan was there so she didn't mind too much.

"Nice dreams darling?" She asked in her soft and slow Rhondda accent. Cassie just nodded, wiping the fairy dust sleep from her large blue eyes. Suddenly realising this was it.

Adventure Time.

Cassie sat bolt upright and began interrogating Nan about where they were going. Her Nan smiled sadly and replied "We're going down Porthcawl, Hun" Before picking the little girl and her teddy bear up and strapping them in the car.

It was cold in the car and smelt funny, like Nan's cigarettes, but Cassie was happy, Nan always bought her a Pick 'n' Mix down Porthcawl and they would walk down to Rest Bay and play on the rocks together. They hadn't been in a while though because Nan had been sleeping lots lately and she had to go to the doctor's to make sure she was getting better. She had baddy lungs. Nan had told Cassie that she might be going away soon though and that no matter what happened; she loved her more than anything in the world.

When they got there, Nan parked in a different place to normal and Cassie wondered if they were getting sweets. Before she could ask, Nan had opened the boot and was doing something weird behind the car. Cassie couldn't see from her booster seat but she could feel the car moving a bit as her Nan fidgeted with something outside, before closing the boot again.

She looked upset getting back in and there was a look in her eye that Cassie had never seen before. She turned the engine on and Cassie noticed a slow hissing noise but didn't have chance to dwell on it.

Cassie's head was starting to feel a bit fuzzy as she stifled a yawn. Nan explained the doctors couldn't make her better anymore. That it was going to be okay. That Nanny was taking them somewhere magical! Where Cassie would still be safe. Where Mummy and Daddy wouldn't be sick anymore and where nothing could hurt them.

Nan undid Cassie's seatbelt and held her in her arms. George was snuggled safely on her chest, and Nan's arms were around her.

Cassie lifted her bleary head.

"Are there lions and tigers there Nan?"

"There's everything you've ever dreamed of, Bach"

Cassie smiled and settled back down with George safely positioned in her arms.

The world was foggy and getting dark as Nan started singing 'Somewhere Over the Rainbow' quietly, just like she used to, when Cassie had had a nightmare, rocking her to sleep.

Everything was slowing down and even breathing was getting hard. She was so tired.

Nan's singing was getting quieter now, like it was coming from far away. The world swam in and out of focus and she squeezed George even closer.

Her little body was going limp, and with her last breath. She whispered in George's ear;

"We're going on an Adventure."

About the author: Cat Hoyle has recently completed a degree in English and Creative Writing from UWIC. Her work has been published in Nexus e-magazine and has been accepted to a print anthology, due for release in Autumn 2011 called 'The C Word'.

SILVER BULLET HONEYMOON

John X. Grey

In Pennsylvania's eastern edge on County Road2003 northwest past the town of Bushkill, Wolf's Lair Hotel Resort and scenic Wolf Lake (emptying southeast by Bushkill Falls into the Delaware River) was Jack and Phyllis Petrov's romantic vacation destination as newlyweds in April 1939. Married at 2:30 P.M. on Friday April 14th inside Gotham, New Jersey's Christ Episcopal Church (Phyllis Harrington's faith) at Garden Street and West 2nd Avenue's northwest corner, the couple drove northwest and north for their one-week Poconos Mountains vacation. Wolf's Lair (1,500' above sea level) boasted 124 rooms, 100 inside the gothic brownstone hotel's five-story building, its grounds containing a big oval swimming pool, four tennis/badminton courts, scenic trails to Wolf Lake one mile southwest or other nearby interest points, and 24 adjacent woodland rental cabins (not counting 50 smaller employee cabins north of the hotel). Pocono Greens, a nine-hole golf course, was also located 2 miles west. The couple arrived at 9:52 P.M. after the arduous six-hour and almost 300-mile drive in Jack's gunmetal-gray/white trim Plymouth P-4 Coupe, having made necessary fuel and rest stops along the way.

"I hope," the bride gave her first impression; "this place looks more inviting in daylight."

Phyllis had changed from a long high-necked white satin wedding gown at church into the blue-gray wide-lapel jacket with matching skirt, white silk blouse and gloves, tan stockings and black satin pumps, stepping out of the passenger's side door opened by Jack after he parked their car in a vacant diagonal space among twenty. She wore her black hair in a wavy shoulder-length bob with its big wide blue clip at the crown. Petrov had on a white suit, shirt, red striped tie, white boating straw hat and brown shined shoes, preferred to the uncomfortable black tuxedo and shoes earlier that afternoon. He scratched at combed-over cropped black hair, removing the stray rice grains thrown on him at the church before picking a few off Phyllis' jacket.

"You said Melanie Brewster recommended it. She's your old friend, not mine."

"She and Mark claimed they had a wonderful time here last summer," the lady retrieved her wide-brim white hat with a blue ribbon off the front seat, "don't forget our luggage, darling. There's no bellhop service after nine. I'm tired enough for going straight to bed."

Jack closed her door, staring at his convertible's rear trunk and seat collectively holding the man's two navy-blue suitcases along with the missus' six-piece white luggage ensemble.

You knew how much she packed for this one-week getaway. A train trip to Niagara Falls could've been our destination if I'd been paying for this.

The private detective knew his new father-in-law, *Gotham Register* newspaper publisher Charles Foster Harrington, was springing for this vacation, giving his daughter time off from her job – whatever Phyllis wanted she got. Petrov was learning the art of marital compromise.

"Coming, dear," Jack brought four of her bags from the trunk, the 6' 2" and 195-pound man following his 5' 7" 132-pound bride of eight hours and five-year a girlfriend. She carried her makeup case and hat box in those gloved hands. He enjoyed her slight hip wiggle walking that white concrete sidewalk and up two short sets of five steps on the main building's hillside, ending at a wide front porch with few lights to the first floor's windows. They entered through heavy carved oak double doors which squeaked on brass hinges and walked toward the half-circle registration desk.

"Yes ma'am, sir, what can I do you for tonight?"

The straw-haired, suntan-faced youth, with residual adolescent acne signs in a blue jacket with gold trim and white slacks, deliberately reversed two words in that question to make a joke, laying aside the *Confidential* magazine he had been reading seated on a wooden rolling chair.

"Our reservations are under Petrov," Phyllis took the lead facing this clerk, "one week's honeymoon starting tonight."

Once all formalities were concluded, night clerk Chip

Mortensen showed the late-arriving honeymooners to Room 510 via the elevator. Jack made a second trip to lock the car, raise its cloth top in place and retrieve his luggage. Their deluxe cream-colored suite had four rooms – a big central bedroom, walk-in closet, front lounge for entertaining and full bathroom with heart-shaped pink tub for two. The Petrovs left their luggage stacked beside the king-sized bed's foot for tonight. Jack changed into special maroon silk pajamas, a gift for the bridegroom from his in-laws, while Phyllis selected her backless powder-blue spaghetti-strap long nightgown with sheer sides. Realizing his bride was tired after today's ceremony and long trip, Jack could wait another night before consummating their union. Phyllis had never allowed anything more than light *petting* from her fiancé since the early November engagement.

Her perfume is intoxicating and I love seeing my lady's exposed chassis horizontal at last, but it'll be more fun and giggles to pop that cherry tomorrow.

Despite deferred carnal pleasures, Jack slept peacefully.

***

Their first full day at Wolf's Lair proved busier than expected with Phyllis rising at dawn, playfully nagging Jack out of bed despite his Saturday habit to sleep until 9:00 A.M. They took a brisk brief morning swim in the hotel's large oval pool, followed by breakfast together wearing white complementary bathrobes over his navy-blue swim trunks and her red skirted-front tank swimsuit, minus the white bathing cap she used earlier, at the hotel's northwest-end first-floor dining room. Jack felt some minor relief there was no bill, considering the nice service dishes for their meal and cloth napkins reflecting posh surroundings.

Mr. Harrington arranged all the expenses. I only had enough saved to visit Coney Island or Niagara Falls.

Phyllis arranged for a couple's tennis lessons since she and Jack had never played the game growing up, before they hiked around hills enjoying romantic views, despite suffering a few mosquito bites near some pine trees. Between a midday dinner and later supper, the Petrovs met Bill and Dolly Adams, a minor league baseball team's pitching coach and his diner waitress wife from Scranton who had saved up for their second honeymoon here. The foursome shared a game of shuffleboard outdoors, followed by gin rummy and bridge – Jack having trouble getting the hang of that latter card game.

"You'll figure each other out," having weathered, brown-haired good looks and the warm smile, gray-suited Bill assured the detective with a back pat as they stood from the parlor's table after the last hand, "it's taken me and Dolly ten years."

"Yeah," the heavyset long flip-curl styled blonde Dolly in the green dress patted Phyllis' left hand at the bridge table, "but with Bill Jr. at my parents' place, I've felt like we've started dating all over again."

After a light supper, the Petrovs and Adamses went dancing in the first floor's east-facing ballroom lit by four sliver chandeliers, containing waxed white tile floors and high rectangular windows showing a faint orange sunset's glow farthest from the western horizon. Jack somehow had fun despite knowing few dances well besides the Charleston. That evening, husband and wife finally consummated their wedlock, and Jack decided Phyllis had been worth waiting for after five years.

But she thinks she'll still work at the paper if becoming a mother. I think mama would've laughed about her optimism, but still liked this daughter-in-law.

Sleeping contented against Phyllis' right side face-down, a right arm draped gently across the lady's bare bosom, and her right hand against his manhood, they had shunned clothing for the first intercourse under silk covers. Tomorrow the Petrovs would attend services at a Reformed Church they passed en route here Friday, even though it was neither Episcopal nor Orthodox as their traditional faiths, followed by nine holes golfing at Pocono Greens.

Even though I don't play often at Galloway and Rutgers northwest of Raritan Hills or own clubs, I hope she likes the game.

By afternoon, Jack and Phyllis suffered a minor argument over strokes at some longer par holes, subsiding after he stopped counting – she hit 92 to his 67. The 37-year-old was no more a golf professional than his semi-athletic 28-year-old wife.

"I'm not sure I want to talk to you now," she changed from a white short-sleeved blouse and knee-length plaid skirt into the shorter sky-blue tennis dress standing before their suite's one full-length oval mirror, "Daddy's the one you should've brought to play golf. I might try it again sometime, but only with other people along. You weren't a good caddy or teacher today."

"Hey, pipe down," Jack wiped his mouth craving a drink, shedding the brown flat cap, tan short-sleeved shirt with brown-checked sweater vest and golf slacks, taking out a white short-sleeved polo shirt and knee-length shorts from one blue suitcase, "I guess I'd expected a girl with your upbringing to have hit balls on links somewhere."

"What's that supposed to mean?" Phyllis turned in her tan bra and panty briefs from that mirror and pulled the dress into place. "A girl with my *upbringing* – just because I come from a well-to-do family, I'm supposed to know polo and croquet too?"

"Look," he tucked the shirt into those shorts and then retrieved tennis shoes and socks, "I didn't mean... let's just enjoy something new together, okay."

"Jack," the pleated short dress in place, she rubbed his shoulders facing him, "this is part of a marital adventure – getting to know each other as friends and lovers. My father never came from money, he earned it. My mother is a different story."

Kissing several seconds as he embraced her, the Petrovs were ready to tackle tennis for the first time.

***

"You need to be less rigid in your backswing," Pierre Laval advised Jack after he missed another practice serve on the court they had reserved two hours that afternoon, the 5' 9" black-haired French-Canadian instructor wearing a blue short-sleeved shirt containing the hotel's name on it and long tan loose pants with polished white shoes, "or you're never going to lob a serve back to me. You, however, *Madam* Petrov, seem almost the natural. Are you certain you have never played this game before?"

Jack and Phyllis faced their instructor opposite the dividing net, three other nearby courts containing couples and groups playing or watching matches. Laval had spent several minutes in demonstrating proper techniques for holding and using their rented racquets, along with the serve and return fundamentals, originally aided by co-worker Janet Van Dyke in a long blue dress and brown sneakers. The French-Canadian seemed self-confident and in great physical shape.

"And you were once a highly-ranked amateur, Mr. Laval?"

"*Oui,*" he smiled and rubbed at the five o'clock shadow, Jack resentment toward the hairy Gallic man building, "I no longer compete but had potential as the youth. Now, I will serve again but without telling to whom."

I don't like this dude. I wonder if I'm bothered by his smooth charm toward Phyllis or the French Latin lover malarkey. I've got no beefs with other hotel staff.

Phyllis returned a serve and Pierre aimed the ball at Jack testing the man's reflexes, but Petrov was momentarily distracted glancing at his wife, her ice-blue eyes intently drawn toward their instructor. The ball struck the detective's right temple and forehead hard, knocking him off his feet. Jack fell across the court, disoriented from the impact for several seconds.

"Oh my God, Jack," Phyllis' voice sounded far away at first as she ran over and knelt at her husband's left, Pierre retrieving the ball bouncing on that pavement after leaping over the net to offer his assistance, "darling, are you hurt?"

"Did anyone get the license number of that streetcar?" Petrov babbled before he shook his head to clear remaining cobwebs, Phyllis examining the reddened spot there after she set her racquet down. "OH, what happened?"

"I apologize, *Monsieur* Petrov. I was not aware you weren't prepared for my next volley to your side."

Blinking blue-gray eyes to regain focus, Jack stared up

at the instructor and saw the smug smile below those dark-green predatory eyes, seeming like a carnivore about to devour its prey. Refusing Phyllis' assistance in standing, Jack's face turned redder and almost matched the ball's impact point when abandoning his wood racquet. Humiliated, he stalked off toward the hotel's restaurant and bar, brushing aside his wife's concerned touch.

"You finish the lessons, Doll," he said, never looking back once, "no point in both of us not having a good time. I need something straight up and it'd better be a double."

"They do not sell distilled spirits here, Mr. Petrov," Laval reminded him as the guest was leaving the court, "but I'm sure you noticed that earlier."

Damn it, the Frog's right. I don't know where the nearest store is and they're all closed on Sundays anyhow.

Jack proceeded to drink glasses of beer alone in the restaurant instead, later cut off by the bartender, when finishing his fourth in an hour, under Pennsylvania's odd consumption laws. He imagined Phyllis laughing and flirting with her handsome tennis instructor sitting on a barstool and later inside his room. Two other men drinking a few feet to the left were discussing recent unsolved deaths around this part of the Pocono Mountains, but he paid little attention to the tale of vacationing visitors here mutilated by what must have been a wild animal in the past ten days. The detective had inherited his deceased Russian father's tolerance for alcohol, but its depressant effects left him sleepy enough to pass out across the king size bed. By early evening, he was awakened when the suite's front door opened, staggering to wait beside that bedroom's half-open door to the lounge. Phyllis walked inside, having changed sometime after her tennis lesson into the blue long-sleeved dress with black flat slippers, her hair in the wide ponytail held by its lone gold clasp. She sensed Jack's presence smelling the beer breath first. He grabbed his wife's left forearm and twisted it behind her back, simultaneously clamping a right hand over the lady's full small lips.

"So, how was the lesson, dear? You not dressed for tennis anymore."

The jealous husband forced his wife toward their bed, releasing Phyllis' arm, spinning her around to face him and shoving the lady to a seated position upon the mattress.

"Jack, you've been drinking too much. What's with you?"

"What's eating me? Explain the wardrobe change, sweetheart."

Without missing a beat, Phyllis took his hands and urged he sit to her left, soon correcting Jack's misconceptions.

"After the lesson, I took a walk around the trails again for fresh air. You were asleep, so I changed in the other room and went out alone."

"Probably with that French éclair – yeah, I saw him making eyes at you."

"Pierre, why no, Jack, I wanted solitude, even turned down visiting Wolf Lake with Bill, Dolly and some other guests. I heard a staff member hint the lake's great for skinny dipping. Do you want to try it later?"

Jack saw her concern for his welfare and happiness in ice-blue eyes that had once stared upon him with disdain when they first met five years earlier at the Raritan Hills Country Club. Of course Phyllis was kidnapped by her reanimated fiancé soon after that and stashed inside the zombie's family crypt a few miles away until the detective rescued her.

She could've had any man in Gotham or the world, but chose a palooka from the wrong side of the tracks. Hell, the gal doesn't mind sharing my little apartment until we find someplace bigger and better.

The man smiled and kissed her with open-mouthed passion. Shaking his head, he added a racier notion.

"Instead of changing into clothes and creeping to the lake, we'll wear just our robes and pool shoes, and leave after dark."

"But it's not sundown yet," Phyllis looked at her thin silver wristwatch on the right arm, "did you want to eat something before we leave?"

"I've got a better idea, *Mrs.* Petrov," his hands unzipped the lady's dress front from the scooped neckline above her apple-sized B-cup bosom, "let's make whoopee until then."

"That *is* a good idea," she pulled his shirt off over the head after shedding that dress, and they gradually became involved together across their bed.

***

At 9:20 P.M., Jack and Phyllis Petrov emerged from Room 510 wearing blue and pink bathrobes, black wooden thong sandals and nothing else. They appeared headed toward the tiny spa on the first floor's southeast corner to anyone encountering them along hallways, inside the elevator or on the grounds, although they met fewer people once outside. After nearly one mile strolling on the dirt path southwest from the hotel, under a full moon's light that made their trip easier, the Petrovs disrobed and unshod, running into lukewarm water, laughing like kids and diving together to disturb its placid surface. Phyllis did not bring any cap for her hair since this was un-chlorinated water. The naked swimming duo was invigorated and Jack soon recovered from his mild hangover. After close to a half-hour skinny dip, the Petrovs emerged and lounged on sandy ground near their robes and shoes, breathing hard and laughing before they rolled into each others arms to continue earlier copulation.

"Jack," Phyllis paused between kisses atop him, "I was worried you were getting steamy jealous for no reason. We should enjoy this time. I'll be on the crime beat and you'll investigate your cases again soon enough."

"Yeah," Petrov agreed, squeezing her ample bare buttocks after the next kiss, "we'll be so busy, I wonder if there's time for starting a family."

Phyllis was initially silent at a subject they had casually discussed during the engagement and less often when dating. She met Jack's disabled veteran brother Ivan, his wife Martina and their five children ages 9 to 17: Philip, George, Natalie, Karin and Theodore (or Filipp, Georgiy, Natalya, Karina and Fyoder in Russian), all living in Queens, and sensed Jack desired a brood of his own.

"I don't know how to answer that," she was always honest with him, he realized, "but the way we've went at it this weekend, I could have a bun baking already."

Content with her answer, accepting their future however it unfolded, Jack aided Phyllis' slip her knee-length pink robe on first, soon both covered and departing that lake.

Why was I jealous before? Petrov walked with his bride arm-in-arm headed toward the hotel, noting an occasional lit resort cabin off to either side, and wondering if they should have asked Phyllis' father to arrange that instead. *She's nuts about me, probably from all those weird dangers we've faced together or other cases I've told her about.*

Considering the staff tennis instructor's subtle interest in Phyllis as casual flirtation, Jack walked at her right and they held hands, until crashing sounds of something in the woods behind them became audible along with growling. The couple turned toward that direction but spotted nothing under moonlight partly obscured by passing clouds.

If it's an animal, I left my gun in the glove compartment half-a-mile away. But I mustn't panic Phyllis...

Suddenly one shaggy form larger than any wolf and running on hind legs burst from the bushes between two trees charging the startled couple. Jack spotted a broken tree branch near his left foot along the trail as Phyllis fled toward the hotel, its upper floor lights visible through trees ahead, but lunging for it he was caught across the right side neck and head by sharp claws. Those gashes, some up to 6" long and a quarter-inch deep, burned as his blood flew through the air. Jack fell into foliage at his left, rolling and tumbling down the small hillside until he finally crashed against ferns near one cliff's edge. He heard Phyllis' distant screams mixed with growls, fearing the thing would slaughter his wife.

Phyllis, I can't lose you after waiting five...years... for our honey...moon...

Jack passed out from shock due to the bleeding claw marks and minor falling injuries. The night regained its stillness as a large shadow crossed his unconscious body.

***

The private detective awakened upon a folding wood-framed cot with thin mattress and pillow. His body still ached from scrapes and bruises suffered falling 30' off the path, but the claw wounds had been bandaged. He sat up and became dizzy, when a husky voice spoke from somewhere beyond his head inside the rustic log cabin.

"Don't try moving around yet, partner," the large, tall man with a thick cinnamon-brown beard and receding wavy hair, dressed in the fringe leather jacket, blue denim shirt and buckskin pants, passed the cot headed toward a heating cast iron stove at the far corner, "you're lucky to be alive."

What happened? Where am I and who's this clown?

Jack's hairy host returned with a three-legged log seat stool and one tin cup of steaming liquid, holding the container toward his face. The injured detective could smell hints of chicken to its aroma.

"Here, drink this," the man advised him once seated, encouraging Petrov to hold the cup if he could, "chicken broth can fix a lot of hurt in people."

The man sampled it with slow sips and found the broth's salty flavor welcome reaching his empty stomach, having eaten little Sunday.

"Thanks, Mister." He winced when talking initially irritated his scratches. "It's good."

"You're more than welcome," the man smiled helping him hold that hot cup, "my name's Brian Holtz. I'm from Clarksburg and have travelled around a piece in my particular business."

"Clarksburg, Tennessee?"

"Nope, the one that's in West Virginia actually."

Jack drank more broth from this large friendly stranger, noticing at the cabin's few square windows it was now daylight outside. He soon felt strong enough to stand, discovering the man had left him naked beneath a red wool blanket, the torn blue robe hanging on a wall peg and the thong sandals nowhere evident here.

"I'd offer you clothes, but don't think mine would fit y'all."

Brian returned the nearly empty cup to a wooden table left of that stove in what served as the one-room cabin's small kitchen area, while Jack left the cot and slowly regained his balance to walk over a dirt floor and retrieve his robe, dried blood on the right side's collar with rips from where that black-furred beast's claws had damaged it.

"And just *what* is it you do, Brian?" Petrov sensed the man was strange, even his smell resembled an animal's den, and noted weapons displayed on these walls – a Winchester rifle, a Claymore sword with red-plaid tassels to its hilt and guard, a long spear with the gleaming silver head, various nets, ropes and two crossbows among them. "Hunting, I'd guess."

"Yep," the man wiped a button nose, gentle hazel eyes studying the guest as he helped the robe-covered Petrov sit at a rickety square table on one of four old simple armless wooden chairs, "you could *say* my life's work is akin to huntin'."

Jack sensed the mischief quality to Holtz's tone as the man produced a brown ceramic jug with its cork stopper and second tin cup from one cupboard. He poured the clear liquid in both cups and replaced the stopper. The detective immediately smelled alcohol.

"What kind is it?"

"Corn whiskey or shine," Brian revealed, "got a kick, but to me it's like soda pop."

Jack sampled the liquid, finding it tolerable when hitting his stomach from all the years he drank hard liquor. The guest finished that cup in seconds, licking his lips.

"So what do you hunt? I don't see any hides or trophies around here."

"This ain't my home," he looked around after finishing his own drink with a sigh, "I'm just squatting here on the trail of something in these parts that's done killed a dozen folks."

"C'mon, what's the mystery?" Jack sat forward nearer his host. "Is the thing that hit me last night doing all that killing?"

"Well, cousin, I've done sized you up to be another hunter, maybe one that lives in some city and doesn't hunt natural things either. You've got the aura about you. I smelled stink from what you've killed afore, something normal human noses can't reckon."

He knows I'm a vampire and monster hunter, not just the private eye?

Jack rubbed at his blue-gray eyes with the left hand and briefly saw a larger shadow from Brian against that wall above a sink with its well hand pump. It was larger than Holtz when even accounting for the stove's bending light. The ears were high upon the skull and rounded above a thicker neck and body, but not on the actual man himself.

"I'm a private eye from Gotham, New Jersey, Middlesex County. Sometimes I take on or stumble into cases involving unexplained stuff in the everyday world."

Jack felt at his bandages when staring toward the front door and remembered he had not traveled to this resort alone.

"Phyllis, oh God, my wife – she's out there somewhere! I don't know what happened to her after I fell..."

Brian restrained Jack with a firm right hand on his robe's back careful of the sore neck's side when they both reached that door. The detective pulled free and faced him.

"I've gotta find her. She could be hurt or even..."

The detective sensed his host's unnatural strength and was becoming used to the man's musky odor inside the cabin's confines, but gave Holtz a stare daring his interference when he imagined Phyllis' mutilated body somewhere in these woods.

"I'll be here if you need me, friend," Holtz told Jack as he exited the cabin for the nearest walking trail five yards away. Stepping on a few uncomfortable sharp rocks in running barefoot, the detective reached the front desk minutes later.

"Mrs. Petrov," front clerk Mickey Chase scratched at his red-brown cowlick-styled hair, before snapping the right hand's fingers, "yes, she's in the dispensary, down the hallway to the right, last door on the right. Sir, maybe you'd better see Dr. Bronstein too."

Jack soon barged into the hotel's medical dispensary in its first floor's southwest corner, where the white dress-clad, raven-haired nurse and a balding brown-haired middle-aged doctor with baggy eyelids wearing a brown suit and white lab coat calmed the concerned husband.

"She's all right, Mr. Petrov," Simon Bronstein M.D. reassured him, "just a bite on her left forearm. I administered an anti-rabies vaccine shot and sent her blood off for testing."

"What happened to her?" Jack sought answers from the doctor and nurse. "We went swimming in the lake last night together and got separated when something attacked us."

"First," Maggie Rogers R.N. was examining the gauze bandage and surgical tape at his right neck and jaw line, "we'd better treat you next."

"Step this way to the examination room, Mr. Petrov," Bronstein ushered him through the admission/records room's left of two doors, "she can't remember much of whatever happened to her. A state game warden found your wife unconscious on a trail this morning one-quarter mile from Wolf Lake."

Jack and Phyllis embraced as he hurried toward her. She sat on the metal exam table in her pink robe, the left forearm's outer side now bandaged.

"Darling, after I fell down that hill, I didn't know what happened to you."

"Jack," she seemed confused, initially staring into space through ice-blue eyes, "I don't recall much after that animal surprised us from the bushes."

"You can get down now, Mrs. Petrov," Bronstein invited her, before looking to Maggie and addressing her first, "I'll remove his bandage but need iodine for all his scrapes and bruises. Whoever bandaged this is good enough at first aid."

"Did it hurt much?" Jack noticed Phyllis rubbing her stomach standing a few feet away to his left in the opaque-windowed white room. "The rabies shot, I meant."

"Yeah, almost as much as the bite that required it." She tried smiling briefly. "Oh Jack, this honeymoon vacation's not turning out very romantic."

"Who knows, sweets?" He reached out to take her right hand, feeling the silver wedding bands touch on her right index finger and his left middle finger. "After last night, maybe the rest of our week has to turn out better."

***

The couple spent their afternoon lounging by the pool, meeting the Fairchilds (Robert and Vivian) from Philadelphia

224

and the Wymans (Eric and Nancy) of Manhattan learning that Bill and Dolly Adams had finished their second honeymoon week yesterday. Jack slept rather peacefully after two aspirins and a beer, but he could feel Phyllis tossing and turning during their third night together as husband and wife, even imagining he heard her growl. Waking around 9:00 A.M. the next morning in white short pajamas, Jack found Phyllis inside the big tub shaving her legs while taking a bubble bath.

"Didn't you do that before our wedding day?"

"Yeah," she paused in running the chrome safety razor along her right calf lifted from the water, "I did, but it grew back sooner than I'd expected."

Smiling at seeing her seated and partially submerged below the suds, Jack noticed Phyllis had removed the arm bandages to reveal smooth tanned skin and no bite marks. He checked his own serious wounds in an oval wall mirror and noted claw mark or scars still red and visible.

"Boy, you sure healed fast."

"I know," she admitted, finishing the right leg, "I take after daddy. He heals faster than mama."

"If you're done," Jack began undressing, "I could use a bath while telling you about the strange man I met yesterday who found me unconscious."

"Please do, darling," Phyllis set the razor aside on a soap dish and retrieved one sponge floating in those suds, "and you can start rubbing my back if you're coming in."

Jack entered the tub and began their romantic bath, noting all of Phyllis' fingernails had become sharper when she playfully scratched his back at one point. She seemed intrigued by the strange mountain man Brian Holtz from Jack's story and they bathed and soaked together about fifteen minutes in the sunken tub. The Petrovs donned robes in returning to the bedroom when hearing a knock at their suite's door.

"Yes," Jack answered it, "can I help you?"

"Charles Percy," the tall, lean man with sandy-brown hair and light-blue eyes in his tan button-down shirt and brown trousers announced, tipping the golden-brown fedora once, "I'm the state fish and game warden for the Wolf Lake area and found

Mrs. Petrov lying between two trees yesterday."

"Pleased to meet you, Mr. Percy, and I'm grateful you helped Phyllis." Jack invited the brown hiking-booted man inside. "In fact, would you join us for lunch downstairs? I'd like to buy your meal and a drink out of gratitude."

"That'd be keen, Mr. Petrov. I just dropped by to see how your bride was doing after her ordeal."

"She's fine, thank you," Phyllis peeked from behind the bedroom's door, "even if I can't remember much about what happened after Jack and I were attacked."

"In that case," Percy wiped at his nose nodding toward Phyllis with concern in the eyes, "I'll wait for you folks downstairs outside the dining room."

Letting the game warden out, Jack joined Phyllis and changed into a light-blue suit, green tie and white shirt with black shined shoes, while the lady picked the short-sleeved lilac dress, tan stockings and black flats.

Maybe he can fill in some gaps; the detective also donned a blue fedora, *for both of us.*

***

Jack and Phyllis Petrov enjoyed their light repast of club sandwiches, kettle potato chips, dill pickle and beers seated with Fish & Game Warden Charles Percy, the 30-year-old man plain spoken and friendly enough. His confirmation of one-dozen strange killings around the area by a wild animal piqued the detective and reporter's curiosity, revealing the strange footprints found around each recent mutilated body.

"I actually saw similar prints near where I'd found you, Mrs. Petrov."

"Please, call me Phyllis," she insisted with a gleam to those eyes, seeming flirtatious at times toward their dining companion, "I owe you my life out there after all."

"And you can call me Jack," Petrov sipped at his beer, licking away the foam from the mouth, "but what sort of animal made the tracks you mentioned."

"That's just it," Percy finished a bite of his sandwich, "they have lupine characteristics from casts the state police made but are larger than any wolf's tracks I've seen."

"And you say each victim was always partially eaten?"

"Yes, Mrs. Pet— I meant, Phyllis," the warden seemed confused by her interest, "but are you sure we should discuss gruesome details when eating?"

"I'm a crime reporter, remember?" She sipped her beer. "I've looked at murder victims working in Gotham, just like my husband the private dick."

When Jack mentioned Brian Holtz, Percy's expression briefly turned sour.

"Yeah, I can *smell* him a mile away. The man claims to be a sort of special game hunter. I think he's just the poacher, but haven't managed to catch him doing anything illegal yet."

"So, you're on the lookout for this animal?" The detective swallowed some food halfway through his question. "And wouldn't know if it's what attacked us the other night?"

"Nope, I never even seen it," Charles finished a sandwich half's crust and pickle in the half-filled dining room, "but the killings started around the three-quarter moon before the full one. Maybe old legends about the moon driving animals and people mad have some truth."

"Why, Charles," Phyllis teased him, glancing at her silver watch, Jack thinking he noted some reddened skin under it around his wife's right wrist, "you sound almost superstitious. Oh, I almost forgot, darling, I've scheduled us another tennis lesson today, hoping you keep your eye on the ball this afternoon."

"You go, sweetie," Jack swallowed some chips and any lingering jealousy he felt toward the French-Canadian Laval, "I'd rather stretch my legs. It was a pleasure meeting you, Charles. I'd offer any help you might need on this case, of course, after what you did for Phyllis."

The two men shook hands in standing from that round table and their completely or half-finished meals and drinks. Phyllis also gave the man one kiss on his left cheek before departing to change for tennis inside her room.

"I'd hate to inconvenience you on a honeymoon, Jack. I'll probably do fine by myself. If I had me that tomato, if you'll excuse my labeling Phyllis, I'd never work on my vacation."

"The offer still stands," Jack sounded earnest, concluding with, "but I wish you luck."

I think I'll visit Holtz again while I'm out walking today.

***

After his short hike from the hotel to Holtz's cabin, Jack inventoried the mountain man's weapon collection, feeling inadequate with only his .38-caliber Colt Safety Revolver and its two extra rounds in the Plymouth's glove compartment. He especially liked the M1903 Springfield .30-06 bolt-action carbine rifle, having trained with one in the US Army at 1918 Camp Custer, Michigan.

"I have some special ammunition for that and my Winchester '73 carbine in the cabinet yonder," Brian Holtz shared some more corn liquor with the visitor as they inspected the hunter's arsenal, "bullets coated with holy water and blessed by a priest, wooden-tipped rounds and even silver-jacketed bullets."

"Are you kidding me?"

"I told you," the man wiped at his button nose after a sip of the true from one tin cup, "I hunt some unusual animals, ever since that buffalo thunder hoof spirit on the Dakota plains back in '87 as I moved east from Montana, born in West Virginia when it was still plain Virginia."

He's pulling my leg. The man doesn't look much older than me even around those eyes. Didn't Virginia break apart during the Civil War?

"Well, I learned the local fish & game warden doesn't like you much."

"Pshaw, the Keystone Cop's got a ramrod up his backside. If prohibition hadn't ended, he'd be after my private still in back too."

Jack admired all of Holtz's weapons, inspecting the special ammunition before he left to rejoin Phyllis for supper in the hotel's restaurant, discovering she had invited Laval to dine with them this evening (hotel staff only allowed if invited by a guest). Jack kept his blue suit on for the occasion, but Phyllis had changed into a sleeveless black satin dress with plunging v-neckline and knee-length hemmed pleats, wearing the black 3"-heeled pumps, silver pantyhose and five pieces of jewelry with red lipstick and painted nails. Pierre wore his navy-blue nautical jacket, red-and-white knit shirt, green slacks and brown wing-tipped shoes. He acted a gentleman with and smiled often at Phyllis while shooting Jack occasional veiled dirty looks.

"I hope you're getting better at tennis after all these lessons," the husband joked, unable to enjoy his well-done steak seeing Phyllis and Pierre had ordered theirs rare with hints of blood, "so maybe you'll show me what I'm doing wrong before bedtime, sweetie."

Frustrated at his renewed subtle jealousy toward the instructor, Phyllis Harrington threw her white cloth napkin onto the table, stood and grabbed Jack by the jacket's right lapel, pulling him from the room and begging their dining companion: "Please excuse us."

The private eye pulled free of her strong grip, the fingernails almost tearing the jacket's fabric, and followed his reporter spouse straight to their suite. Some shouting ensued after Jack closed the front door and it continued inside their bedroom.

"I saw the way your peepers were eyeballing that swarthy cream puff, Doll."

"Pierre is charming and considerate, because that's part of his job teaching tennis."

"God, why did I even bother when Roger Benson kidnapped you in '34 after your daddy hired me, just so we'd end up together like this? I should've never taken the case."

"I thought you were attracted to me because I reminded you of that lady you lost to Mr. Sloane in 1925. Wasn't your business short on funds that month too?"

"Right, you and Annie were two of the most stubborn broads I've ever met." Standing with his back to the bed, Jack loosened that tie before grabbing Phyllis' shoulder straps. "And I know you wore this and painted yourself up for *Laval*. You're hot to trot after him. Why?"

Phyllis pulled free before backhanding Jack's left-side jaw, knocking the man onto his back across their bed stunned by her strength. Switching off the lights, the brunette stripped her dress and underwear, pouncing upon the dazed man and almost tearing his clothes away. They made love with Phyllis on top, as Jack noted moonlight streaming in from the window flanking their bed. Mrs. Petrov gradually appeared hairier, her ears elongating to become pointed atop the head, before she resembled the thing they encountered after skinny dipping two nights ago.

Oh my God, what's happened to her? She's a...monster.

The man was pinned to the mattress and pillows under hands with claws now cutting into his skin, her ice-blue eyes glowing through that semi-darkness. Jack heard someone open their suite's door using a key, as Phyllis turned to watch for the footsteps coming through the parlor. The bedroom's door then opened, its wall light switch was flipped on, and Pierre Laval stood there jingling a key ring in his left hand.

"*Mon Cherie*, I see you have finally completed the change triggered by my love bite the other evening. But your man must not be killed inside this hotel. Too many complications will result then, no?"

The man now looked hairier than when seated downstairs at the small dining table, his dark-green eyes also visibly glowing here now.

"Laval, you did something to Phyllis, made her a *monster*?"

"Very perceptive, *monsieur* detective," Laval moved to open a taller narrow window left of the bed, "but we will take you outside and feast on your body tonight. Didn't those vows you recited for her say – until by death parted?"

Jack felt Phyllis tense atop him as Pierre moved closer and began removing clothing to change into something resembling Mrs. Petrov. Before he could escape her grasp, the detective watched his wife tackle Laval, rolling around in battling across the room's red carpet, colliding with other nearby furniture. Seconds later, they crashed through that left-side tall window still grappling, exchanging bites and snarls. Petrov stood from the bed and quickly dressed before he walked to the window and felt a westerly breeze stir torn curtains as he peered down to find no sign of either pointed-eared creature below.

Where'd they go? Laval was the thing that bit Phyllis' arm and attacked me?

The detective left his suite to report the broken window and his wife as missing inside the hotel. Before returning to 510, Petrov fetched his revolver and wore it concealed in the brown shoulder holster, lightly sleeping across the king-sized bed and remaining dressed. Phyllis and Pierre never returned there that night.

***

"Open up, Holtz," Jack Petrov pounded on the rustic cabin's rickety lashed-plank front door just after dawn, "we need to talk!"

After a few more blows, the detective stepped back when Brian Holtz cracked the door open, staring at his unexpected visitor with bleary hazel eyes, possibly affected by alcohol from the night before.

"She's changed – your wife, I meant."

"How the hell could you know about...?"

Still wearing yesterday's clothes, Jack barged into the single-room dwelling past his half-awake host in a red-striped stocking cap and long yellowed white nightshirt, looking around the weapons there as that heavyset hunter explained his last statement.

"I can sense the presence and proximity of those creatures, being similar in nature." Brian joined Jack, knelt to his right at the carved cabinet holding ammunition the detective was shown before. "I've never met your wife, but know *two* beasts now prowl the area."

"Damn it, you don't have any pistol ammunition," Jack fumbled through trays and boxes stacked before him, pulling his revolver to show the hunter what he needed, "and this is all I'm packing. Back home I've got connections for the ammo I'd need..."

Petrov paused and stood, staring at his gun, before Brian

arose to pat his back twice.

"To kill her, I reckon you was about to says."

NO, she's my wife. We've been together for years even before marriage. I love her more than life. I can't just...

"She's not your blushing bride now, Jack, but the hungry beast passing for a lady," Holtz walked to the wall mounting where those Springfield and Winchester rifles hanged on pegs, "just like the thing I've been huntin'. I'm supposing it *changed* her into what you've seen from bitin' the little lady, for you to come here a hollerin' after my help."

"I've killed what the world calls monsters before, Brian," Jack faced him with clenched fists after holstering the pistol, "all the way back to one night in a snowy north Russia wilderness of 1919."

"I reckon to being right about you," the man slapped his right knee, "smelled that on your body when I found it bleeding and unconscious on the hill."

"Okay," Jack took the Springfield off the wall and aimed it around the room after making certain the rifle was unloaded, getting the feel for a weapon he had not used in 21 years, "first we kill the bastard who bit my Phyllis the other night. If it's a sort of curse I heard about, maybe the attacking monster's death, if he's the curse's founder, might free her."

Brian Holtz stared at him with genuine pity, suspecting otherwise, before he took hold of the Winchester and fetched suitable ammunition for their hunt.

"I've heard tall tales about men becoming animals too, even killed a few in my day, but *these* creatures change form and hunt at night especially during full or three-quarter moons."

"So," Jack examined two silver-coated Springfield ammunition five-shot clips, "you'll help me kill this thing and save my wife?"

"Sure, Jack," Brian took the army rifle back, explaining, "but you get on back to the hotel and see if she's turned up after last night. I'll arrange what we need. Then, meet me here tonight before sundown. Bring the little woman along to meet me if there. We'll chain her onto my bed for safety before getting the polecat that bit her."

Petrov agreed to Holtz's plan and left after a half-hour there. He reached the Wolf's Lair but learned Phyllis had never returned since last night. The management was also cross about a broken window and damaged furniture in Room 510, before Jack sought peace in drinking some beer that afternoon.

Oh God, I'm not much of a prayerful man, he stopped at the hotel's second floor small chapel used in wedding ceremonies, kneeling to beg the Almighty, *but please bring my Phyllis back to me alive and well.*

***

Phyllis Petrov awakened sometime during daylight from illumination streaming through the curtained window beyond her feet, lying tied to a single bed with strong ropes, the tight red bandana gag around her mouth. She wore one white terrycloth bathrobe and nothing else, soon struggling against separately bound wrists and ankles, occasionally screaming despite any sound being muffled. As the sun beyond the window's closed white drapery dipped lower, the woman heard a door open somewhere to her left in another room. Seconds later, Pierre Laval stepped through this bedroom's single exit and closed it, dressed in white tennis attire and carrying three green tennis balls and the racquet in those hands.

"Forgive me, *mon amour,* I was detained at my job with other guests."

The brunette continued struggling to escape as Pierre stored his racquet and balls inside the closet left of a mirror-topped dresser, and then removed the shirt to reveal a tan complexion, hairy chest and arms with their supple muscles, rubbing his mouth while staring at her.

"Perhaps I should have left you *au naturale* as a beautiful sight after work."

He sat on the bedside and smiled at the captive before untying her robe and pulling it apart to view Phyllis' thrashing nude form, *petting* the lady briefly as she resisted.

"You will accept me, Mrs. Petrov. Tonight, I kill your husband outside the resort in my bestial guise and gain a lovely widow freed from her encumbering mate."

He's insane. Where are we? Oh, Jack, I can't even warn you about the danger.

"But that awaits us after dark, *Cherie*." He began undressing near her and looked around the bedroom (in what she would later discover was his quarters among rows of cabins below the hotel's north side). "Now we make *amour* in our human guises for the first time. We did it last night after I'd beaten you unconscious, but while both still *Loup Garou*."

Phyllis screamed louder and fought harder against his sexual assault, but outside that blue with white trim cabin the partly cloudy April afternoon turned to early evening and no sound was overheard. She wished Jack could prevent the horror occurring here and tonight. After twilight, Pierre left by the back exit still naked, transforming into the *Loup Garou* he had been ever since suffering the unnatural bite when age twelve in rural central Quebec.

No, I can't let him hurt Jack too.

Screaming through the gag almost to the point of howling just after she heard the similar sound from somewhere in surrounding wooded hills, Phyllis Petrov pulled harder on those ropes lashed to bedposts, her body's muscles tensing and flexing as skin around them became hairier with the darkness. She finally freed herself using the new primal strength. The second creature caught that first one's scent outside the cabin's rear door and followed mere minutes behind him. Confused by the animal hormones after forcing Jack to have sex, and then knocked unconscious battling Laval outdoors and brought here, Phyllis would now *kill* the tennis instructor for making her into a monster.

***

Jack Petrov dressed in his green and brown plaid suit with green tie and brown shoes, the only items he had resembling hunting camouflage, while Brian Holtz wore the buckskin tan tunic and pants with boots when both men met inside that man's cabin. Jack took the Springfield and two clips of silver-coated ammunition, while Brian carried the Winchester, a crossbow and long spear, the spearhead and bolts containing silver points. Setting out at 6:05 P.M., the men never noticed Fish & Game Warden Charles Percy in his tan and green uniform shadowing them from inside the woods off the nearest walking trail to that cabin. Armed with his .40-caliber Whitney-Burgess carbine rifle, the official kept both hunters in sight most of the time.

"Look," Jack knelt between two shrubs in the woods roughly somewhere between Brian Holtz's cabin and the hotel, "one creature has been this way."

Brian knelt and sniffed at those prints, before standing to inform Petrov: "They're two or three days old at least. Come on."

The detective made more noise moving through vegetation than the larger hunter, being unfamiliar with the outdoors growing up on Long Island and in Detroit. They soon approached a wide nature trail Jack recognized as the spot where he was attacked. He examined the tracks still visible from that encounter, as Brian found others nearer the woods heading toward Wolf Lake.

"These are newer," the hunter discerned, "almost as if we're meant to find them. They're distinctive and heavy, possibly deliberate."

The hunters reached the lakefront area minutes later, as Jack recalled the fun time he had in that water with Phyllis. A less-than full moon shined off its placid surface as they discovered the large human-sized wolf tracks reached one dead end.

"That's peculiar," Brian Holtz leaned down beside a tall tree's trunk, as Jack walked a few steps away seeking other signs from the creature, "it looks like he stopped here, but—"

Suddenly a dark blur emerged from vegetation above when Holtz spotted the climbing impressions in tree bark too late, struck across the scalp by razor-sharp claws and soon tackled onto the sandy ground's short grass. Despite seeming dazed, the hunter wrestled against that black-haired predator, having lost his carried rifle in the foliage from the initial attack and unable to reach the spear or crossbow slung across his back. Jack raised his rifle to shoot, but man and monster were intertwined too close together battling across that ground. The man-sized wolf then took a heavy rock and smashed Holtz's head repeatedly before he could avoid or block it, until lying on his left side in claw-torn clothing and bleeding from various injuries.

"Okay, you hairy son of a gun," squeezing the trigger, Petrov aimed at his target's head, "taste my bullets."

Another gun's firing sounded and Jack had the rifle shot from his hands, its stock striking him in the jaw as the impacting bullet hit the weapon's right side.

Prone and defenseless near the lake's edge, unable to see in moonlit darkness where that shod had come from or who fired it, Petrov was pounced upon by the wolf creature and fought to keep its fangs from touching him, despite the claws tearing at his suit and inflicting wounds on arms and torso from this predator with familiar dark-green eyes. After several seconds, Jack was surprised when a second black-furred wolf-like thing tackled his opponent and fought that beast. Soon, the intense melee was joined by a third animal – the large brown bear with blood stains across its head and body. As the battle moved nearer the woods, Jack crawled away to retrieve his borrowed Springfield, until another unseen gunshot knocked it further from his grasp.

Who the hell's shooting at me and why?

He pulled his concealed pistol and crouched near a large rock on the shoreline, watching to the right as a shadow emerged from the trees carrying one rifle in both arms. When the figure was within ten yards, Jack recognized him as Charles Percy. In the monster fight, the first black creature held its own against the bear, but seemed annoyed by the other wolf's attacks and often knocked that wolf-thing aside with gentler swats than any being inflicted.

"Charles, shoot them, not me! But not that one – I think it's my Phyllis."

Petrov moved from aiming his gun at the warden toward the creatures, uncertain which one to attack first.

"Sorry, Jack, but I've been flying under false colors." Percy fired a quick shot to disarm Petrov when he was turned slightly left watching those things still fighting nearer the trees yards ahead of them. "I found out about *Monsieur* Laval days ago. He persuaded me we could come to an arrangement, once I threatened him with the silver-bladed knife after he was caught in the steel net trap I'd laid around here."

The detective grasped his right hand in pain where the bullet had grazed the thumb-index finger junction, seeing the Springfield just a few steps away as that bear broke off from the main fight and charged the warden with the wolves pursuing closely and still fighting each other.

"I keep busy hunting a rogue animal killing people in the area," the warden fired his .40-caliber rifle at the bear's head, only grazing the left ear, and quickly reloaded to aim again, "until *Monsieur* Laval is no longer useful to my plan. I kill him, substitute another carcass and become the local hero."

Jack dove for that rifle Holtz had given him and fired it at Charles Percy, damaging the Whitney-Burgess' breech and ruining his second shot upon the bear. The man screamed when he was tackled and mauled by the large animal's bites and claws, the first wolf again attacking that bear and still fighting its fellow monster.

Great, I know one of them is Phyllis. But can I spot Laval's green eyes even with Army marksmanship eyesight instead of her blue ones?

With four shots remaining in the rifle's first clip, Jack stood and fired, pulling the rifle's bolt back hard each time. The first bullet struck the bear's right side neck; the second penetrated one human-sized wolf's left shoulder and the third its skull, but that thing pulled the other wolf against it to take a final bullet through the chest together. All three hairy bodies laid in a huddle, bleeding from battle injuries and silver bullet wounds. Percy had been mauled to death by that bear's claws and teeth.

I thought the one attacking that bear had Laval's eyes.

Petrov used the rifle's barrel and his left foot to turn the first human-sized wolf over from lying on its side, clearly seeing each bullet hole, especially one above the dark-green eyes, as he identified Pierre Laval – the dead body reverting to its human form. The bear breathed heavily while face down and now resembled Holtz sitting beside Percy's mutilated corpse.

He turned over the last shallow breathing creature with dread and saw Phyllis' lovely ice-blue eyes staring from within a black-furred face, her chest bleeding.

No, Laval used my wife as a shield when I aimed for him. She needs Dr. Bronstein before it's too late. Oh God, I'd almost forgotten – today's April 19 – my birthday.

The 38-year-old detective removed his jacket to cover Phyllis' body covered by the claw marks Laval inflicted, along with rope burns around each wrist and ankle and where that bullet had passed through her upper chest above the heart.

"I'll carry her," the injured Brian Holtz stood slowly, Percy's blood still covering his face and hands and bleeding from the neck wound missing the carotid artery, "they're finished."

"No, I'll do it. She's *my* wife."

Nodding, Holtz retrieved his tattered buckskin clothing he had shed becoming the bear, fashioning a crude loincloth secured around the waist. Jack cradled Phyllis in his arms, leading their way to the hotel. Dr. Bronstein was summoned from his cottage for emergency wound repair on Mrs. Petrov in the dispensary. The next morning Jack led local and state police, called by hotel management, to the spot where a naked Laval and mauled Percy remained near each other. Brian Holtz was treated for his wound, not especially harmed by silver bullets, gave a helpful statement for clearing Jack of criminal charges, and disappeared never to be seen in the area again.

***

"Charles, Noel, I'm, sorry," was all Jack could say, meeting his in-laws on Thursday at Sussex, New Jersey's St. Claire's Hospital (nearest to the resort), "the bullet wound was repaired and transfusions given, but she's not responding."

The stone-faced publisher looked more ashen and his hair seemed grayer than ever, as the white-haired frail wife leaned against her husband in visiting their daughter's private critical care room. Jack waited outside, each man wearing a black suit now and Mrs. Harrington the black long dress and veiled round hat. He could not tell them yet his part in unintentionally shooting their only daughter as a *Loup Garou*.

She's dying and doctors here don't know why. Bronstein repaired the damage with no complications at the hotel. Phyllis may have been poisoned by the silver bullet.

Sitting in a wooden chair outside his wife's room, Jack would witness her death two days later on Saturday, April 22, 1939. Laval's shooting ruled self-defense and Percy's death blamed on him (the body reportedly infected with undiagnosed rabies); Petrov gained little satisfaction having slain the monster which claimed the woman he loved on their honeymoon.

About the Author: John X. Grey is the pen name of Edwin Ray Haney from Southern Ohio, and has been published with short fiction and poetry in more than forty different anthologies from a half-dozen small presses since 1999. For more about the writer and his fiction work, please see his Amazon.com author's page amazon.com/-/e/B004E or his Weebly.com page and blog theanticelebrityjohnxgrey.weebly.com). Grey is also now working toward getting one of his ten genre novels eventually self-published.

Lightning Source UK Ltd.
Milton Keynes UK
177097UK00001B/36/P